The Girl with the Uninvited Ghost

A Pandemonium Mystery: Book 1
CYNTHIA VARADY

All That Glitters Is Prose

For Matthew and Odin. The two great loves of my life.

Chapter 1

M ahogany brushed a hot pink curl from her eyes and checked the compass. Seelie Park's sodium lights bathed the area in a yellow glow, nullifying the silver radiance of the full moon. A soft breeze, scented with jasmine blossoms, cooled her bare arms. Inside the compass's domed enclosure, a needle fashioned from the wing bone of a Jersey Devil spun wildly. Compasses crafted from a Devil's bones never failed to locate magical dead Folk, but Mahogany had doubts about the accuracy of this one.

She tapped the glass and sighed. The needle slowed, swayed back and forth, and gave a final wistful rotation. It pointed toward the dark street west of the park. Pandemonium's clock tower chimed twice, signaling safety for the magical people in town. The bell's resonance reverberated through the moon-glazed night, waking a dog who gave a series of irritated barks at the troublesome clock.

"Finally," Mahogany said, gazing in the needle's direction. "Bazgul, come."

A football-sized tarantula skittered out of the yellow-black shadows, carrying something in its mandibles.

"You ate before we left the house." Mahogany tried to give the spider a warning glare, but her love for indulging the lesser demon supplanted her temporary annoyance. Bazgul had come to her when she was a child. He'd appeared in her crib as a giant spider and had stayed by her side ever since. Most children would have rejected an eight-legged companion. For Mahogany, it was love at first sight.

Bazgul tilted his fuzzy head. The lifeless baby bird grasped in his mandibles scraped softly over the short-cropped grass. The street lamps' yellow light glinted in his eight eyes. It was as close to a pout as Bazgul could manage.

Mahogany placed her hands on her hips. "Don't look at me like that. You know I can't say no when you beg. Be quick."

The demon-spider threw his head back, releasing the baby bird. The tiny carcass cartwheeled into the air like a beanbag thrown by a drunk during a game of cornhole. Bazgul's mandibles separated into a gaping maw filled with razor-sharp teeth, and the dead bird tumbled into his waiting jaws. With a satisfied crunch, the bird disappeared. Bazgul scampered to Mahogany and climbed her leg, shrinking as he went. By the time he reached her shoulder, he'd deflated to the size of an everyday tarantula.

"All right, buddy," Mahogany said, heading towards the dark street. "Let's go find us a dead wizard."

She was new to the job of magical relics collector. Agalia Sorrowsong, the curator of Pandemonium's History Museum, had offered her the position six months ago. When a magical person passed away, their enchanted objects needed to be collected before they fell into the wrong hands. Code for humans. Cedric, the previous collector, had expired during a routine pickup. One devious sorcerer who'd been visiting Pandemonium when he'd died had a penchant for booby traps. Cedric, an 80-something-year-old human, had stumbled unwittingly into a hallway filled with enough firepower to make Laura Croft rethink her career choice. Poor old Cedric had wound up decapitated and eviscerated before a pack of hungry wolves finished off his corpse. This horrific death sent the local authorities, primarily non-magical Folk, into a tizzy.

After Cedric's death, Agalia set her sights on Mahogany. At first, the offer surprised her. Agalia, an old-school sorcerer, had never shown Mahogany, a human, any kindness. Agalia informed Mahogany that the Guild forbade magical Folk from becoming relic collectors because of their high status in the community. Plus, the job didn't take any real brain power. A stumbling block Agalia knew Mahogany wouldn't struggle with. The only qualifications needed were the knowledge that magic was real, being human, and delivering the items desired by the Guild of Myth and Magic.

Mahogany jumped at Agalia's job offer despite the risks of bodily harm. She welcomed a break from her dull routine of selling herbs at Haughty Hemlock. Plus, the idea of breaking into magical Folk's homes gave her a thrill.

The needle shifted and swayed as Mahogany navigated through the deserted street. In a final flurry of motion, the bone needle rotated several times and stopped. The house was one of four brownstone apartments typically rented by summer tourists.

"Okay, Bazgul, this looks like one." Mahogany scowled at the prospect of an out-of-town wizard dying in a rental. Mahogany knew the magical residents of Pandemonium's quiet village and was curious about what she might encounter inside. She took a deep breath to quiet her nerves at the thought of ending up like Cedric. Giving a final cursory glance to the sleeping street, she approached the dark house, tiptoeing to keep her bootheels silent on the sidewalk.

She tiptoed up the stone steps to the sturdy front door and reached for the polished brass mail slot, intending to send Bazgul through to slip the lock. The door creaked inward an inch as her fingertips grazed the metal flap.

Mahogany froze. She'd never arrived at an unlocked house, much less an open front door. Magical people were a paranoid bunch. Leaving one's home open for anyone to enter uninvited didn't happen—unless you were a witch in the woods who enjoyed the taste of lost children.

The door creaked, sending a chill down Mahogany's spine. She stepped up to the threshold and pushed the door wide, suppressing the feeling that something abysmal awaited her.

"Hello?" she half-called, half-whispered into the dark entryway.

She received no answer, which both relieved and frightened her. Mahogany summoned her courage and slipped through the door, shutting it with a soft click.

Dim light trickled through two narrow rectangular windows flanking the door, partially illuminating the front hall. Mahogany could make out a coat rack piled with heavy tweed jackets. Beyond that, shadows lurked at the edge of the glow. The oppressive aroma of dying flowers, dust, and kerosene clouded the air.

Mahogany wrinkled her nose and grasped the silver pentagram necklace she'd worn as long as she could remember. "Bazgul, light."

The demon spider emitted a blue-green glow, brightening the foyer.

Near the entryway's center stood a squat, round table holding a vase of wilting roses. Their drooping flowers kissed the dusty tabletop on crooked stems. Inset bookcases lined the walls—the shelving bowing under the weight of their contents. Teetering piles of books had bled from the overstuffed shelves at the edge of the worn parquet floor, stacked in haphazard heaps.

Mahogany took another step into the cluttered foyer, and something crunched under her turquoise cowgirl boot. She glanced down, revealing a shattered antique hurricane lamp.

Her dread rising, Mahogany took in the foyer again. Her first impression of an untidy wizard vanished. The mess was more than clutter. Someone had deliberately trashed the place. Books lay in disarray, as if flung from their shelves, their spines broken and pages torn. A painting of the Massachusetts witch Trials hung near the stairs and bore a giant slash, splitting the canvas in two.

"Bazgul, I have a bad feeling."

The demon spider shifted on her shoulder, mandibles chattering.

"I want to get out of here too, buddy, but we have a job." Mahogany took a deep breath, settling her nerves. She pulled a crumpled paper from her pocket and smoothed it against the thigh. Black ink emerged from the blank sheet, pooling in the center before sending out liquid tendrils, forming the list of objects.

"A figurine of an Egyptian cat containing—" A moan from a room to her right cut her words short.

Fear gripped Mahogany's stomach. "Hello?" she called into the ransacked house.

A moan answered her, and she followed it.

Mahogany found herself in what appeared to be a study. Silver moonlight mixed with the yellow of the streetlamps streamed through a large arched window facing the street. Two red velvet sofas flanked an enormous stone fireplace, between which sat a low coffee table. Above the mantel hung a massive, gilded mirror reflecting the room. Even more rows of books lined the walls.

As she glanced around the study, Mahogany found it in the same disarray as the entry hall—books flung from their shelves, pictures ripped from the walls, broken glass crunched underfoot.

"Hello?" she called again. She tiptoed to the center of the room and peered between the large couches. A pair of dirty sneakers, more gray than white, peeked out from the edge of the coffee table.

Mahogany crept over to the dirty sneakers and found them attached to the feet of a young man. His pale skin glowed against his dark, untidy hair. A wide halo of blood encircled his head. Nearby, a heavy, granite bust of Mother Shipton lay on its side—a dark red stain with several strands of hair clung to the sculpture's bottom edge.

The young man moaned again. Mahogany stepped over a large crystal vase and moved to his side. A dozen or more red roses lay wilting on the floor.

"What happened?" she asked. "Who did this to you?"

The young man opened his eyes. "I don't ... I didn't see."

Mahogany placed a shaking hand on his chest. "It's okay. You're going to be fine." She reached into the back pocket of her jeans for her cell phone, her heart hammering against her ribs. She'd never stumbled upon anyone dying. Most of the houses she'd visited in the last half year had been occupied by elderly Folk who had died of natural causes. But nothing like this.

"Mike," the young man groaned. "You need to help him."

"Who's Mike?"

At that moment, a metallic glint caught the corner of Mahogany's eye. She turned from her phone and spotted the body of a bearded older man on the opposite side of the coffee table. Behind a pair of round glasses, his unblinking eyes stared straight ahead—pupils dilated in death. Over the top of the coffee table, the hilt of a long, jeweled dagger protruded from the wizard's back.

"Mike, I presume," Mahogany said to the dead wizard. A chill crept up her spine as she gazed into his dead eyes.

Bazgul hissed and tensed on her shoulder, his blue-green light snuffing out. A floorboard behind Mahogany creaked.

The hair on Mahogany's neck rose, and she craned, peering over her shoulder. A figure clad in a dark hoodie stood over her, a fireplace poker gripped in their raised hand.

Bazgul leaped from Mahogany's shoulder, growing in size as he sailed through the air, and landed on the obscured face of the hooded figure. The figure screamed before crumpling to the floor—Bazgul clinging to their face. In the distance, sirens cut through the night.

Mahogany stared open-mouthed at the writhing, hooded figure before gathering her wits. Jumping to her feet, she raced towards the exit. Bazgul hopped onto the leg of her jeans as she passed. She reached the front door, yanked it open, and escaped into the warm summer night.

Chapter 2

The soles of Mahogany's boots hit the sidewalk with a wooden clomp. She raced across the street and dove behind a parked car. Her breath came in ragged gasps, and her mind whirled. What had just happened? Had someone just tried to bludgeon her with a fireplace poker? The cool metal of the car door bled through her shirt, calming her. She peeked over the car's hood but quickly hid behind it as three police cruisers skidded to a halt in front of the row of brownstones.

Nearby, in the darkness, a trashcan crashed into the sidewalk with an aluminum clang, scattering discarded glass bottles and soda cans. The cacophony made Mahogany's heart race anew. At the opposite end of the block, she glimpsed a dark figure sliding around the corner to the south, heading towards Pandemonium's downtown.

Mahogany closed her eyes and tried to slow her breathing. The urge to run pulled at every fiber of her soul. She'd been in the house with an assassin. All the other relics she'd collected had been from wizards who died of old age or spells of their own making gone wrong, not murder.

After half a minute, Mahogany peeked through the driver's side window at the ruckus across the street. Blue and red lights flickered off the block of sleeping houses. A uniformed officer stood in the doorway Mahogany had fled through only moments before.

"Do you think they caught the murderer?"

Mahogany turned her head so quickly that her neck cracked, sending a tingling pain up her scalp. Crouched beside her was the injured young man from the study. He stared at her and repeated his words when she didn't respond. "Did they catch him?"

He wore a pale green t-shirt that hung on his thin frame, accentuating his narrow shoulders and pointy chin. If the shape of Henry Cavill's jaw was the bar for male virility, the person squatting next to her fell short on the hunky spectrum. From this angle, she could tell he was tall, over six feet at least. His wide-set, deep blue eyes searched hers.

Mahogany placed her head on the cool glass of the driver's window, her neck throbbing. "This can't be happening." Annoyance replaced her previous terror.

"I know. It's baffling," the young man said, returning his wide-eyed gaze to the police cars.

"This is just my luck." Mahogany dusted off her hands and crept along the length of the vehicle toward the park. The last thing she needed was for the police to question her. Even though Mahogany was confident she could lie her way out of the situation. However, she'd rather keep well clear of the cops if possible.

She got to the end of the car and scampered, keeping low as she made her way to the next vehicle parked on the street. She sensed the young man following and groaned internally. Mahogany peered over her shoulder and found him crawling along the gutter, keeping pace with her. Mahogany crawled to the end of the block before standing. She forced herself to walk at a relaxed pace despite the cold sweat dripping down her ribcage. She crossed the street and headed for the park.

"Wait," the young man yelled after her.

Mahogany paused and peered at the young man. He dashed into the street, not bothering to look for traffic. As he reached the street's broken yellow line, the headlights of a large van illuminated the night.

The young man froze, his mouth forming a circle of shock. The van barreled towards him. Tensing for impact, the young man squeezed his eyes shut. Yet, the impending blow never came. Instead, the van passed through him like he didn't exist, which was debatable at this point in his afterlife. Can one truly exist without a corporeal body? What is the definition of existing, anyway?

He checked himself over, his eyes wide in disbelief. "What just happened?" he screamed. "What's going on?"

Mahogany sighed and faced the frantic young man still standing in the street. "You're a ghost," she hissed. "You died back there." She motioned toward the brownstone.

"No," he said, shaking his head. "No way. I'm right here with you, standing in the street."

Mahogany glared. "How else do you explain that van driving through you?" She loathed ghosts, especially talkative ones. The young man looked a couple of years older than her, but dumb as a brick.

His face crumpled. "I'm too young to die."

"You're too dead to cry," Mahogany said, her tone softening. She turned on her heel and continued to Seelie Park, Bazgul chattering in her ear.

"Wait," he said, running to catch up with her. "I, I'm dead, and you can see me. That means you were there when I died."

"Unfortunately," Mahogany said through gritted teeth. She didn't have time to babysit a disgruntled spirit. She had work to do, and now, with the cops involved, her job just became a thousand times harder.

"This also means you're stuck with me until someone avenges my death," he continued.

"I'm aware." They headed into the park, and Mahogany made a beeline for the parking lot. She strutted up to a sunshine yellow Vespa and jammed the helmet over her burst of pink curls.

"So, how are we going to solve my murder?" he asked, glancing at the scooter. "Nice bike, by the way."

Mahogany glared at the ghost before mounting the Vespa and starting the engine. She revved the throttle a few times before zooming out of the parking lot and onto the street, leaving the gangly specter alone. A moment later, he bounded to a halt on the back of the scooter, causing Bazgul to hiss from his perch on Mahogany's shoulder.

"That was exhilarating!" the spirit yelled into Mahogany's ear. "Did you know we're tethered by an invisible cord? I've never gone bungee jumping, but I imagine that is exactly what it's like, only horizontally instead of vertically. I'm Guy, by the way. Guy Miller. What's your name?"

"Mahogany," she answered through gritted teeth. She knew she couldn't simply ditch the ghost. The haunted never got off that easily.

"Like the wood? That's interesting.

It wasn't her real name. That piece of information had never been given to her. Mahogany is what she was called. Neema had given her the nickname for being 'about useful as a piece of wood,' or so she was told. It wasn't the best nickname, but Mahogany had grown to like the moniker, mostly since she'd never met another person who shared the name. Plus, mahogany was a beautiful wood, and its deep brown color matched her dark skin.

"Are your parents carpenters?" Guy asked.

"I wouldn't know." Mahogany longed for solitude. She'd gotten on just fine for the last twenty years with only Bazgul as a friend. She didn't need or want a ghost hanging around until someone solved his murder. That could take years or, well, forever. She hoped the police had already apprehended the responsible party.

"You don't know what your parents do for a living? Did they not raise you? My maternal grandmother raised me. She's non-magical, so I didn't start learning the craft until a year ago, when Mike started apprenticing me." His face fell. "I can't believe someone murdered us. My poor gran is alone now. By the way, Mahogany, what?"

Mahogany answered by revving the engine again, speeding them toward the home she shared with Neema, her abductor.

Chapter 3

Neema sprinted up the stairs of the modest two-story Craftsman home. She shook out of her dark pea coat and kicked off her shoes, stripping to her undergarments. She pulled on her fuzzy blue bathrobe, cinching the tie around her thickening waist. There wasn't much time before Mahogany returned home.

After a couple of calming breaths, Neema's racing heart slowed. She padded down the stairs to the kitchen, put the kettle on, and grabbed a mug. The adrenaline still flooding her system made her hands shake, and the mug clattered on the tile countertop.

Things had escalated quickly after she'd received the first letter. Much too quickly. While she'd expected something like this for the last twenty years, the reality still shocked her.

Neema grabbed a large mortar and pestle from the kitchen and took it into the apothecary through the adjoining door. She deftly picked the herbs needed for her spell and added them to the thick porcelain bowl, glancing at the pool of silver moonlight spilling through the large plate glass storefront. She needed the full moon's light for the spell. For that, she'd have to work quickly.

The kettle gave a soft, breathy whistle as she reentered the kitchen. Despite being alone, she quickly stifled the flame, not wanting to hear the kettle's full cantor at this late hour. Neema poured the boiling liquid into the mug and tossed in a tea bag. As suspected, Mahogany's Vespa purred into the drive a moment later. Neema settled her ample rear against the kitchen counter, grabbed the mug with now steady hands, and blew the steam from the steeping tea. She glanced thoughtfully at the herbal concoction, half pulverized in the mortar.

Mahogany threw open the kitchen door and stomped inside, slamming it behind her. She kicked off her boots, and the wooden heels thudded against the tiles. She flung off her backpack, which landed with a solemn sigh of fabric and zippers.

Bazgul leaped from her shoulder, landing on a cat tree by a bank of windows next to the back door. He made a tight circle before settling, his gaze scanning the drive for signs of nocturnal life.

Neema winced at the sudden onslaught of sound. Mahogany didn't share her desire to keep quiet in the dead of night.

"You're home early. How did it go?" She peered over the mug at her adopted daughter, a quizzical eyebrow raised, the smooth olive skin crinkling. For a woman in her mid-fifties, Neema has the complexion of a woman nearly a decade younger. She knew it hadn't gone well. She'd witnessed that much, but the exact details were vague.

"You're up late," Mahogany said, ignoring Neema's question. She stomped to the refrigerator and yanked it open.

"I needed the full moon." Neema glanced at the deflated backpack. "What happened? Where are the artifacts?"

"I decided against doing my job and brought home a ghost instead." Sarcasm dripped from Mahogany's words as she gestured toward the back door, her face twisted in an angry grin. She grabbed the milk bottle and popped the top with her thumb. The cap made a series of neat flips before clattering to the floor. She tilted her head back, taking a deep drink straight from the bottle.

Neema bit her lip. Although Mahogany had reached her early twenties, she occasionally acted like a petulant teen.

"Wait, what?" Neema shook her head and set the tea aside. "A ghost?" This was even worse than she first thought. Neema glanced in the direction Mahogany had gestured, but saw nothing. "I thought everyone was supposed to be dead when you arrived."

Mahogany took a final swig and roughly placed the milk into the fridge, sloshing a few drops out of the narrow neck. "That's how it's supposed to work. The wizard was dead, stabbed, but his apprentice took his last breath while I was there."

"Stabbed?" Neema blanched. When she saw Mahogany enter the brownstone, she had hoped Mike's fast-food lifestyle had simply caught up with him. Things were much worse than she had thought. So much worse.

Neema picked up the mortar and pestle and began grinding the mixture vigorously, thankful that the motion hid her shaking hands. She needed to get this spell finished.

"Are you sure he didn't just fall on the blade? Like a catastrophic accident? Or maybe a murder-suicide pact?" Neema said, her tone hopeful.

"Not unless he was double-jointed and stabbed himself in the back." She took a heavy seat at the kitchen table. "And his apprentice dropped the bust of Mother Shipton on his head hard enough to kill himself."

Neema turned to their bust of the Prophet Ursula Southeil, who had turned a king and his men to stone after they failed to pass her test. She made the sign of the horns to ward off evil. "Using the Prophet to take a life will only bring calamity."

Mahogany tracked something only she could see, and her eyes narrowed. "Are you sure you didn't kill the old guy, and then some-one killed you?" she asked. Her gaze settled on the hutch against the kitchen's far wall—its shelves filled with thick tomes on magical herbalism.

Neema waited, guessing that the apparition was answering Ma-hogany's question.

Mahogany's face pulled down in a frown as she listened to some-thing only she could hear. "Guy says he didn't do it. He heard Mike yell and ran to investigate. Then someone hit him from behind." She lowered her head to the table and sighed. "That must have been the same person who attacked me."

Neema resisted the urge to rush to Mahogany and check her for injury. She gripped the mortar and pestle harder. "Well, you seem to have made it out in one piece." Cold indifference laced her words.

Mahogany peaked over at Neema from the tabletop. "Please, don't gray your hair over me. Someone almost brained me with a fireplace poker, but Bazgul rescued me. A bite from a demon, even a lesser one, is not pleasant. It's probably festering as we speak."

From his place on the cat tree, Bazgul raised his head and chat-tered.

Mahogany turned to face him, her face a mask of shock. "What do you mean you don't know if you bit them? They sure screamed like you had."

Bazgul chattered again, and Neema swore his fuzzy black visage sagged with guilt.

"You closed your eyes?" Mahogany shook her head.

"Perhaps they have arachnophobia?" Neema offered. Bazgul, while a puppy dog at heart, had a way of causing a visceral response in most people.

Bazgul turned to face Mahogany and chittered again before dissolving in a red-brown haze and slipping upstairs.

"So much for festering wounds." Mahogany glared at the cat tree.

"Don't be too hard on him." Neema retrieved her abandoned herbal mixture and set the bowl on a windowsill bathed in a patch of bright moonlight. She cupped her hands over the bowl and closed her eyes. Tendrils of magic snaked through the soles of her feet and up her body. She willed the energy through her hands and into the herbs. As a wortcunner, Neema could perform magic, but her spells depended on an herbal medium.

"That ought to do," she muttered, turning to Mahogany. "Ghosts can be tricky to get rid of. His murder will have to be solved for him to move on, unless..." she hesitated, weighing her words carefully. "Unless he has unfinished business."

"Nope. No unfinished business. At least I don't think so," Guy said. He'd migrated to the kitchen and currently had his head shoved into the steaming kettle. His voice was tinny as it bounced around the metal interior.

"I can't think about that right now." Mahogany pinched the bridge on her nose. "I need those objects before Agalia and the Guild get impatient."

Neema cringed inwardly at the mention of Agalia Sorrowsong. She was one of those witches who gave their ilk a terrible reputation. The magical community both feared and respected the museum curator's curses, which were legendary. It would serve Mahogany well to stay on Agalia's good side.

Then there was the Guild of Myth and Magic. Composed of elders from varying magical groups, the Guild watched over Folk, ensuring magic stayed where it was supposed to—out of the hands of humans. Coming to their attention negatively was something to be avoided. Neema worried that if Mahogany screwed this collection up... Well, she didn't want to think about what might happen.

"I wish you'd taken a job with lower stakes." She sighed and glanced at the spell marinating the moonlight. "Let's get this sorted before anyone gets their knickers in a twist. I'll go with you."

"You don't have to do that," Mahogany turned to face Neema, her expression horror-stricken. "It's my job and my problem."

An emotion akin to regret rose in Neema's chest, but it dissipated almost as quickly. She'd kept Mahogany on a short leash most of her life, and with good reason—six months into the job and nearly murdered. There was no way Mahogany was returning to the brownstone without backup. Neema had tried to dissuade Agalia into offering Mahogany the position, but there was no arguing with the old witch once she'd set her mind to something.

Neema turned to the counter and busied herself with a few stray dishes in the sink. "Don't be ridiculous," she said, over her shoulder.

"With two of us, it will be faster. Perhaps your ghost can help us locate the items. What do you know about him?"

"Too much," Mahogany said, her voice tight. "He won't shut up. And he's not my ghost."

"Did you mention his name is Guy?" Neema asked, drying her hands on a floral hand towel. "Is he cute?"

"Guy is about as far from cute as one can get." Mahogany stared through the doorway into the apothecary, her eyes narrowed. "How about the wizard? What was his name? Mick? Mork? Mack?" she called.

Neema fought the urge to peek into the apothecary, knowing she'd see nothing but shelves lined with jars filled with herbs.

"The blue?" Mahogany said, a single eyebrow cocked high. "Was he a Lord of the Rings fan?"

Watching Mahogany appear to talk to herself was unnerving, and Neema rolled her shoulder to dispel a chill building at the base of her neck.

Mahogany addressed Neema without taking her eyes from the empty doorway. "The old wizard was called Magoris Idrus the Blue, which has got to be the dumbest name I've ever heard."

"Well, I ought to hit the hay. You should get some sleep, too," Neema said suddenly, faking a yawn. "We have another long night ahead of us."

Mahogany watched Neema disappear up the stairs. The fuzzy robe's hem swished around her calves as her hips swayed.

"Wait, I thought you said the wizard's name was Mike."

"Oh, that's just his nickname. He went by Magic Mike," Guy said, floating into the kitchen.

Mahogany burst into peals of laughter, a rare sound. "Like the stripper movie? Oh, that's good." She thought of the dead, chubby wizard with the long gray beard and sobered.

"It was a nickname from his younger days in Boston. Some human gave it to him because he couldn't remember Magoris," Guy said, gazing around the kitchen. "What's in there?" He pointed to another doorway at the opposite end of the kitchen.

"The living room," Mahogany asked, her voice distracted. Her gaze settled on Guy, and she saw him for the first time. His hair was a much lighter shade of brown than it had looked on the street, and his dark blue eyes were an unsettling shade of sky blue. Overall, he wasn't ugly or cute, but ordinary and forgettable.

He walked up to the refrigerator and placed his hand on the front. A moment later, it phased through the stainless steel door. An excited yip escaped Guy's mouth. Mahogany watched with mild amusement as Guy disappeared into the appliance.

"This is so weird," came his muffled voice. "I bet this is how clouds feel when an airplane passes through them. If clouds weren't water vapor and had a central nervous system."

A yawn gripped her jaw, forcing it open. "Neema's right. I need to get some sleep."

Chapter 4

"What's on the list?" Neema asked. She and Mahogany stood in the book-stuffed study where Magic Mike and Guy had lost their lives. Dried pools of blood graffitied the antique Persian rug. The waning gibbous moon slipped through the study's arched windows, bathing the room in its cool glow. In the distance, the clock tower tolled twice.

Mahogany pulled the crumpled list from her pocket. "Let's see. There's a six-inch black cat statue with Amenhotep III's liver, a tin-type of Lizzie Borden, a fourteenth-century anelace with a jeweled hilt, and a leather-bound Book of the Dead."

"Does your ghost have any idea where the items might be?" Neema asked, gazing around the study. Mahogany noticed that her line of sight stayed above the bloodstains.

"He's not my ghost," Mahogany said, clenching her jaw.

"By the way, what's an anelace?" Guy asked. He stood in the doorway to the study, casting a wary eye into the room.

"It's a long dagger from the Middle Ages, almost a short sword. They were fashionable for the English nobility to wear," Mahogany said. She stepped over the bloodstain left by Magic Mike as he bled out and picked up a picture frame sitting on the brick mantelpiece. Behind it stood a small black statue of an Egyptian cat. "Got one." She handed the figure to Neema, who placed it in a waiting tote bag.

"Oh, the dagger. Yeah. That was part of the binding," Guy said. "I'm pretty sure it had been in Mike's family for generations."

"Binding?" Mahogany asked. She set the photo back on the mantel and turned to Guy. Bazgul skittered along her arm and onto the mantel, where he climbed up the large, gilded mirror reflecting the room.

"What's this about a binding?" Neema asked as she adjusted the tote bag on her shoulder.

"Magic Mike was about to bind me to someone," Guy said. He entered the study, skirting the wall nearest the door, and disappeared through a bookshelf.

"Gods," Mahogany murmured, her teeth gritted. She exited the study and followed Guy's nasally humming into the kitchen. "Binding you to whom?" Mahogany asked.

Guy stood inside the kitchen sink. His torso sprouted from the water-stained enamel. "That is a good question. Mike didn't say," he said and walked through the sink and into the counter. His head and shoulders disappeared into the cupboards above, while his lower half remained hidden in the dishwasher.

"Mike didn't tell you who the binding was for?" Mahogany said, and raised a skeptical eyebrow.

Neema joined Mahogany in the kitchen doorway. "Why would Magic Mike do that? Binding a person to another without full knowledge could be disastrous."

"Mike said the less I knew, the better." The closed cupboard door muffled Guy's voice. "He said the person had something to do with the woods, a forest, or something treey. And cold weather. Snow or maybe sleet? I can't remember the details."

"Wizards are so annoying," Mahogany said. She turned to Neema. "Magic Mike didn't tell him who or why or what he planned to bind Guy to, only that the less he knew, the better."

"That makes about as much sense as a witch with a white cat," Neema said. "Mike was an odd creature. Was the binding completed?"

"Hard to say," Guy said. "The blow to my head wrecked my memory of the night."

Mahogany sighed. "He doesn't know. Let's get this done." She gazed at Guy's narrow torso and rolled her eyes. "I'll take the entry hall."

Several hours later, Mahogany and Neema stood at their kitchen table, admiring their haul. "That's everything except the anelace," Mahogany said. They have looked in every crevice, nook, and corner of the brownstone, but they couldn't locate the anelace. A half hour before the sun was scheduled to make its appearance, they had returned home with the Guild's list nearly complete.

Guy floated through the table and stood in the middle of the objects retrieved from the brownstone.

"Are you going to make a habit of this?" Mahogany asked, her brow knitting into a frown.

"I might," Guy said. "There's something quite liberating about shedding my corporeal form."

"Gods, you're insufferable," Mahogany muttered.

"Plus, being inside an object lets me see recent events that happened to and around it," Guy said.

A small smile crept over Mahogany's lips. "Such a romantic. I bet you said that to all of your girlfriends."

"Ew, gross," Guy said, making a face. "I'll have you know, I am, er, was a complete gentleman with my romances."

Mahogany ran her gaze over Guy's upper half. His rumpled shirt, sloppy hair, scrawny frame, and pasty complexion would have kept him off the cover of GQ. The word nerd didn't do him justice. All he needed was a pair of thick-rimmed glasses and a graphic t-shirt depicting something D&D-related to polish off the look. She doubted he'd had many opportunities to be a 'gentleman.'

"Where do you suspect the anelace might be?" Neema asked. "Do you have any idea what it looks like?"

"No," Mahogany said, "but they're hard to miss. They're practically swords, and according to the Guild's list, this one has a jeweled hilt." As the words slipped from her lips, Guy and Mahogany locked eyes.

"The murder weapon," they said in unison.

"Someone killed Mike with a magical relic?" Neema asked. "That means the police have it."

"Well, how in the fiery pits of Hades am I supposed to get that back?" Mahogany demanded. She took a seat at the table with a heavy sigh.

Guy gave a wry smile. "Your womanly charms?"

Mahogany pinched the bridge of her nose, trying to squelch a headache blooming behind her eyes. "Don't the cops lock important objects, like murder weapons in evidence lockers?" she asked. "Inside police stations, where all the police hang out with guns and mace and TASERs and stuff?"

"You could always ask Ralph Evens for help," Neema teased, her eyes twinkling.

Mahogany threw a glare at the older woman. "I'm open to any other options."

Neema gave Mahogany's shoulder a reassuring squeeze. "We'll only use Ralph as a last resort. I've got a port-o-hole or two lying around that will work perfectly. We'll figure it out."

Chapter 5

The sound of breaking glass startled Mahogany awake. She stretched, rubbed her puffy eyes, and rolled out of bed as a garbage truck rumbled down the street. She pulled the silk sleeping cap from her head and groaned as she caught sight of her reflection in the mirror hanging on her bedroom door; her bright pink curls stood in matted clumps around her head. So much for getting a quick start this morning.

"Greetings and salutations," said a cheerful voice.

Mahogany jumped as Guy materialized through her bedroom wall, wearing a dopey grin.

"If you're going to stick around, you need to work on bringing me coffee in the morning," Mahogany said. She threw the covers back and headed to her closet.

"Move objects? Is that possible?" Guy held his hands in front of his face and looked them over. "That would be incredible. It would be like I never died."

"Except I'm the only person who can see or hear you. Not quite like being alive," Mahogany said. She grabbed items suitable for public consumption and headed to the bathroom for a much-needed shower. "Oh, and if I catch you in the bathroom at any point, I will perform an exorcism."

Guy, who had followed Mahogany to the bathroom threshold, tilted his head in thought. "Exorcisms only work on demons inhabiting humans, by the way." He folded his hand across his narrow chest. "You know what you could do? Solve my murder."

Mahogany shot Guy a look that would have caused great bodily harm had he a body to hurt.

"Got it. Privacy is paramount." He attempted to wink, but it looked like he had something in his eye, and fired two finger guns at her before sinking through the floor.

Mahogany rolled her eyes and headed for a shower.

Mahogany headed downstairs to the kitchen with a relaxed sigh. Having washed away the grime of the previous day left her feeling renewed. Her freshly styled curls bounced with vigor. She skipped into the kitchen. Her silver pentagram bobbed jauntily on its chain as she beelined for the coffeepot. Liquid black joy greeted her with its earthy aroma. She inhaled the intoxicating scent and poured herself a large mug. She added copious amounts of sugar and milk, taking a quick swig straight from the bottle before placing the frosty jug back in the fridge. As she stirred her restorative brew, Neema strode into the kitchen waving a white legal-sized envelope.

"Here's the port-o-hole I mentioned."

Mahogany's mood fell. How could she have forgotten about the anelace? With a groan, she took another sip of her light brown coffee. Despite the several spoonfuls of sugar, it tasted bitter.

"You better get a move on if you're going to break into the headquarters of Pandemonium's finest," Neema said, offering the envelope. Mahogany took it with a wan smile.

"How are you going to get into the evidence locker?" Guy asked. He'd stuck his head into the coffee carafe. "If I close my eyes, I can almost taste it. Huh, Madagascar, shade grown. Nice choice."

"Not me, we," Mahogany said, nodding to Guy and Bazgul, who had crept onto the kitchen island from his cat tower. "You two are going to help me, but first, I need food."

***

"This is cute. Magic Mike didn't let me out much while we were here." Guy said, joining Mahogany on the wide sidewalk in front of Hot Brews. Large baskets filled with bright blooms hung along the edge of a slanted awning, sheltering several small tables from the bright morning sun. Two large windows encased in polished wood filled the front facade, which was opened on warm summer nights, allowing a fresh breeze to cool the space. Like most of Pandemonium, Hot Brews resembled the owners' country of origin. Here, a Parisian-style café.

"How long were you in town before..." Mahogany trailed off, diverting her gaze from Guy, suddenly uncomfortable. She wasn't used to talking to the recently dead. It had never occurred to her that a ghost might mourn their death. She placed her helmet on the Vespa's seat parked at the curb and fluffed her curls back to life.

Bazgul scampered from the back of her shirt to her head, nesting in her kinky pink hair.

"About a month," Guy said, seeming to miss Mahogany's near snafu.

"Did he ever mention why he'd brought you to Oregon from Ohio?" Mahogany headed for the café's glass door.

"No, he was pretty tight-lipped about everything," Guy said, floating after her.

As they entered the café, Guy's mouth dropped open. Uniformed police officers occupied nearly every table in the small café. "Why is this place filled with cops?" he whispered out of the side of his mouth as if anyone but Mahogany could hear him.

A tall, hunky officer half waved at Mahogany from a table against the wall. He had blond hair cut into a tight crewcut and a round baby face dusted with the last vestiges of adolescent acne.

Mahogany groaned internally. Of course, Raph would be here. She usually popped in for an afternoon treat, avoiding Ralph and his breakfast muffin and a cup of green tea. But her need for police intel on the station couldn't wait. Ralph and Mahogany had dated briefly in the teens, but the spark hadn't been there for her. She wished she could have said the same for Ralph. He'd been pining after her ever since.

Ralph's biceps bulged against the hem of his blue police uniform shirt. He lowered his hand, turning back to his bran muffin and crossword with the expression of a scolded puppy.

Mahogany pretended she hadn't seen Ralph and got in line behind several more officers. She placed her back to Ralph and the rest of the cafe, pretending to study the chalkboard menu behind the counter. The last officer in line glanced over his shoulder and smiled.

It died on his lips as his gaze fell on Bazgul. The officer blanched and stepped around his compatriots, placing several feet between himself and the lunatic with a massive spider perched on her head.

"Good morning, Mahogany, Bazzy," said the beautiful blond woman beaming behind the counter. "It's so good to see you. What'll be this morning? Hot cocoa? Steamed milk with vanilla syrup? Oh! I know. A chocolate croissant and a strawberry smoothie." She practically bounced out her ballet flats as she spoke.

A bitter taste rose in Mahogany's throat at Evelina's nickname for Bazgul. "That sounds fantastic, Evelina," she said, rethinking how often she visited Hot Brews. The way she had ticked off Mahogany's favorite orders set a stone in her stomach. Had she become a regular without realizing it?

"My pleasure," Evelina said, her effervescent personality bubbling over. Mahogany took a small step back, so none of the giddy fairy's sparkling personality spilled onto her shoes. Evelina moved behind the counter with the grace of a prima ballerina. Each lock of her golden hair gleamed like spun gold. Her complexion appeared ageless, with no visible scars or fine lines. Her willowy frame looked like a strong wind might blow her over, yet she hefted the thick glass blender as if it were featherlight.

"Will you be joining us or taking it to go?" Evelina asked. Her hand poised to pour the smoothie into a pint glass.

"Better make it to go," Mahogany said. "I've got business elsewhere."

Mahogany cleared her throat as Evelina placed the order on the counter. "Heard any gossip about the police station recently?"

Evelina's bright smile pressed into a conspiratorial frown. "Oh, I love gossip. What kind are you searching for?"

Mahogany peered around at the uniformed patrons. "I don't know. This place is packed with cops. Have any of them mentioned the station? Like weak spots?"

Evelina raised a perfectly sculpted eyebrow and tapped her pointy chin. She grabbed a mint from a dish on the counter and offered it to Bazgul. The demon spider took the striped candy in his mandibles with the gentleness of a flower fairy depositing dew on gossamer. Mahogany frowned, hoping Bazgul didn't get sticky crumbs in her freshly washed hair.

Mahogany sighed when Evelina didn't answer. "Did you hear about the wizard getting stabbed the other night?" She sipped her smoothie, her taste buds singing at flavors intangible. How was it possible for an item of food to taste like sunshine and laughter? Okay, maybe being a regular here wasn't such a bad thing. The food was, well, magical.

"I heard about the murder the other night, but I didn't catch the details. How do you know it was death by stabbing?" Evelina leaned her elbows on the counter and rested her sharp chin on her manicured hands, her violet eyes growing wide.

Mahogany glanced around, making sure no one was in earshot. "I was there. I got a message that a wizard had died, so I headed over. It turned out someone had murdered him. Then the cops arrived." Mahogany pulled the chocolate croissant from its white paper bag and took a bite. Her mouth flooded with joy. Flavors reminiscent of fresh rain and first kisses danced on her tongue.

"What about me?" Guy whined. "Someone murdered me too."

"Jeez, Mahogany. Are you all right?" Evelina asked, her rosy cheeks fading to a less radiant shade of pink.

"I know, but you're not what's important," Mahogany said, her eyes flickering to Guy.

"Who are you talking to?" Evelina asked, peering over the counter at the floor. "Do you have an imp with you?"

"The murdered apprentice," Mahogany said, rolling her eyes toward Guy.

Evelina threw back her head and laughed, exposing her beautiful swan-like neck. "Oh, man. You have a ghost. That's perfect. What's their name? Are they cute?"

Mahogany ignored Evelina's questions. "I need to get into the evidence locker. I'm pretty sure that the last magical relic I need is in there."

Despite pressing her bow-shaped lips together, a hiccup of laughter escaped Evelina. "You are in luck. Last week, I overheard a pipe burst in the station near the evidence locker. They had to keep the windows open and get some of those giant dehumidifiers to dry the place out. Maybe you could get in that way?"

"That's a lot of information to glean from customers," Guy commented, raising an eyebrow. A glint of newfound respect sparked in his sky-blue eyes as he peered at Evelina.

Mahogany counted to ten in her head. "She's Fae. When humans eat Fae food, they can't help but talk. It's like truth serum," she said to Guy. Mahogany turned back to Evelina. "That sounds perfect. Do you have any idea where the evidence locker is?"

"Sorry, no." Evelina shook her head, her blond locks shimmering like liquid gold, and she turned to welcome a new customer. "Welcome to Hot Brews. What can I craft for you?"

The customer placed their order and sat at an empty table to wait.

"How much do I owe you?" Mahogany said, grabbing her coin purse.

"After that story, you get the friends and family discount," Evelina said, waving away Mahogany's money.

Mahogany raised her smoothie in thanks and turned to leave.

"Oh, Mahogany, one more thing," Evelina said. "Watch out for Detective Sawyer. She's the new homicide detective who transferred from Southern California. You're going to want to stay off her radar."

"Thanks again," Mahogany said, turning toward the door, colliding with a tall young man distracted by his phone. Her smoothie slipped from her hand and cartwheeled through the air. The man reached out with animal-like reflexes and caught it before it hit the tiled floor.

"I'm so sorry," he said, handing her the plastic cup. "Are you all right?"

Mahogany stared into the man's deep hazel eyes, and something in her chest hitched as if hooked like a mermaid on a fishing line. In her stomach, a hoard of butterflies bumped and collided. Her head tingled, and her breath caught in her throat. For an unknown amount of time, Mahogany stared at the man, unable to speak.

In her ear, Bazgul chattered, conveying his annoyance. The sound brought Mahogany back to her senses. The man's gaze landed on the demon spider, and he smiled, surprising Mahogany. Bazgul's spidery form usually elicited the polar opposite in humans. Mahogany regained her voice. "Yeah, sorry," she managed and skirted around him and out the café door, embarrassment warming her cheeks.

Suppressing the urge to look over her shoulder at the man, Mahogany headed outside and gazed across the street at the police station. The large, formidable building had once been a hotel for new residents of Pandemonium as they fled persecution. Towns like Pandemonium emerged across the New World as Folk found themselves imprisoned, banished, and executed for witchcraft and devil worship. It was too easy for some crazed human to accuse women of signing covenants with the devil or eating babies—both preposterous notions. However, having wings or horns was a much easier target.

"So that's why the place is crawling with cops?" Guy said, looking from the police station to the café. "That makes sense."

"Detective Sawyer," called a young plain-clothed man. He jogged down the station's steps to meet a tall woman with dark curly hair exiting a royal blue Dodge Charger.

Mahogany studied Detective Sawyer. Unlike female detectives on television who ran after perps in stilettos, Sawyer wore sneakers with her sharply ironed work trousers. Immediately, Mahogany respected Sawyer for her sensible footwear. She gave her beloved turquoise boots a gentle dust before crossing the street.

"How are we going to find the evidence locker?" Guy asked as they casually walked up the street along the side of the station.

Low awning windows lined the building at street level. Two-foot-deep window wells surround each. Metal grating, designed to keep out vermin, was bolted over the wells.

Mahogany pulled her phone from her pocket and pretended to answer a text as she glanced past the phone to the window grates. "There's no way for me to get in there. It'll have to be you two," Mahogany said, her mouth barely moving. "Guy, I need you to pop inside and see what's in each room."

"I see," Guy said. He stepped up to the grate, sank into the room below, and reemerged a few seconds later.

"It's filled with filing cabinets."

They moved to the next window, which contained an empty office. The one after that was a break room.

"Last one on this side," Mahogany said, still pretending to play with her phone. They had reached the back corner of the building. An alley separated the station from the next building on the block.

Guy disappeared through the grate and returned moments later. "This is it!" Guy raised his hand for a high five. Mahogany frowned and rolled her eyes.

"Right. I'm not solid. Okay, boss, what's the plan?"

"Locate Magic Mike's evidence box and lead Bazgul to it with the port-o-hole," Mahogany said.

Guy frowned. "Poor Bazgul. He never learned to read? What a shame."

"Move. Let's get this over with before we attract attention," Mahogany said.

A woman carrying a baby stopped to stare briefly at the strange fuchsia-haired girl standing in the alley with a giant spider perched on her shoulder. She gripped the child to her chest and hurried up the street.

"Too late," Guy chimed and disappeared into the evidence locker. A few minutes later, he floated back through the wall.

"What took you so long? Did you find it?" Mahogany's impatient energy flushed her dark cheeks.

"Sorry. I found my box next to Magic Mike's." Only then did Mahogany notice that Guy's cheerful disposition had darkened—his narrow shoulders slumped, and the gleam vanished from his blue eyes.

A pit of empathy knotted in Mahogany's stomach. "I'm sorry. This can't be easy."

Guy nodded—his blue eyes fixed on a faraway point. "The box is in the middle row, bottom shelf. The only box without water damage."

Mahogany relayed the directions to Bazgul. "Do you understand?"

In response, Bazgul began shimmering. His body became translucent until it dissipated into a red-brown mist. The demon mist rose from Mahogany's shoulder and traveled through the grate, where he rematerialized on the other side. Mahogany crouched and passed a small, black fabric-like object through the grate. Bazgul took the scrap in his mandibles and crawled through the open window.

"I died early in my training and didn't get the chance to learn much about demons. Why a spider?" Guy asked, shaking himself from his introspection.

"Bazgul is a lesser demon and can take the shape of most small animals," Mahogany said, pretending to be on a phone call. "Spiders are his favorite because they freak out humans."

"What about being attached to a human? Demons rarely do that unless they possess them."

Mahogany shrugged. "Bazgul came to me when I was a baby. At least, that's the story Neema tells me. She came to get me from my crib and found me and Bazgul snuggled together. He's been by my side ever since."

The tinkling of Bazgul's claws on the window glass ended their conversation.

"Okay, team. Let's get home and see what's in that box," Mahogany said.

Chapter 6

Mahogany entered the kitchen and took the second port-o-hole from the envelope. She slapped the small circular object onto the kitchen island, and a small, black hole appeared in the granite countertop.

She reached into the hole, which expanded to accommodate her arm, and felt around. Frowning, she pulled her arm from the port-o-hole, holding an object sealed in a clear plastic evidence bag.

"A wallet?" Mahogany turned the bag over in her hands to read the label. "Guy Miller? Crap. Bazgul placed the port-o-hole on your box instead of Magic Mike's."

Mahogany turned to Guy, who stared wide-eyed at the wallet in her hands.

"Were both of your boxes next to each other?" A ball of irritation formed in Mahogany's chest.

Guy shook his head, bringing himself back to the present. "Uh, yeah, I guess so. I got distracted by having my life reduced to a single box in a police station basement." His voice had an acidic quality Mahogany didn't think he was capable of.

"Perfect. This day keeps getting better." Mahogany tossed the wallet back into the port-o-hole. A distant thud echoed through the hole as the wallet joined whatever else was in Guy's evidence box.

Neema breezed into the kitchen from the apothecary and headed straight for the steaming coffee shop on the counter. "Oh, I see you made it into the evidence locker." She glanced at the small, black hole in the countertop. She filled her mug and took a sip, eyeing Mahogany. "Isn't this a good thing? Why do you look as if someone danced over your grave?"

Mahogany sighed, narrowing her eyes at Guy. "The port-o-hole is on Guy's box, not Mike's."

"So flip it over and pull Mike's box through," Neema said with a shrug. "You've been using port-o-holes since you were a kid. Flipping one reverses the other. Instead of reaching into Guy's box, you'll reach out of it."

"That is clever." Guy moved to stand beside Mahogany as she scratched at the edge of the magical portal with her nerve-chewed index finger. She peeled it off the counter, flipped it with an irritated flourish, and slapped it back onto the granite.

Mahogany released a sigh that made Bazgul retreat to his cat tree and shoved both arms up to her shoulders into the elastic port-o-hole.

In the police evidence locker, two knit-covered arms appear from a black circle, no larger than a nickel, on the side of the white document box. The dot stretched, fitting snugly around the arms. They fumbled, searching blindly for Mike's evidence box. The unseeing hands grabbed hold of the first container they found and pulled it through the hole. Once the box had disappeared, the gap shrank to its original size, appearing as a small mark on the container's side.

Mahogany, Guy, and Neema stared at the cardboard container. Bazgul, having lost interest, gazed through the kitchen window as he perched on his cat tree, hungrily eyeing the neighbor cat as it sunned in a patch of morning light near Mahogany's Vespa.

"Now what?" Guy said, eyeing the red evidence tape securing the lid to the body of the box.

"Hang on," Neema said. She hurried from the kitchen to the living room. She returned after a few moments and held out a short, bone-handled knife with an onyx blade.

"I know what that is!" Guy said. "It's a spectare, which is Latin for observe or look at. It allows you to open all sorts of items and reseal them without detection." Guy puffed himself up as if he'd just answered the winning question on Jeopardy. "Historically, the spectare was a favorite object of fraudulent executives and suspicious spouses."

Mahogany took the spectare. "I was beginning to wonder if Magic Mike had taught you anything." She sliced through the tape and peered into the box. The bagged anelace lay across the top of the other items collected from the brownstone's crime scene. Dried blood crusted the sharp blade, making Mahogany's stomach roll.

"Well, that was easy." Mahogany lifted the jeweled dagger from the box, pushing down the queasy feeling. A chill from the icy blade seeped through the bag and into Mahogany's hand, and it ran up her arm, lodging in her heart. She gasped and dropped the anelace, where it clattered to the counter.

Neema frowned, a look of concern lining her smooth face. "What's wrong?"

"Something's wrong with the anelace." Mahogany shook her head, as if clearing a fog. The ache in her heart slowly dissipated.

Next to Mahogany, Guy swooned, his knees buckling.

"Are you all right?" Mahogany raised an eyebrow at Guy's fallen form.

"I think being close to the murder weapon is affecting me." Guy got to his feet, placed his hand through the evidence bag, and closed his eyes. His translucence form shimmed and took on a reddish hew. Black splotches appeared on his hands and face, pulsating and rippling. "The murderer felt a tremendous amount of rage. It left an imprint on the blade."

"Guy says the murderer tainted the anelace with their murdery rage," Mahogany said, filling Neema in. "That's a lot of bad juju." Mahogany rubbed her hand, which still ached, and hoped that whoever cursed the magical blade was long gone. She had no desire to have another run-in with them. Almost getting her skull cracked open with a fireplace poker was enough.

"Poor lamb." Neema removed a small brown vial from one of the kitchen cupboards. "Maybe the scent of chamomile will help calm his nerves." She opened the vial and placed it on the counter. "Inhale deeply," she said to the kitchen. "Wait, he can inhale, can't he?" she inquired, turning to Mahogany.

"Seems so," Mahogany said, watching as Guy stooped over the vial, puffing like a runner after a marathon.

Neema smiled at the space over the vial and turned to Mahogany. "We need to get started on the replica before anyone notices the box is missing."

"Gods, this is so much more work than just collecting relics from dead Folk. Where's the clay?" Mahogany eyed the anelace with suspicion.

"I have some in the storeroom," Neema said, heading back into the Haughty Hemlock. "Back in two shakes."

Beside her, Guy continued to huff the chamomile fumes.

"Better?" Mahogany asked, a speculative eyebrow raised.

"Much," Guy said. "I don't know if it's a placebo or if I can smell it, but I feel much more centered."

"Fantastic," Mahogany said, rolling her eyes. She peered back into the box so she wouldn't have to look at Guy. A flat, yellow envelope caught her attention. Curious, she read the label. "One photograph?"

"Photograph? What kind of photograph?" Guy stopped huffing and peered over Mahogany's shoulder. "Maybe it's a clue to solving my murder."

"The description says it was in Magic Mike's hand when the police found his body." Mahogany slit the envelope's seal with the spectare and slid out a glossy 4x6 black-and-white photograph of four individuals. Two had black Xs marking out their faces, while a third had their face circled. The last person's image remained untouched.

Mahogany frowned and moved the image to catch the light, hoping to reveal the faces beneath the Xs. She could just make out a woman with long, dark hair adorned with a crown of roses. The other was a young man wearing tea-shade spectacles and a short beard.

"That looks like Magic Mike," Guy said, pointing to the marked-out face of the bespectacled man with the beard. If he'd been able to breathe, he would have exhaled directly into Mahogany's face.

"How do you know?" Mahogany said, her gaze glued to the woman with her face circled. A white patch sprouted from the young woman's hairline, despite her youthful appearance.

"He always wore round glasses like that. It was his signature look." Guy shrugged. "His beard is shorter, and he's about fifty pounds lighter and twenty years younger, but that's Mike."

Mahogany had a similar notion about the woman with the white patch of hair. She was younger and thinner, but without a doubt, the woman was Neema.

Guy shifted his pointing finger from Mike. "She looks a lot like Neema. Except for the poliosis, it could be her twin."

"She dyes it," Mahogany said. "It's even in her eyebrow now."

"Wait, so that is Neema? If that circle means what I think it means, she's in danger."

"Unfortunately, I agree with you. It looks like whoever killed you and Magic Mike is after the people in his photograph."

"What about her?" Guy pointed to the woman with the flower crown and crossed our face. "Is she a murder victim, too? And her?" Guy jabbed a finger through the woman with the unmarred image.

"Maybe she's the murderer," Mahogany said.

"What do you think that says?" Guy pointed to the wall behind the figures.

Mahogany brought the photo close to her face and squinted. The letters H, S, and O peeked from between the group's shoulders and heads. "No idea. It could be anything."

Neema's footsteps echoed over Haughty Hemlock's hardwood floor as she returned to the kitchen. "Sorry, that took so long. I had quite forgotten where I put the clay."

Mahogany slipped the photo under the envelope and smiled. "That's all right."

Neema stopped in her tracks and squinted. "What's wrong with your face?" In front of her, Neema held a black trash bag in both hands. A clump of something heavy strained against the plastic.

"What do you mean?" Mahogany asked.

"You smiled. You never smile," Neema said.

"I do, too," Mahogany said, an edge in her voice.

Guy snorted. "No, you don't. You are the most unsmiling person I've ever met, and I'm from Columbus, Ohio."

Mahogany glared at Guy. "I am not unsmiling."

Neema hefted the trash bag on the counter with a grunt. "Gloves!" She snapped her fingers. "I nearly forgot. Be right back."

As Neema's ample rear disappeared through the doorway, Mahogany slid the photo out from under the envelope and snapped a picture with her phone. She shoved the image back into the envelope with shaking hands, resealed the tape with the spectare, and tossed it into the evidence box.

"Here we go," Neema said, reemerging from the apothecary. She handed Mahogany a pair of surgical gloves. "Let's get started before it gets late." She put on the gloves and opened the garbage bag. Neema ripped off a sizable chunk of gray clay. "That ought to be enough." She held the clump out to Mahogany.

Mahogany took the clay and began kneading it on the countertop while she studied the shape of the anelace.

"I don't get it," Guy said. "It's just clay."

"It's replica clay. It has the magical ability to create exact replicas. A replica created with this magical clay could even undergo carbon dating and match the actual object." Mahogany rolled the clay into a cylinder, matching the anelace's length.

The bell over the door of the shop jangled. "Duty calls," Neema said, snapping off her gloves and tossing them on the kitchen island. "Use tongs to get that thing out of the bag." She motioned to the murder weapon. "It's far too nasty to touch." Neema disappeared into the apothecary. "Welcome to the Haughty Hemlock. How can I help you?"

Mahogany grabbed the silicone-tipped tongs from an earthenware jar near the stove and used them to pull the dagger from the evidence bag.

She began with the hilt, sculpting each jewel until the clay anelace matched the original in shape and size.

"Impressive," Guy said, admiring the sculpture.

"I got an A in art."

Guy smirked, but Mahogany's stony visage remained deadpan. He rolled his eyes. "Now what?"

"We wait," Mahogany said. "In a few hours, the clay will set, and it'll take on all the properties of the original; color, texture, weight."

"Blood?" Guy said, his lip raising in a sneer.

"Yes," Mahogany said, her eyes drifting to the macabre stain. "Even the blood."

The bell over the apothecary door jingled again. "Mahogany, dear, can you please come and assist me?" Neema called through the doorway.

"Coming." Mahogany pulled off the gloves. The fingers of one caught the tacky clay blade. The force pulled the drying clay toward the edge of the counter, where it slipped toward the floor. Instinctively, Mahogany caught the clay dagger and carefully placed it back on the counter.

"That was close," Guy said.

Mahogany nodded, her heart hammering in her chest. "Too close." She tossed the used gloves into the garbage and headed into the Haughty Hemlock.

An hour later, Mahogany admired her handy work. The replica had set and was the exact likeness of the medieval anelace.

"Fascinating," Guy said. "If it weren't for the blood lust singing from the real blade, I wouldn't be able to tell them apart."

"That's the plan." Mahogany picked up the replica, sealed it in the evidence bag, and placed it back in the document box.

⸻ ⚘ ⸻

Across town, Pandemonium's newest detective, Teresa Sawyer, entered the evidence locker and approached the spot where she had placed the evidence boxes connected to the brownstone murders. However, the one she needed wasn't there.

The detective sighed deeply and returned to the clerk, muttering under her breath about the lax procedure of small-town police.

In the cozy kitchen connected to the Haughty Hemlock, Mahogany maneuvered the sealed document box back through the port-o-hole. A heartbeat later, a small, unassuming blotch on the box labeled Guy Miller stretched wide, and Magic Mike's missing evidence appeared through the growing hole. Two hands gripped the handholds on either side of the box and placed it on the shelf before disappearing. The hole once again retook its unassuming posture just as the clerk and the detective returned.

"Do you mean this box?" the clerk asked, pointing to a container set askew with the others.

"Are we the only people here?" Detective Sawyer gave the locker a scrutinizing glance.

The clerk nodded; one eyebrow cocked high on his forehead. "Yes, detective."

Sawyer frowned. "I'm sorry for the mistake."

The clerk took his leave, and the detective cut the tape and placed a bagged SLR camera into the box.

Chapter 7

Mahogany entered Hot Brews. The scent of intoxicating baked goods and steamy coffee lulled her nerves. She ordered an iced chai and sat pondering her predicament with Guy. The squeal of steaming milk and snippets of partially overheard conversations drowned the spiraling thoughts in her racing mind, and she zoned out. When Evelina took an empty seat at the table when her shift ended, Mahogany jumped.

"Lost in thought?"

"Maybe a little," Mahogany said and rolled her anxiety-stiff shoulders.

"How's your cute ghost?" Evelina asked, glancing at the table's empty chair.

"He's not mine, and he's not cute," Mahogany answered. She took a noisy sip of her chai. The sharp spicy flavor hitched in the back of her throat and she almost coughed. The half-melted ice clinked softly against the glass.

"Hey! I am too cute. I had had several dates with a beautiful young lady from here before my murder, by the way. Karrie Samuels. Do you know her? Her brother hated me," Guy said. He stared pensively into the distance, his eyes misting over. "Karrie might have been the one."

Mahogany buried her face in her hands and groaned. "Of all the women in Pandemonium, you had to choose Jeff Samuels's little sister. He's probably the person who murdered you." She shook her head. "Jeff's a complete psycho."

"This is worse than I thought." Evelina pressed her bow-shaped lips into a line. "I can see I did the right thing in poking around."

"Poking around what?" Mahogany said from behind her hands.

"I did some research on how to get rid of ghosts. There are two principal ways to send murdered apparitions on their way." Evelina shifted in her seat to better face Mahogany.

In the empty seat, Guy perked up, a worried frown pulled his eyebrows together. "I'm not sure I like the sound of this," he said and turned his attention to Evelina.

"I'm listening." Mahogany peeked through her fingers.

"The first is banishment, which doesn't send them to the other side but dissipates their soul through the cosmos." Evelina made a poofing motion with her hands as if she were a magician making a rabbit vanish into her hat.

Guy's mouth dropped open, and what little color his pasty, translucent skin held drained from his face. "Pump the brakes, Blondy," he said, holding his hands up in front of him.

"Tempting." Mahogany glared at Guy from behind her fingers.

"That method," Evelina continued, "takes a year to complete."

"A year?" Mahogany almost shouted, slapping her hands on the table. Several customers glanced in their direction.

Guy smirked ruefully and crossed his arms.

"What's the other way?" Mahogany managed through gritted teeth.

Evelina scrunched her face apologetically. "Solve the ghost's murder."

"Ha," Guy barked and attempted to slam his hand on the table, but it went right through it. He tipped forward, losing his balance. "I've been saying that since day one," he said, recovering.

Mahogany shook her head, pink curls bouncing. "I don't know the first thing about solving murders."

"Sure, you do," Evelina said, giving Mahogany a soft shove on the shoulder. "We watched all those detective shows as kids. We're already armchair mystery-solving pros. All we need to do is translate what TV has taught us into real life."

"We?" Mahogany raised an eyebrow. She had a distinct memory of sneaking away from the city council meetings Neema used to drag her to as a child. They were usually held in one of the resident's homes. Mahogany was always quick to sneak away and find the nearest television, settling into whatever prime-time mystery was on air. She also remembered these whodunnit soirees as solo missions. "You were there?"

Evelina nodded. "I followed you." She tapped her lip, her eyes distant. "All this time, I figured you knew I was there."

Mahogany silently considered Evelina's words. "No, I hadn't realized. Did we ever talk?" The notion that her covert sojourns hadn't been all that secret floored her.

"Well, yes, and no. I wanted to see what you were doing, so I followed you. You were more interesting than the other kids at those boring council meetings." Evelina brushed the words away like they were obvious.

"Well, thank you for the offer, but this is my problem. I can take care of it on my own," Mahogany said, her head reeling. She'd never known that Evelina found her interesting. Most of the kids in Pandemonium had bullied her, following the lead of their parents, who saw humans as lesser than magical folk.

Evelina crossed her arms. Her eyebrows arched high on her forehead, and her bow-shaped mouth puckered. "There is no way I'll let you do this alone. It's way too massive. An out-of-town wizard and his apprentice get murdered at a rental in Pandemonium, and my best friend almost gets killed as collateral damage?" She shook her head. "No way. I'm in for the long haul."

Mahogany wanted to ask what else Evelina had learned about the case, but the phrase 'best friend' had thrown her. She didn't consider anyone a friend, much less a best friend. She could certainly do worse than Evelina. Something hard shifted in Mahogany's chest as she regarded the pretty blonde Fae. She could use her help, but that would mean group work, and Mahogany had always hated team sports.

"Still." She shook her head, frowning. "I don't want to drag you into my problems."

Guy snorted. "Problems? I'm the one with the problem. Dead before my time—the love of my life was ripped away. My chance to be a great wizard snuffed out before it began." He folded his thin arms over his hollow chest and frowned at Mahogany, blue eyes liquid with emotion.

"You don't have to drag me into anything. I'm coming with you because I want to." Evelina placed a warm, perfectly manicured hand over Mahogany's nervous-chewed fingers.

"Why? Why don't you treat me like everyone else?" The warmth of Evelina's hand seeped into Mahogany's fingers, sending a tingling sensation through her arm to her chest. It was the polar opposite of what the cursed anelace had done.

Evelina blinked at Mahogany, her expression blank. "I like you. I always have. Plus, I'm a nonconformist. I don't care about the opinions of others. Also, if you bothered to notice, our generation doesn't fall in step with the older Folk. When we were kids, people bullied you, and now you expect the same treatment, but that's not the case." She smoothed her luscious blond hair out of her face and nodded to the counter. "On a lighter note, have you met the new guy?"

Mahogany stared at Evelina, at a loss for words. Had she been walking around for the last fifteen years, imagining no one liked her?

"New guy?" Mahogany said, happy to change the subject. She followed Evelina's gaze. The man she'd bumped into as she'd left Hot Brews that morning stood at the counter ordering hot cocoa. He wore his dark hair cropped short. A well-fitting pair of jeans and a t-shirt sporting The Animals' album cover, *House of the Rising Sun*, promised a toned body beneath. The new guy turned, his hazel gaze found Mahogany, and he smiled. A deep dimple pierced one of his golden cheeks.

That hooking sensation from early ignited in Mahogany's chest, pulling her towards him. She tried to smile back, but found her cheeks numb and unresponsive. An electric zing ran down her spine, making her head buzz, and warmth filled her belly in an explosion of nervous butterflies.

"I bumped into him this morning," Mahogany said, her voice far away.

"His name is Tony," Evelina said. "He just moved to town. Beautiful, isn't he?" She raised her hand and waved. Tony nodded with an amiable smile, grabbed his order, and headed over to join Evelina and Mahogany.

"Tony, this is my friend, Mahogany. Mahogany, this is Tony. He works over at Backmasking Records." Evelina gestured to Tony, who locked eyes with Mahogany, making her stomach tingle. The tug of the hook increased, making Mahogany's eyes water. Then, as soon as it began, the tug disappeared, leaving a tender spot behind.

"We've met, sort of," Tony said, pulling the chair out that Guy occupied. "How was your smoothie?"

Still acclimating to his spectral form, Guy floated momentarily before falling to the ground.

Tony sat and a sneakered foot poked into Guy's back. Guy giggled and shifted away from Tony's intruding foot.

"Did the air just kick on?" Tony peered under the table, frowning. "My ankles are catching a draft."

Evelina smiled and mouthed "ghost" to Mahogany, who shook her head slightly.

"There's probably a vent pointed at us," Evelina said, covering for Guy's ghostly chill. "My feet just got cold too."

Tony scooted his chair under the table and took a sip of his cocoa with a frown. "Where's your spider?"

"Um, Bazgul's at home napping. It's been an interesting few days." Mahogany managed, her cheeks still numb.

Bazgul chose that moment to materialize in a puff of red-brown vapor on Mahogany's lap. She gave a tiny yelp of surprise and took a quick drink of her chai to cover her shock. Bazgul had never appeared without being summoned before.

Evelina's gaze dropped below the table and landed on Bazgul, her eyes growing wide.

"I've never seen a *Brachypelma smithi* get that large before," Tony said.

Startled, Mahogany glanced at Tony. Evelina was right. He was beautiful.

"Bachy-what?" Evelina said, prizing her gaze off Bazgul.

"It's the, uh, Latin name for, um, orange-kneed tarantulas." In Mahogany's lap, Bazgul's weight condensed, followed by something damp seeping through her leggings.

"Oh," Evelina gasped. She sat back, a sly grin pulled at the corners of her mouth. "That's interesting. Do you know the Latin name for a South American bullfrog?"

Tony shook his head and turned to Mahogany. "I have a few tarantulas at home. You should check them out sometime."

The wet patch expanded, and she was sure Bazgul had just peed on her. "Sure." The spot in her chest where the hook had imbedded surged with pain before disappearing again. "That would be great," she croaked, trying to sound nonchalant.

Chapter 8

Detective Teresa Sawyer regarded Agalia Sorrowsong. The museum curator was of indeterminate age, but if the detective had to guess, she would say the woman was in her early sixties, give or take ten years in either direction. Agalia's hair was the color of ash lined with silver that sparkled in the cramped office's single, incandescent bulb. Soft lines branched from the outside corners of her eyes, and the barest hint of laugh lines creased the sides of her mouth. Beyond that, her skin was flawless.

Sawyer sat opposite Agalia in an uncomfortable chair. A large desk stood between the detective and the curator, piled high with papers. She'd toured the museum earlier as she waited for Agalia to finish a phone call. The collection contained a wonderful display of artifacts dating back to prehistory, long before the Spanish had arrived in the New World. Contemporary art created by local artists also graced the walls and display cases.

Agalia held a photograph of a gilded short sword taken by the crime scene unit. "It's called an anelace," Agalia said, returning the photo to the detective. "They were popular with the English gentry in the late medieval era. It appears to be a beautiful specimen. Where did you say you found it?"

"It's part of a murder investigation," Sawyer said. She took the photo and placed it in an inside pocket of her blazer. When she'd transferred to Pandemonium, she had hoped to turn down the volume on her career. The grind of murders, sexual assaults, kidnappings, missing children, and gangs had taken their toll on the detective's health. After fifteen years on the force, she started having panic attacks. Yet, unwilling to throw her career away for more gentil work, she put in for a transfer to a small town. She crossed her fingers that this murder was a one-off and not something that would be a regular occurrence.

"Oh, dear," Agalia said, her eyes widening. "I expect you're referring to the murder the other night?" She shook her head and clicked her tongue. "The town used to be so safe. Things like that don't happen here. Do you have any leads?"

Sawyer didn't respond to the curator's inquiry and left the question hanging between them. "Have you ever run across a weapon like it before?"

Agalia nodded. "You don't work as a curator for as long as I have without seeing your fair share of deadly antiquities." She sat back in her chair. "Someone once imported a Renaissance-era cannon as a means of home protection. Set the darn thing up on their lawn. You can imagine how that went."

The detective raised an eyebrow but said nothing.

"You're new here," Agalia continued, "but I'm sure you're well aware of the eccentricities of Pandemonium's residences. A piece like this is a dime a dozen around here. Although, most of them are replicas." She nodded to the detective's coat. "I'd wager that is a genuine artifact. The provenance might be traceable."

Sawyer thought about Pandemonium's reputation as 'Halloween Town' and its strange denizens. Being from Southern California, she'd encountered her fair share of freaky people, but this place took the cake. Most of the population dressed like fairy tale creatures, roaming the streets like it was the scariest holiday all year long.

"Provenance?"

A polite smile crested Agalia's thin lips as she took the tone one might employ when speaking to a child. "The line of ownership. We have impressive archives in the basement filled with ownership documents on pieces like your murder weapon."

Detective Sawyer raised an eyebrow. "I never said it was the murder weapon."

Agalia raised her hands defensibly. "Let's not play coy, detective. What other reason would you have to inquire about the anelace if it wasn't attached to a crime?"

Sawyer returned Agalia's prim smile and matched her condescending tone. "You'd be surprised." She stood. Her legs and low back thanked her for abandoning the horrible chair. "I will be in touch about searching your archives if necessary." She held out her hand, and Agalia took it.

"Of course, detective. Call again anytime," Agalia said, inclining her head in a parting nod.

As she exited, Sawyer almost tripped over Mahogany, who waited just outside the office.

In the hallway, Mahogany examined the frayed cuticles of her left hand and chew-reddened fingertips. She might need to invest in some of that nasty-tasting nail polish if her stress level stayed at this level.

"Did you know this place has dinosaur fossils? Like big ones?" Guy's lanky figure seeped through the wall in the hallway inches from Mahogany. At that same moment, Detective Sawyer exited Agalia's office, and the obnoxious apparition and steely crime solver collided.

Guy giggled as if a brood of puppies licked his toes. Inversely, Teresa Sawyer gasped and shivered slightly, her eyes wide.

"You all right?" Mahogany asked. Against her thigh, the anelace sang—the vibrations telegraphing through her bones. The sensation reminded Mahogany of the tattoo she'd received on her shoulder. The rapid-fire needle had sent shocks through her shoulder blade and down her arm.

"I'm fine," Guy said. He turned to look at the detective. "I like her. I've passed through hundreds of people in the last few days, and none felt like that."

Mahogany suppressed the urge to gag and did her best to divert her eyes from Guy's unwelcome presence.

Detective Sawyer shook her head. A rosy blush colored her olive complexion. "Just a cold spot. It's gone now."

Mahogany feigned interest. "Old buildings, am I right?"

The detective glanced down the hallway before she locked her gaze on Mahogany. "You must be Mahogany, the curator's assistant."

"That's me," Mahogany said. She forced her hand outward and offered it to the detective. She hoped the movement appeared natural.

"Mahogany, what?" the detective asked as they shook.

"Pardon?" Mahogany asked. She released the detective's hand and resisted the urge to wipe her sweaty palm on her leggings.

"Your last name?" The detective said. She leaned toward Mahogany, her gaze intent.

"Oh, I don't have one," Mahogany said. "My adoptive mother doesn't believe in them."

Sawyer's face pulled together in a severe frown. "What does it say on your birth certificate?"

Mahogany's heart picked up speed. A trickle of sweat slid down her side. "Lost in a house fire."

"Why didn't she order another one?" The detective stepped closer to Mahogany. Her breath smelled of cinnamon.

"We tried, but the city hall with the hard copy lost all of its older documents in a flood."

"That's a lot of natural disasters. Was the flood around here?" Sawyer reached into the inside pocket of her blazer and pulled out a small notebook and a pen.

"No. Massachusetts. Outside of Boston. I don't remember the name of the city. We moved here when I was an infant." The tote bag slid back on Mahogany's thigh as she leaned away from Sawyer. The anelace left a static tingle as it traveled across her hip.

Sawyer's pen scratched at the pad. Mahogany imagined the sound resembled a person clawing to escape a sealed coffin. When she'd finished her notes, Sawyer snapped the pad shut with a deft flick of her wrist.

"Here's my card. I'm new to Pandemonium, and it's good to get to know people who might help me navigate the area," Sawyer said, trading her pen and pad for a business card.

"Sure thing," Mahogany said, taking the card. Sweat gathered between her shoulder blades.

Sawyer leaned back, her intense gaze softening at the edges. "What's in the bag?" She nodded to the tote on Mahogany's shoulder.

"Are you always this nosy?" Mahogany said.

The detective smiled. "Occupational hazard. Sorry."

"It was nice to meet you, Detective Sawyer, but I have business with Agalia." She stepped around the detective and stood on the threshold of Agalia's office while Sawyer's keen eyes tracked her.

"Of course. Nice to meet you, too." Sawyer took two steps toward the gallery and then stopped. "One last thing. You probably heard about the murders the other night."

Mahogany nodded. "It's a small town."

"Did you know the victims?"

"I didn't. The brownstones are rentals. They're pretty busy in the summer with all the tourists. Pandemonium is great for travelers because it's a hub to the beach, wineries, and woodland hiking," Mahogany said. "Plus, we have that playful Halloween vibe."

More words had come out of her mouth in the last five minutes than had all week. The sweat gathering along her spine trickled south, hitting the waistband of her pants.

"Yeah, I've noticed the constant LARPing. What's that all about?"

Mahogany gave a noncommittal shrug. "Just keeping the Pacific Northwest weird."

Pandemonium had received its Halloween Town moniker decades earlier. Large amounts of what humans perceived as people in perpetual costumes were indeed Folk living without hiding their true forms. If a tourist ran into what appeared to be a goth with fangs, they had better wear a turtleneck and eat copious amounts of garlic because they were looking at a real, blood-sucking vampire.

"Hmm," Sawyers said with a slight nod and took her leave.

"Wow. She's intense," Guy said. "Why don't you have a last name?" He followed Mahogany into Agalia's office.

Inside the office, the sweet smell of flowers grew more pungent, only now they carried a sour odor of decay.

"That took longer than expected," Agalia said. Instead of looking at Mahogany, the curator shuffled through papers on her desk. "I needn't remind you that you are still on probation."

The surrounding room expanded, growing twice its size. The hard, wooden chair the detective couldn't wait to vacate transformed into a plump armchair welcoming Mahogany to take a seat. She resisted the urge and trained her eyes on Agalia.

"There were complications, but everything's sorted now." Mahogany took the tote from her shoulder and placed it on a stack of files on Agalia's desk.

Agalia waved her hand in the air. "Complications followed Magoris. I guess you're hardly to blame." Agalia found what she searched for in the pile of papers and handed a sheet to Mahogany. "For services rendered."

Mahogany took the pay stub and the attached check. "You knew Magoris?"

"Everyone in the magical community knew Magoris by reputation," Agalia said, casting a withering glance at Mahogany.

"I hadn't heard of him," Mahogany said. She folded the check and placed it in the waistband of her leggings.

Agalia's eyes blinked rapidly, a cheerless smile frozen on her lips. "That's not surprising," she said. "You didn't receive a proper magical education, being human."

Mahogany nodded, trying to ignore the slice of Agalia's words. "What was his reputation?" She knew Agalia couldn't resist showing off what she knew, especially to a lowly human.

"Well," Agalia began, leaning back. The designer office chair gave a smooth exhale. "Magoris was top of his caliber and showed a lot of promise from an early age, then the scandal occurred."

"Scandal?" Mahogany said.

"What scandal?" Guy asked from behind Mahogany.

"I don't like to gossip or speak ill of the dead," Agalia said.

Mahogany stifled a snort, failed, and coughed to cover her blunder.

Agalia raised an eyebrow and leaned forward, lowering her voice. "When he was in his early twenties, a close friend died of mysterious causes. Many thought he'd helped cover up her murder, but neither the Guild nor the police could prove anything." She shrugged. "The inquiries stopped, and Magoris went off the grid."

"That might explain why we traveled so much," Guy said.

Mahogany's thoughts drifted to the photograph containing both Neema and Magic Mike. Was Neema part of the scandal?

"Thanks for the check," Mahogany said, turning toward the door.

"Thank you for gathering everything. I assume the list is complete?" Agalia lifted the tote bag with a grunt and examined the contents.

"Yep," Mahogany said over her shoulder. "Magoris was murdered with the anelace."

"I suspected as much. It explains why the detective is so interested in it." Agalia reached for the anelace and stopped. "Oh, I see. That's a powerful curse. I'll have it purified." She dropped the tote on the floor behind her desk and returned to shuffling papers.

Chapter 9

The blare of Mahogany's alarm startled her awake. She fumbled with the clock for a moment before the insistent beeping quieted. She fell back to the pillow, heart pounding against her ribcage. The near-erotic dream lingered in her consciousness, becoming fuzzy around the edges.

She and Tony had sat together on a bench in Seelie Park. The air was so thick with butterflies that it appeared like a field of flowers had taken flight. Their fragile bodies bumped and glided on beams of the setting sun scented with the blush of jasmine blossoms.

Tony turned to her, his hazel eyes sparkling in the fading summer light. He placed a golden hand on Mahogany's umber cheek and pulled her in for a kiss. As their lips touched, a thrill ran through her, making her toes curl. Her breath caught in her throat, and she pressed herself into his warm frame. Tony took his free hand, grabbed Mahogany's waist, and pulled her into him until she couldn't tell where he ended, and she began.

She repositioned herself, wrapping her legs around Tony's waist. His mouth moved from her lips to her neck, kissing and love-biting, causing Mahogany to gasp in pain and excitement. How long had it been since another being had touched her like this, touched her at all?

Tony pulled back. His finger nimbly slipped the buttons on her blouse. The evening breeze caught Mahogany's neck and chilled the area where Tony had left his mark. She closed her eyes, relishing the glow of the moment.

The dream played in her mind like a film slowly exposed to the light, fading until only a ghost of an image remained. Mahogany swiped a hand over her face, wiping the sleep from her eyes. Next to her on the pillow, a very toad-like Bazgul hunkered, the soft purr of a contented snore drifted into her ear. A puddle smelling of ripe pond water dampened the pillowcase beneath him, wetting Mahogany's neck.

"Good morning, sunshine," Guy said as he materialized through her bedroom door. His radiant smile froze on his face when his gaze fell on Mahogany's bed. "That must have been some dream. You're completely tangled in your blankets," he said. "By the way, what's up with Bazgul?"

Mahogany gazed down. Indeed, the blankets were in a kerfuffle around her legs. "Guy," she said, scrubbing her eyes with the heel of her hand, "what's the rule?"

Guy's gaze fell to the floor. "Never float through a closed door without permission. My apologies."

Mahogany scrambled out of the covers. "Well?"

"I'll just go then." Guy pointed over his shoulder at the bedroom door.

"Great." It had been three days since Guy's murder, and Mahogany found adjusting to his chipper presence challenging. She needed to have at least one cup of coffee before engaging in chitchat, and several more before she could feign happiness.

Guy floated back into the hallway. "There's coffee when you're ready," he called. Mahogany's bedroom wall, muffling his voice.

Mahogany sighed but didn't respond. She opened the closet and shuffled through her clothes, irritated by everything she saw. With another heavy breath, she settled on a pair of dark leggings, a sweater tank top, and a loose belt. She then headed to the bathroom to wrangle her kinky hair into submission.

With an appraising look in the mirror, Mahogany straightened her pentagram charm and headed downstairs. The loving scent of coffee greeted her as she entered the kitchen. She beelined to the steaming carafe and filled the waiting mug on the counter.

"So," Guy said, startling a yelp out of Mahogany. "I thought we could go check out the wishing well by the old beach road."

"Did you?" Mahogany said, delivering enough milk into her coffee to bleach it tan.

"Since my brief stay in Pandemonium as a living person didn't allow me to see the sights, I thought you could be my guide," Guy said, his tone chipper. "After all, where you go, I go."

A small pit of resentment formed in Mahogany's chest. Biting back a comment, she heaped an amount of sugar into her mug sufficient to make a hummingbird fall into a diabetic coma. She studied Guy with a measured expression as she stirred the light, sweet substance.

"If you don't like the wishing well, we could check out the stone circle or the cemetery. Maybe there are other ghosts there?" Guy smiled, but Mahogany didn't see any warmth in it.

She sipped her milk-cooled coffee and remained silent.

"If I could go alone, I would, but there's that pesky thing about me being your ghost and all." Guy's smile raised his cheeks a little further.

"I'm well aware of the proximity issue." Mahogany thought about all the times she'd tried to ditch Guy. Each time, he'd snapped back to her like a leashed dog.

"What do you say? Wishing well, cemetery, or ancient stone circle? I'm also open to suggestions."

"I have a better idea." Mahogany threw her head back and gulped the mug's contents in one go.

"What's that?" Guy asked, a frown creasing his pale forehead.

Mahogany slammed the empty mug onto the counter like an old west gunslinger preparing for battle. "We're going to solve your murder."

Guy gave a wide grin and clapped his hands. "Yeah!"

She strode over to where her trusty turquoise boots waited and shoved her feet into them with renewed purpose. Guy needed to be sent to wherever the afterlife intended for him—some place far from here where he could boar undead wizards with his inane conversations.

From the corner of her eye, Mahogany glimpsed Neema in the living room at the writing desk. She placed a crumpled envelope in one of the desk's small drawers before locking it with a skeleton key.

"Good morning," Mahogany said.

Neema jumped and shoved the key deep into her dress pocket. "I didn't hear you," she said in a breathless voice, a blush creeping up her neck.

"Sorry." Mahogany stared at Neema, trying to work out the last time she'd seen her blush, and came up empty.

Neema looked at her bare wrist. "Gods, is that the time? I have so much to do before I open the store." She rushed through the kitchen and into Haughty Hemlock.

"Well, that was weird," Mahogany said, shooting the writing desk an intrigued glance, her lips pursed.

"What's she got locked in there?" Guy folded his ghostly arms over his chest.

"I know one way to find out." Mahogany copied Guy's stance and glanced from him to the desk.

"How's that?" Guy's forehead puckered, and he raised a speculative eyebrow.

Mahogany nodded from Guy to the desk. When Guy still didn't pick up on what she was putting down, Mahogany threw her hands into the air. "You're impossible." She left Guy standing in the kitchen, tiptoed into the living room, and examined the drawer.

In her haste, Neema hadn't entirely deposited the envelope into the drawer. One white corner poked from the gap where the drawer fitted into the desk.

Mahogany peered over her shoulder. From where she stood, she could see the stairway leading from the kitchen to the bedrooms, but little else. Neema hummed tunelessly in the apothecary, and jars clinked as she readied the store for opening. Seizing the moment, Mahogany grabbed the envelope's corner and shifted it from side to side, maneuvering it out between the gap.

"Oh, I see what you mean," Guy said, joining Mahogany at the desk. "You want me to look inside the drawer?"

Mahogany had eased the envelope halfway out. A pink rose stamp adored the top right corner with a postmark from Pandemonium's post office. She could make out half an address written in unfamiliar blocky lettering.

The kitchen floor groaned, freezing Mahogany in place—the envelope gripped tight in her perspiring hands. Neema's heels clicked across the kitchen tile. A cabinet creaked, followed by the clink of a ceramic mug as Neema set it on the counter and began filling it with coffee. Mahogany held her breath until the Neema clicked her way back into the store.

"Close calls love you," Guy said. "You better hurry."

"Thanks for the pro tip." Mahogany yanked hard, praying to the gods that the paper wouldn't rip. The deities on high must have found this little game of cat and mouse interesting because the envelope slipped free a second later.

Mahogany glanced at the foreign handwriting, while Guy peered over her shoulder.

"That's the brownstone's address," Guy said. "Why in the world would Neema have this?"

Deep furrows lined Mahogany's forehead. "She must have taken it when we collected the relics. Do you recognize who it's from?"

Guy read the return address. "Thaddeus Spike? Never heard of him."

"There's a reason Neema took this. We just need to figure out why, but first, we have another task."

"What's that?"

"Do you like libraries?" Mahogany asked. She tip-toed back into the kitchen and grabbed her backpack and slipped the envelope into her pocket. "Pandemonium has one of Oregon's premier libraries."

"Oh, I love libraries!" Guy said and clapped his hands like a child at a birthday party when it was time for cake.

"Then you're in for a treat." She headed for the door, giving Bazgul's cat tree a cursory glance. She hadn't seen the giant spider since she'd woken up. Mahogany frowned, exiting the house before Neema could put her to work.

Chapter 10

"This is one of Oregon's premier libraries?" The disappointment in Guy's voice brought a modicum of pleasure to Mahogany. "It's so small and ugly."

The library stood squat and unimpressive against the rest of Pandemonium's low, exotic skyline. Red brick and spray stucco, painted in a dull shade of gray that was as close to a non-color as paint could get, made up the library's exterior. The building was at odds with the more ornate constructions keeping it company on the block. It would seem the city's planning council viewed librarianship as a utilitarian function, replacing the Corinthian columns of Joseph Carnegie's legacy with what could only be called '1970s shoe factory chic.'

"Don't be so hard on the old place. Sure, it looks like it comes from off-the-rack blueprints, but it's what's inside that counts," Mahogany said, killing the Vespa's engine. She'd parked the yellow scooter next to a show-stopping cherry-red Harley.

"Well, the bike's nice, at least," Guy said. He patted the Vespa's seat. "Don't worry, little buddy. Maybe you'll grow up to be a Harley, too."

Mahogany gave an irritated grunt and headed toward the library's smoky glass doors. They slid open with an electric swoosh, and a surge of cool air rolled out to greet them.

A few parents browsed the children's section with toddlers in strollers or carriers, but other than that, the library remained quiet. Mahogany headed straight to the oversized, semi-circular reference desk at the library's center, with Guy in tow.

"Good morning," Priscilla Wembley said. Priscilla, Pandemonium's librarian, wore her electric blue hair spiked about her head in a tight pixie cut. Her form-fitting black leather pants and a fashionable red jacket would have been more at home on the set of an action movie than in a place of learning. Inked on her neck was a tattoo of a skull with crochet hooks crossed below it, followed by the phrase, "Hooker for life." Despite being of the werewolf persuasion, Priscilla was less fierce than others of her ilk.

Guy gave a low whistle. "Well, I guess we know whose Harley that is outside."

"Hi, Priscilla. I have a strange request." Mahogany held her phone with the image she'd taken of the photo from the evidence locker. "If I wanted to learn more about this photo, how would I do that?"

Priscilla took Mahogany's phone and studied the image. "Do you know anything about it?" she asked.

"It might be from the Boston area about twenty years ago," Mahogany said. "The boy in the photo is Magoris Idrus." Mahogany pointed to Magic Mike's crossed-out face.

Priscilla handed the phone back to Mahogany. "Well, there can't be too many magical Folk who share the same name as the murdered wizard from the other night." She gave Mahogany a knowing look. "Let's see what a general search digs up." She tapped away at her computer keyboard and scrolled through the returned hits.

Mahogany glanced around the library as she waited. Thick wooden beams ran from the ceiling to the floor, creating a vast colonnade. Low bookshelves sat between the beams, allowing a full interior view. Several tables lined with computers took up the back half of the library. Comfy chairs and boxes of toys cluttered the children's area near the front of the space.

"I would ask how the new job is going, but I think I know the answer," she said without taking her eyes from the monitor.

Mahogany smiled. "It's been interesting." A flash of light reflected off a picture frame behind the reference desk caught Mahogany's eye. A young girl flanked by a man and a woman adorned with matching hats beamed. The snowy landscape and their cold-blushed cheeks told of a fun winter's day.

"Is that you?" Mahogany asked, and nodded to the picture.

Priscilla turned to the photo. "Yes. Every year we'd go out to Mount Hood and play in the snow. Sometimes they'd take me out of school early. It always felt like we were breaking the rules."

A tinge of sadness at the thought of all the winter trips she'd missed with her family made Mahogany's chest ache. Whenever the holidays came, she wondered what her family's traditions might be; did they do all the regular human things like carve turkeys, hang stockings, or trick-or-treat? She feigned a cough, trying to relieve the ache.

Priscilla turned back to the computer screen, a slight smile lifting the corners of her mouth. "Well, here's something interesting," she said. "That was way too easy."

"What?" Mahogany leaned over the tall counter to peer at the screen.

Priscilla waved Mahogany to join her behind the desk. Mahogany crouched next to Priscilla to better see the monitor. Mahogany could feel the warmth radiating off the librarian, even through her leather jacket. Werewolves always ran hotter than other Folk.

An article archived from a newspaper in Boston showed the same photograph as the one in evidence. Next to the image, the story read: Mysterious Accident Leaves Local Teen Dead, Friends Questioned.

The article mention Magic Mike was along with Kassandra Frost, Aurora Kingsley, Thaddeus Spike, and Dorcia Frost.

"Thaddeus Spike. That's the name on the envelope," Guy said over her shoulder. "And I bet Kassandra and Dorcia Frost are relatives. Maybe sisters? Cousins? But which one's Neema, and why did she change her name?"

"Can you print this out for me?" Mahogany asked, contemplating the same questions Guy had posed.

"Absolutely," Priscilla said. She tapped at the keyboard, and a large printer near the desk hummed.

"Now, where to?" Guy asked as they exited the library.

Mahogany slipped the helmet over her head. "If we're going to solve this, I need to know what you and Magic Mike did while in town."

"He didn't let me out much. I spent most of my time planning for the binding spell," Guy said with a shrug.

"What about Karrie? Where did you meet her if you didn't get out much?" Mahogany turned the key, and the Vespa hummed to life.

"We met outside the brownstone. She was walking her dog." Guy took a seat behind Mahogany. "We'd sneak away; me to avoid Mike and her to avoid her brother."

"Any idea where Mike got up to?" Mahogany said, ignoring the softening of her heart at Guy's secret romance. Her mind tickled at the steamy Tony dream, and a blush warmed her cheeks.

"I'm not sure where he disappeared, but he usually smelled of cider and fried food," Guy said.

"I know just the place," Mahogany said, pulling the Vespa out of the library parking lot.

Chapter 11

Mahogany navigated her Vespa into a parking space outside Tipsy O'Lush's.

"This is where Magic Mike spent his last days?" Guy gazed at the half-timbered construction. Its white-washed stucco sections, partitioned by half-exposed wood beams, lent to the building's fairy-tale aura. "It's gorgeous," Guy said, tilting his head back to admire the two-story structure. "Way better than the library."

"If we're searching for an old wizard, the local pub is the best place to begin. Plus, it has the choicest cider in the state," Mahogany said, securing the yellow scooter.

They headed across the parking lot, and a din of unrest pulled their attention. On the sidewalk in front of the pub marched a gaggle of protesters holding signs and chanting: "End Halloween!"

"What on earth?" Guy said as he and Mahogany took in the unlikely spectacle. "Do they mean Halloween as in the last day of October?"

"Excuse me," Mahogany turned to a Fae couple standing nearby. "What's all this?" She pointed to the protesters.

"They're trying to end Halloween Town, as in Pandemonium," said the first. He rolled his shoulders, making the large, transparent wings on his back bob. "They want to eject the freaks." His pointed ears twitched as he spoke.

"By freaks, he means magical Folk, sweetie," said the second. He grabbed the hand of the first, and they turned and headed into the pub.

"Wow," Guy said. "The irony is almost too much to fathom."

"That's humans for you," Mahogany said out of the side of her mouth. "They've traded their pitchforks in for picket signs, but nothing's changed. They move here because Pandemonium is a fun, quirky town, but then they feel the need to transform it into a suburban nightmare." She cast a disdainful glare at the group. She'd spent the last twenty years longing for a normal life; public school, sleepovers, and a mom and dad tucking her into bed at night. However much she'd wished for the trappings of mundane human life, she had never wanted to change Pandemonium. Leave it in her rearview perhaps, but change it? Mahogany pursed her lips and turned toward the pub's front entrance.

Inside, Mahogany and Guy found a cozy table near the pub's back wall. Red-shaded lights hung from the ceiling, casting a rosy glow about the place. Exposed wood beams, black with age, gave off a brooding atmosphere. Framed photos spanning nearly a hundred years littered the walls, illuminating Pandamonium's rich history.

"Tell me everything you remember in the days leading up to your murder," Mahogany said.

Guy gazed around the dim room. "I spent a lot of time alone, working on the binding spell. Mike left for hours at a time, coming back smelling like cider."

"What about food? Did he bring anything back to the brownstone?"

Guy tapped a finger against this chin, his eyes squinting in thought. "French fries and roast beef sandwiches."

"Like that?" Mahogany pointed at a server carrying a sizable tray on their shoulder. Piles of fries and steaming sandwiches stuffed with hot roast beef ladened the plates.

Guy examined the tray, his eyes growing wide. "Yes, that's it exactly!" He closed his eyes. "I can almost taste it." A dreamy smile crept across his face. "Great work," he said, his eyes popping open. "You found a lead. I'm so proud of you."

Mahogany ignored him, although her chest filled with confidence she hadn't experienced before. "Did he bring sandwiches home the night you died?"

"Yes. Earlier in the evening."

"Do you think he met with someone?" Mahogany peered around the room, searching for anything that seemed out of the ordinary. A tall order considering this was a pub in a magical town filled with magical Folk.

"I'm not sure," Guy said. "Maybe that Thaddeus Spike guy from the letter. He seems to be everywhere."

"That's what we need to find out."

"You said it yourself that Karrie's brother Jeff is a psycho. He hated me. Even threatened me a few times," Guy said, tapping his chin. "I think he should be at the top of our suspect list. He used to follow her to our meeting places and harass us. Real stalker vibe. We had to get stealthy."

Mahogany thought about the attractive yet meek Karrie Samuels. Her brother had frightened off every potential suitor in Pandemonium. It made sense that she would set her sights on an out-of-towner. They were the only people ignorant enough to give her the time of day.

"Yeah, but why kill Mike too? I get why he'd want to brain you over the head, but Mike?" Mahogany shook her head. "It makes no sense."

"What if Mike surprised him when he came to murder me?" Guy offered.

Mahogany tilted her head in thought. "Maybe? Okay, so far, Jeff Samuels seems like a good suspect."

"Then there's Neema and the photo," Guy said. "Someone in that might be responsible."

"We need more research before we jump to conclusions," Mahogany said.

Guy opened his mouth to say more when Evelina breezed into the pub. She seemed to exude a luminescence akin to a sunrise in the dim interior. Half of the tables turned to peer at the lovely Fae. After a moment, her gaze lit on Mahogany and she approached the table.

"What are you doing here?" Mahogany asked as Evelina took an empty seat.

"I'm helping you solve the murders." She smoothed her shining hair and straightened her bright floral blouse.

"How did you find me? I didn't tell anyone I'd be here," Mahogany said. A bud of irritation tingled at the base of her skull. She still didn't know how she felt about Evelina helping her solve Guy's murder. In her experience, group work never turned out well.

"Simple deduction," Evelina said, leveling her gaze at Mahogany. "Where else would an old wizard go?"

"The local pub," Mahogany said, rolling her eyes.

"Plus, they have the best cider in the state." Evelina pushed a neon green flier across the table to Mahogany. "Did you get one of these?"

DOWN WITH HALLOWEEN! Screamed the flier.

Mahogany cringed. She hated writing done in caps. It was such a middle-aged white woman thing to do. "Is this from the protesters?" She picked up the flier for a closer look.

"Can you believe the nerve? Wanting to purge Pandemonium of its most winning quality. They've got a petition out there for a special election to get one of them on the city council."

"Wow, they're serious," Guy said, peering at the flier.

"They're having a recruiting meeting tomorrow. We should go. Maybe we'll find some leads to the case there," Evelina said.

"Murder is one heck of a way to get your point across." Mahogany said and pondered the motivations that would drive a person to murder. She'd been mad before, but not that mad. "Why murder two out-of-town wizards? None of it makes sense."

"Hey, if customer service has taught me anything, you should never underestimate a white lady with a grudge," Evelina said, "and they're all white out there."

Mahogany shrugged. "While I agree, the motive is thin. It could be political—murder some magical Folks so you prove your point that they bring a dangerous element to the town."

"Oh, that's good!" Evelina said, her sparkling violet eyes growing wide. "I hadn't thought of that. Now we have to go to the meeting tomorrow."

At that moment, the door to the pub opened, and in walked Brian O'Malley, the town cobbler. A woman followed close behind. She wore a large, black-brimmed hat pulled low in the front, concealing her face. Brian spoke with one of the Walsh brothers at the reception desk by the front entrance before he and the unidentified woman headed upstairs to the inn above the pub.

"That's interesting," Evelina said, tracking the couple as they vanished for what appeared to be an afternoon romp. "Have you ever seen Brian O'Malley with a woman before?"

"I've never seen Brian O'Malley with anyone, much less a date," Mahogany said. The pub flooded with light again as another customer entered the establishment.

"Oh, good. Tony's here." Evelina stood and waved her arms in the air.

"What are you doing?" Mahogany hissed, glancing toward the door. Tony's tall, well-built frame strode toward their table and heat flooded Mahogany's chest and face. First Evelina and now Tony. How large was this group project going to get? At the sight of Tony, the dream she'd had of the two of them in Seelie Park came into sharp focus. A swath of sweat prickled across her scalp, and she thanked her luck that the pub's dim light concealed her growing embarrassment. She could almost feel his hand on her face, his lips on hers, his fingers undoing her—

"Why, Miss Mahogany," Guy said, affecting a southern drawl. "I believe you are blushing. Good thing you put on extra deodorant this morning."

Mahogany shot Guy a look that made him throw his hands up in defense.

"I told Tony to meet us here," Evelina said, retaking her seat.

"Why?" Mahogany said, horror-stricken. "He's new to town and a human. Won't the fact that he's living among magical Folk break him?" It seemed like a legitimate excuse, even if not entirely accurate, but the idea of telling Evelina about her crush on Tony tightened her chest with anxiety. She wasn't ready to share that tidbit just yet.

"You're human, and you're fine," Evelina said, shrugging Mahogany's words away. "Not to mention, we could use some eye candy since I can't see your cute ghost." She nudged Mahogany with her elbow and winked.

"He's not my ghost," Mahogany said, her left eye beginning to twitch.

Chapter 12

"Hey, I hope I didn't miss too much," Tony said.

"Not at all. I just got here," Evelina said. She kicked out a chair for Tony to take. "Mahogany. Why don't you fill us in?"

Tony's smooth golden skin and deep-set eyes radiated a warmth that traveled across the table and seeped into Mahogany. The hooking sensation stabbed into her chest briefly before fading. Nerves fluttered in her stomach, making her queasy. She took a deep breath and told Tony and Evelina about Jeff Samuels and how he'd threatened Guy over dating his sister, Karrie. She also mentioned that Magic Mike had frequented Tipsy's. Maybe someone here had more information about what he was up to in town.

Tony sat up straight in his seat. "How did you find all this out?"

"Insider tip," Mahogany said, side-eyeing Guy, who beamed at her.

"Otherworldly more like it," Evelina said.

"What do you mean?" Tony asked.

"Nothing," Mahogany said through clenched teeth, glaring at Evelina.

Tony eyed them but didn't press the issue. "Jeff is a piece of work, especially where his sister is concerned. I've only lived here for about a month, and I've seen him harass people. I can see Jeff losing his temper and taking it too far. Can you describe him? The murder victim?"

Mahogany glanced at Guy. "White, about six-foot, skinny, brown shaggy hair, bright blue eyes, a few freckles on his nose."

"And he dated Karrie Samuels?" Tony asked, the corner of his eyes crinkling in thought.

Mahogany and Evelina nodded.

Tony whistled through his teeth and sat back in his chair. "I've seen the two of them together. You mentioned his name was Guy?"

Guy sat forward and leaned his elbows on the table. "He saw me and Karrie together?"

"Guy Miller. He was twenty-five. From Columbus, Ohio," Mahogany said.

Evelina glanced at the empty chair at the table and smiled sadly. "If this Magic Mike ordered meals from here regularly, then one of the Walsh Clan is bound to remember him. Let's ask." Evelina waved to the server, and he came over. "Hey, Mick. Did you see an older, chubby guy with a long white beard in here recently?"

Mick snorted. "You just described half of our clientele." He spoke in a lilting Irish accent, one generation removed. It was an adopted effect for the tourists, but had become a habit. Few questioned the accent—it went with his flaming red hair and beard.

"He was here every night for a couple of weeks ordering two roast beef sandwiches with a side of fries," Mahogany said. She felt Tony's eyes on her as she spoke. The budding sweat on her scalp bloomed anew under his gaze. She hadn't felt an attraction like this in ages and had quite forgotten how to master herself.

Mick set the table with square bar napkins before answering. "Aye, I remember the fellow. He was the one who got himself stabbed a couple of days ago."

"Did he only come in to eat?" Evelina inquired.

"No, he'd have a pint with the gent over there." Mick gestured to a thin older man, whose sinuous build told of avid athletics in his youth. His graying hair, while still full, had receded in the front. A thick, salt-and-pepper coat of whiskers covered his neck, chin, and cheeks, which cried for a close shave. "He's got a room upstairs," Mick said, nodding to the stairs the cobbler and mystery lady had disappeared up minutes before.

The whole table turned to peer at the wizard nursing a pint, his head bent toward the table.

"Do you know his name?" Evelina fluttered her long eyelashes at Mick.

Mick smiled back. "Thad."

"Thad?" Mahogany asked, her heart quickening. "As in Thaddeus?"

"That's right," Mick said. "Are you ready to order?"

"A round of your finest cider for the table," Evelina said, flashing her best smile.

"You got it," Mick said with a wink.

"And a blooming onion, too, please," Tony added.

Mick nodded and left to fill their order.

"They make an excellent stout here, too," said Tony.

"Only drink the cider. Anything else crafted by a leprechaun is bad news," Evelina said. "It's safer and less likely to give you a hangover. You've heard of Rip Van Winkle, right? His is a cautionary tale. Whatever you do, stay away from whiskey." She shuddered. "That New Year's Eve will live on in infamy."

"Leprechaun?" Tony laughed, watching the imposing members of the Walsh Clan behind the bar. "Aren't they a little tall for leprechauns?"

"Leprechauns are bigger in the States, literally and figuratively," said Mahogany. She shot Evelina a look, silently pleading with her to stop the mythical being talk. "However, they have a few little ones that help with the brewing." She waved her hand nonchalantly, hoping Tony would think she and Evelina were joking.

Tony turned to look at Mahogany. A slight frown creased his forehead. "Huh. Learn something new every day."

"I might have found another clue." Mahogany pulled the letter from her pack and placed it on the table, hoping to steer the subject away from fairy tale creatures and back to the investigation. "It's addressed to Magic Mike from a Thaddeus Spike."

"To Magic Mike?" Evelina said, picking up the envelope for a closer look.

"Where did you find it?" Tony asked. He held his hand out, and Evelina handed him the letter.

"The crime scene," Mahogany lied. She didn't want to involve Neema just yet.

"You've been to the crime scene?" Tony's face lit up like a child who had received an invitation for a free unicorn ride.

"It's still sealed," Evelina said, flipping the envelope over.

"I was too busy to read it." Mahogany thought back to her research in the library.

"No time like the present," Evelina said. She ripped open the envelope and slipped the letter free.

"My first federal offense." A wistful smile lifted the corners of Tony's beautiful mouth, making him even harder to look at. "My mom would be proud."

"You have a strange mom," Evelina said as her gaze roved the page.

"Well?" Mahogany leaned forward, wishing she could see through the paper to the writing on the other side.

"It's blank," Evelina said, turning the page over.

"What do you mean?" Mahogany slipped the letter from Evelina's hand. Sure enough, the paper was void of writing.

"Why would anyone send another person a blank piece of paper in the mail?" Evelina frowned.

"Maybe it's a hidden message?" Tony said.

Mahogany and Evelina peered at him; their expressions quizzical.

"Go on," Evelina said when Tony offered nothing more.

"When I was a kid, my brother and I wrote messages with baking soda and water. When it dried, the paper looked blank but rub some lemon juice over it, and bam!—hidden message revealed."

"Huh," Evelina said, "and here I thought you were just a pretty face."

Tony smiled. "I'm full of surprises."

"There's lemon at the bar," Mahogany said, trying to ignore the budding flirtation between Evelina and Tony. She pointed to the polished bar at the center of the pub, where a plastic tub of ice sat packed with lemon wedges.

"A black light will work too, and it won't ruin the paper if we're wrong," Tony said. He pulled his key chain from the pocket of his well-fitting jeans. Among the keys was a thumb-sized black light. "These make parties a lot more interesting." He pressed the button on the side of the cylinder, and a blue-purple light hit the table, displaying how badly the Walsh Clan wiped down their tables.

"Oh, gross!" Evelina said, pulling her hands off the table as if it was a fire-breathing dragon.

Tony flashed his winning smile and motioned Mahogany to hold out the letter.

She did as he bade. While the black light had revealed the failings of the burly pub owners to provide a clean establishment, it did not unlock any hidden messages, and the page remained stubbornly blank.

Evelina crossed her arms over her chest, pursing her lips, and Mahogany sighed.

"We just need to find the right key to crack the code." Tony shrugged. "It could be heat, smoke, or a different type of light."

Mahogany nodded, put the letter into its envelope, and stowed it in her pack again. "I'll keep trying."

Mick returned with their order. Cider sloshed over the rim of Evelina's glass and hit the scuzzy table with a wet slap.

The Fae inspected her glass with appraising eyes and scowled. "Ah, Mick. This glass has lipstick on it." She pointed to the offending pink lip print.

"What? Not your shade?" Mick chuckled and walked away.

"This place sucks," Evelina said and pushed her full pint glass into the middle of the table.

Tony ripped a large section of the breaded onion from the bloom and dipped it in the spicy horseradish sauce. "What doesn't kill you," he said.

"Cheers." Mahogany lifted her glass, which wobbled slightly in her nervous hand, and she hoped no one noticed.

Tony joined her and said, "To Guy and Magic Mike."

"To Guy and Magic Mike," Mahogany said.

Evelina sighed, toasted with them, and they all drank heartily. Mahogany hoped the alcohol would drown the butterflies in her stomach.

"I'm gonna be sick," Evelina said and made a soft retching noise, pushing the glass aside again.

Guy shrugged and plunged his face into the glass, sighing with relish.

"So, what's our next move?" Tony asked, leaning close to Mahogany as they eyed Thaddeus. The scent of rain and salty air made Mahogany painfully aware of Tony's aftershave.

"You smell nice," Evelina said as if reading Mahogany's thoughts.

"Thanks. I picked it up at the Haughty Hemlock." Tony raised the neckband of his shirt and sniffed.

"Is this one of your signature scents, Mahogany?" A sly half-smile grazed Evelina's lips.

Mahogany scowled. "We're planning, remember?" she said, bringing the conversations back to the investigation. The tug in her chest pulled again in the direction of Tony. It indeed was one of her scents. She remembered creating the aftershave only a few weeks ago.

"You made this?" Tony asked, sniffing his shirt again. "It's one of my favorites."

One of his favorites? How many aftershaves did one guy need? And, if he'd come into the Hemlock several times, how had she never run into him before? Mahogany wondered. Before she could answer him, Evelina gasped and jumped out of her chair. "I'll be right back." She disappeared into the thickening lunch crowd, leaving Tony and Mahogany alone, almost.

"He's pretty cute," Guy said. "Why don't you ask him out? It's obvious you're attracted to him."

Tony took another large bite of his blooming onion and scooted the plate closer to Mahogany. "Help yourself," he said. "I don't want to be the only one smelling of onion."

"Ooh," Guy said, sounding like a ghost for the first time. "You know what that means. Now you won't be able to smell his stinky breath when you two get closer." He attempted to wink, but it came off looking like he was suffering from a facial tick.

Mahogany forced a smile, plucked a petal from the onion's bloom, and popped it in her mouth. The combination of crunch and soft-cooked onion made her stomach lurch. She realized she'd forgotten to eat. To ram this realization home. Her stomach burbled, and a rosy glow colored her cheeks.

"Yeah, they're the best in town," Tony said with a knowing smile. "Have as much as you want. We can order another if needed."

Mahogany both enjoyed and admired Tony's calm manner. He obviously wasn't crushing on her like she was on him. Every move she made felt forced and awkward.

"I got it!" Evelina whispered breathlessly, plopping back into her seat.

"Got what?" Mahogany said around a mouthful of deep-fried onion.

"Thad's room key."

"What? How did you do that?" Tony asked.

"I checked the registration book at the front desk to see which room was his and then swiped the key when Mick two wasn't looking."

"Mick two?" Tony asked, raising a dark eyebrow.

"One of the Walsh brothers. I forgot his name. They all look alike," Evelina said. "Come on."

Chapter 13

Mahogany, Evelina, Tony, Guy, and the blooming onion weaved through the growing lunch crowd to the stairs leading to the guest rooms.

"Mahogany and I will go up, and you stand guard," Evelina said, motioning to Tony.

"Are we sure about this?" Mahogany raised a skeptical eyebrow. A fine mist of nervous sweat beaded on her upper lip. "This is escalating way faster than I'm comfortable with."

"Oh, Mahogany," Evelina patted Mahogany's hand. "We'll be finished before you know it."

"It's not you two that's worrisome," Guy said. He eyed the gloomy Thad on the other side of the bar. "Will you finish before *he* knows it?"

Mahogany couldn't argue with Guy's logic. "Why does Tony need to stand guard if there's no need to worry?" she nodded toward Tony, who watched them intently.

Evelina shrugged. "It's just a precaution. We're covering our bases. Hedging our bets. Hoping for the best, but preparing for the worst."

"Gods." Mahogany threw her hands in the air. "If I agree to go with you, will you stop with the horrible clichés?"

"Absolutely," Evelina said with a wink. "Tony, I'm calling you now."

Tony nodded and set his cider and the half-eaten onion on a low shelf running along the wall. He leaned against it with casual confidence and answered his cell before the first ring could finish. An old tintype photo gleamed behind a dusty frame hanging above where they stood. A ghostly blond family dressed in hardcore gothic attire stared with dead eyes into the camera. Mahogany rolled her shoulders, trying to dispel the sensation of being watched.

"I'll keep you on the line," Evelina said. "Tell us if Thad is heading to his room."

"You got it," Tony nodded, phone pressed to his ear. He furrowed his brow, as if listening to an intriguing story from the other end.

A pang of jealousy fluttered through Mahogany's chest. When had Evelina and Tony exchanged phone numbers?

"You better get on that," Guy said over his shoulder, floating up the stairs. "She's way ahead of you."

Mahogany scowled after the apparition and followed him to the tavern's second floor.

"Which room is Thad staying in?" Mahogany asked in a hushed tone when they reached the second-floor landing.

Evelina checked the key in her hand. "Room Five."

The worn wooden stairs creaked under their feet, making them cringe. However, the din from the pub drowned out any evidence of their illegal ascent.

Two hallways bisected the landing—one running perpendicular to the stairs, the other continuing straight.

"Which way?" Evelina asked, swiveling her head to peer down the hallways.

A brass plaque mounted on the corner of the intersection caught Mahogany's eye. "Over here." She motioned and Evelina followed. Near the end of the hall, a polished brass five adorned a blue door. The path continued beyond the door to another short hallway where more guest rooms lay.

Evelina reached a trembling hand forward, fumbling with the key.

"Here." Mahogany took the key. Despite her pounding heart, her hands were steady. She slipped the key home and opened the door, and they both stifled a gasp—Thad had turned what should have been a quaint room decorated in rustic Irish decor into a makeshift darkroom. Black and white photos hung from a clothesline zigzagging across the room. Thad had removed the heavy tartan quilt from the bed and hung it over the room's only window, blotting out the bright summer sun. The scent of photographic chemicals tainted the air.

Remembering herself, Mahogany grabbed Evelina by the arm and shoved her into the room. She scampered in behind her, and closed the door with a much too loud click, slipping the bolt home.

"What in the world?" Evelina muttered, stepping into the room. She ducked beneath the photos as she went. "Mama Walsh's head is going to explode when she sees this."

"There might even be another murder." Mahogany imagined the imposing Walsh matriarch. Mama Walsh took great pride in her inn. Where her boys failed downstairs in the pub concerning cleanliness, she made up for it with the guest rooms.

She peered at the photo closest to her. An image of Haughty Hemlock's storefront lay in glossy black and white. In the shop's window, Mahogany and Neema hung a sign announcing an herbal tea sale.

A tingling sensation formed at the back of Mahogany's neck. Is this what it was like to have a stalker? "I feel violated."

Guy snorted. "Says the person who just unlawfully entered someone's hotel room."

"There are more over here." Evelina pulled a photo from the line and handed it to Mahogany. Guy and Magic Mike carried heavy suitcases into the brownstone. "Is that Guy?"

"See," Mahogany said, handing the photo back to Evelina. "He's not cute."

Evelina took the photo and studied Guy's image, her eyes soft with emotion. "He's nerd chic. I kind of like the lanky look. If I'd had a chance, I would have been his friend." She re-clipped the picture to the line.

"At least someone appreciates me," Guy said with a snort.

"He says thanks," Mahogany said, studying another picture of her at Hot Brews with Bazgul perched on her head.

"There are a lot of you and Neema," Evelina said, her voice colored with concern.

Mahogany nodded. Indeed, there were a lot. An unsettling amount. "Why take these?"

"Photos? What sort of photos?" Tony's voice drifted out of Evelina's phone.

"Gods, I'd forgotten you were there," Evelina said, clutching her neck in surprise. "There are photos of Guy and Mike along with Mahogany and Neema."

"That's creepy," Tony said, worry deepening his voice. "Maybe you two should get out of there. We don't know who we're dealing with. Thad might be the murderer."

"This one is from Columbus." Guy pointed to a photo near the darkened window.

"He followed you across the county to Pandemonium?" Mahogany said. "If he's the killer, why wait?"

"Maybe he wanted to get you all in the same place?" Evelina cast a dark look at Mahogany.

Fear percolated up Mahogany's spine. If Thad was the murderer, what would he do if he caught them in here?

"Come look at this," Guy said. He'd moved to a small desk littered with writing implements—envelopes, paper, and stamps scattered over the worn desktop.

"What is it?" Mahogany's curiosity outweighed her growing fear, and she stooped under the clotheslines, joining Guy.

A sealed envelope lay on a pile of blank paper. The same block lettering and pink rose stamp adorned it as the letter in Mahogany's backpack. Only this one was addressed to Neema.

"Thad's on the move." Tony's urgent voice sprang from Evelina's phone. "Get out of there. He's with one of the Walsh boys and looks super grumpy."

Mahogany grabbed the letter and shoved it into her back pocket. She and Evelina hurried back to the door, dodging the drooping clotheslines.

They stumbled out the door and into the hall. Heavy footsteps creaked their way up the stairs.

"I'm not sure what happened to the key," the Walsh brother said. "I'll keep searching."

Thad grunted in response.

Mahogany's once steady hands now convulsed. Adrenaline surged through her, curdling the blooming onion in her stomach. She fumbled the key around the lock, dropping it twice before shoving it home. She wrenched the key to the right, and the lock clicked into place.

Evelina grabbed Mahogany's backpack and hauled her around the corner, out of sight. They pressed themselves against the green door to room six, holding their breath.

Thad and the unnamed Walsh brother's heavy footfalls crested the stairs to the landing and headed toward them.

The skeleton key rattled in the lock.

"I'll take it from here," Thad said, his gravelly voice scraping around the corner and into Mahogany's ears.

The Walsh brother muttered a goodbye and headed back to the bar. Thad waited until the tall leprechaun retreated into the pub before entering his room.

Mahogany and Evelina waited for Thad to slam the door shut before dashing past and into the safety of the pub.

"That was way too close," Evelina said, her cheeks red.

"It'll be days before my heartbeat returns to normal," Mahogany huffed, her pulse thrumming in her head. "We need to get out of here and discuss clues and suspects."

"We can use my house. I live alone," Tony said, popping the last piece of blooming onion into his mouth.

"That's perfect," Evelina said, fanning her face. "I have some treats for Bob."

"Who's Bob?" Mahogany asked, a dark eyebrow climbing her forehead.

"Bob is Tony's cat," Evelina said, smiling.

Guy tutted. "She already knows about his cat and is bringing him treats. Your window is closing." He singsonged the last part, sending a knife of irritation slicing through Mahogany.

Evelina looped her arm through Tony's, and they started toward the door. Guy shook his head and floated after them.

"Can we make a murder wall?" Tony asked. "I've always wanted to make a murder wall."

Mahogany swallowed a groan, and with a surreptitious glide of her hand, she set Thad's room key on an empty table as she passed.

She'd almost reached the door when the sound of someone blowing their nose with gusto got her attention. Mahogany glanced toward the offending noise. A forlorn young woman sat crying into a shot glass at a table on the other side of the pub.

The woman was none other than Karrie Samuels, Guy's paramour.

Chapter 14

"Karrie?" Mahogany asked, her voice low. "I'm not sure you remember me. I work at Haughty Hemlock." Karrie often stopped by the apothecary on her dog-walking route. Neema sometimes had treats for Karrie's canine charges, but Mahogany hadn't engaged her, preferring Bazgul to the yipping dogs. Much like Mahogany, the mousey blond woman didn't socialize. Her brother saw to that, scaring away most people who would befriend her.

Karrie tilted her chin and glanced at Mahogany, swaying slightly. Her puffy eyes swam behind pools of tears. The young woman's shoulders slumped under the weight of her grief. "Uh, sure. You're that weird chick with the giant spider."

"That's me. Do you mind if I sit?" Mahogany sat in one of the empty chairs around the table, not waiting for an answer.

"Help yourself," Karrie said, her head bobbing like a boat at sea. Mahogany could smell the potent Leprechaun whiskey seeping from her pores.

"Can you tell me about your brother and Guy Miller?" Mahogany said, getting to the point. Her tone was subdued, which was difficult with the lunch crowd clamor.

At the mention of Guy's name, Karrie's face crumpled, and tears overwhelmed her, pouring down her cheeks.

"Mahogany? What's going on?" Evelina asked. She and Tony approached the table, watching Karrie Samuels sob on Tipsy O'Lush's dirty table.

"I found Karrie Samuels," Mahogany said, pointing to the sobbing woman.

Karrie's head hung lower and lower until her forehead rested upon the sticky table.

Evelina tutted under her breath and reached for the shot glass half-filled with whiskey. "This won't do." She marched to the bar and returned with a stack of napkins and a pint of cider.

"This will lighten your spirits instead of dragging them to Hades." She slid the pint glass across the table.

Guy materialized and leaned against the wall behind Karrie. His gaze trained on the floor.

Karrie lifted her head, took a sip of cider, and nodded. "Thank you."

Evelina sat, raised a hand to pat Karrie's snot-streak arm, and thought better of it. "There, there," she said, patting the crying woman's snot-free shoulder.

"I'm so sorry to ask this." Mahogany's cheeks tingled with emotion at Karrie's reaction to Guy's name. "Was there any bad blood between Guy and your brother?"

"Are you with the police?" Karrie asked.

Mahogany, Evelina, and Tony exchanged a look.

"We're private investigators," Evelina said. "Guy's family hired us."

Mahogany frowned. Was impersonating a private detective as bad as impersonating a police officer? She knew the latter was illegal but hadn't a clue of the legality of the previous.

Karrie nodded. "His grandmother, you mean. He didn't have any other family."

"Right, back in Columbus. She couldn't make it out herself, so she asked us to help," Mahogany said, her stomach tightening. In for a penny, in for a pound.

"Well, we'd only known each other briefly, but he was perfect." Karrie blew her nose loudly into a napkin and then dropped it on the table with a soggy thud. A sob escaped her, and she buried her face in her hands.

"When was the last time you saw your brother?" Mahogany pressed.

Karrie shook her head. "I'm not sure. Jeff might be at his girl-friend's place, but I haven't heard from him. He mentioned he planned on being at the End Halloween meeting tomorrow after-noon. He's working with Nancy Roberts to get some sympathetic people on the city council to, you know, clean up Pandemonium. Nancy's the head of the operation. She's pretty intense."

At Karrie's mention of 'cleaning up Pandemonium,' Evelina no-ticeably bristled, and Mahogany shot her a warning glance.

"Any idea who Jeff is dating?" Tony asked, taking the tone one might expect of a fictional detective from an overly dramatic televi-sion series. Mahogany hoped he wasn't laying it on too thick.

"No." Karrie shook her head again. "He doesn't share personal stuff with me."

"How was he with Guy?" Mahogany asked.

A single tear trickled down Karrie's cheek. "Jeff hated Guy, but that was because he didn't give him a chance. He knew Guy was into magic and the occult." She shrugged and eyed Mahogany's pink hair and Evelina's pointy ears. "You know, Halloween Town stuff, but Guy was so nice. He liked me despite Jeff." Her teary eyes darted from Mahogany to Evelina to Tony. "There's no way Jeff could have killed anyone. Is there?"

Mahogany took Karrie's icy hand and squeezed. Her stomach lurched at the dampness, and her eyes went to the soggy tissue laying heavy on the table. "We don't know, but we'll find out," she said, recovering herself.

"Thanks for that," Guy said once they were outside.

"For what?" The sun radiated a steamy heat that came in waves off the asphalt parking lot. The scent of fried food drifted from Tipsy's, making the air seem hotter. Mahogany noticed the afternoon heat had driven off the protesters.

"For holding her hand," Guy said. "Karrie and I had something real. It didn't get far, but it meant something." Guy sighed. "I hope her brother didn't murder me and Mike. That would be worse than awful."

Mahogany nodded, considering the implications of a relative killing the person you loved. "I hope not, too, for her sake."

Tony turned toward Mahogany, an eyebrow hitched high on his forehead. "Who..." he started, but Evelina cut him off.

"The poor girl," she said and grabbed Tony's arm, attempting to steer him farther into the parking lot.

Mahogany's face grew warm. She'd have to be more careful about speaking to Guy in public. People might think she was a few pumpkins short of a patch.

He turned from Mahogany with a slight shake of his head. "Who needs a ride to my place?"

Evelina skipped to Tony's car and popped open the passenger door.

"I have my Vespa." Mahogany nodded to the sunshine yellow scooter.

"Sweet!" Tony said, nodding with appreciation at the motorcycle's diminutive cousin. "I've always wanted a Vespa."

Mahogany's stomach fluttered with nerves. He liked her spider and her scooter.

"You can follow me," he said, jumping behind the wheel of the blue Honda Civic.

"Lead the way," Mahogany said.

Chapter 15

Mahogany entered Tony's cozy bungalow and hesitated. The front entry led to an open floor plan, joining the kitchen to the living room. A tile counter wrapped its way around the kitchen, separating it from the living room. The vaulted ceiling met with a set of French doors that opened onto the lush garden. A hallway off the living room led to the rest of the house. Mahogany had expected the mid-century normalcy of Tony's home. What she hadn't expected were the walls and bookshelves littered with occult artifacts.

"This is your house?" she asked, pulling off her boots and setting them next to a pile of shoes near the front door.

"It's my family's home. My uncle passed away about a year ago, and I asked to be the caretaker." Tony walked to the kitchen. "Can I get you anything?"

Mahogany moved to a bookshelf next to the pile of shoes and picked up a carved owl statue no larger than her palm. The tiny figure gave off subtle magical vibrations. She wondered why Cedric, her predecessor, hadn't been called to Tony's after his uncle had died. After all, Tony was a human, and the Guild collected magical objects for safekeeping after Folk crossed to the other side.

Tony emerged from the kitchen with chips and guacamole. He motioned to the owl statue in Mahogany's hand. "That's Oleander. My uncle's familiar."

Mahogany turned the statue over in her hands, at a loss for words.

Tony smiled as if reading Mahogany's thoughts. "My family is semi-magical. Seers mostly. My great-grandmother on my father's side traveled with a circus doing tarot readings." Tony headed into the living room and put the chips and guac on the coffee table.

Mahogany followed Tony with her gaze. On a bookshelf near the French doors sat two large glass tanks, each holding a beautiful, orange-kneed tarantula. A smile lifted the corners of her mouth. Bazgul would love this place, although she'd have to watch him. He might want to make a snack of the spiders.

"Bob, here kitty, kitty," Evelina singsonged. She took a bag of treats from her purse and shook them. A large black tabby trotted out from wherever he'd been napping and gave a long, loud meow.

Mahogany regarded Evelina. Had she known that Tony came from a semi-magical family and had failed to tell her?

Evelina shook a few of the treats into her palm and offered them to Bob. The cat sniffed them for a long minute before gobbling them up. She peered over her shoulder at Mahogany, as if sensing her unspoken question. "I wouldn't have invited him to Tipsy's otherwise. He knows I'm a Fae."

Mahogany narrowed her eyes and clicked her tongue.

Tony shifted, his gaze moving between the two young women. "I grew up in the Bay Area. San Francisco," he started by explanation.

"My uncle lived here, and when he died, none of the other cousins wanted to move, so I offered to take care of the place."

"I suppose he knows about Guy too?" Mahogany said, placing Oleander back on the bookshelf. She felt she needed to get all of their secrets out in the open. If Tony knew that magic and mythical beings existed, it would make working together that much easier.

"Evelina mentioned that she's Fae. Wait. You don't mean Guy, the murder victim?"

"He's her cute nerdy ghost," Evelina said.

Tony's face lit in a broad smile that lifted his cheeks, crinkling his deep-set hazel eyes. "One of the murder victims is haunting you? That's so cool! I mean, not cool for him, or you, I guess." He closed his mouth, cheeks reddening. He snapped his fingers. "That's who you were talking to in the parking lot. Is he here now?"

Evelina stood and brushed her palms on her leggings, removing flecks of cat spit and treats. "Don't forget Bazgul. Not only does she have a ghost haunting her, but Bazgul is her demon familiar. It's a double whammy."

Mahogany glared at Evelina, not ready to forgive her for her lack of transparency. She wished she agreed with Tony, but she didn't find Guy to be a cool addition. She glared at a section of the living room wall Guy had disappeared through as he meandered about Tony's house. "Yeah, he's here. He goes everywhere with me. But I wouldn't call him cute or cool unless you like being followed around by someone who doesn't understand the concept of privacy."

Realization dawned on Tony's face. "Of course! The ghost is your insider tip. That's how you knew so much about the crime, but back up. Bazgul's a demon?" He shook his head and whistled low under his breath. "That *is* a double whammy. My spiders are just plain old arachnids."

"Bazgul, come," Mahogany said, unable to fight the urge to show off. She'd never felt the need to impress anyone before, especially with Bazgul.

The demon spider appeared a moment later in a red-brown haze atop one of the glass terrariums and gazed down at the spider inside.

"Bazgul seems to like them," Evelina remarked, nodding to his intent inspection of the terrariums. She flopped onto the couch and helped herself to chips. "You said that you inherited from your father's side?"

"Bazgul," Mahogany said, her tone warning. "Play nice."

Bazgul raised a bristly leg at his mistress as if to say, I know, I know, and continued his inspection of the terrarium

"My family helped settle Pandemonium, then my great-great-grandfather fell in love with a human, and the family dis-owned him." Tony took a seat on the couch, scooped up a handful of chips, and started munching.

A glint of pleasure surged through Mahogany when Tony placed several feet between himself and Evelina. "It must be nice knowing so much about your family," Mahogany said. She wandered over to the mantel, which overflowed with framed family photos. Above it hung a large framed concert poster of Led Zeppelin from The Fillmore in San Francisco.

"It has its twists and turns. Knowing my ancestors hated their kid enough to disown him for loving someone stinks, but it's not uncommon with magical Folk. Or humans. The circumstances are just different. They don't want to see their family powers dimin-ished." Tony shrugged. "At least I get to live in an incredible house filled with magical objects, in a stunning and unbelievable town, and meet fantastic people." He smiled at Evelina and Mahogany, his gaze lingering on Mahogany long enough that heat flooded her cheeks.

Mahogany cleared her throat. "Should we look at the letter we swiped from Thad's room?" She pulled the envelope from her bag and tore it open.

Tony and Evelina leaned forward to have a look.

"It's blank," Tony said.

Mahogany sighed and dropped the irritatingly empty page and envelope onto the coffee table before grabbing a chip. Her stomach rumbled. The small amount of blooming onion from Tipsy O'Lush's wasn't nearly enough to satiate her hunger. She dipped the chip into the guac.

"This is delicious. Did you make it?" Mahogany asked, grabbing another chip and loading it with more guacamole.

"Special California recipe. I used to work in a taqueria. I have many food secrets up my sleeve," Tony said. He proceeded to one of the many bookshelves and browsed the titles. "My uncle might have some books on magically coded messages. I'll research and see what I can find."

"Perfect," Evelina said and clapped her hand. "Now, let's make a murder wall!"

"I have just the thing." Tony disappeared down the hall and returned, pushing a large, old-fashioned blackboard on wheels.

"Where did you get this?" Evelina ran an admiring hand over the flat black surface. "This is real slate."

"It was my uncle's. He used to teach at Hippolyta," Tony said, referencing the girl's school run by Amazonians and named after their fallen queen. "When they upgraded the classrooms with whiteboards, he asked to bring a few keepsakes home."

"Do you have chalk?" Evelina inquired, a silly grin lifting her cheeks.

"Sure do. What color doth the lady wish?" Tony grabbed a cardboard box off the shallow wooden shelf below the smooth slate. An assortment of neon-colored chalk glowed at them.

"Oh," Mahogany said despite herself. "Pretty."

"Impulse buy," Tony said with a shrug. "I like shinies."

Mahogany chose a bright purple stick while Evelina grabbed the shocking orange.

"Where do we start?" Evelina said, tapping her lip with an index finger.

"With the victims," Mahogany said. In the center of the blackboard, she wrote Magic Mike's and Guy's names.

"Then the suspects," Tony said.

"Jeff Samuels," Evelina said, "and the wizard Thad, for sure." She added Jeff and Thad to the board above Mike and drew lines connecting them. Along the line connecting Jeff to Guy, she wrote 'jealousy.' For the line between Jeff and Mike, she wrote 'collateral damage.'

"What about Thad? We don't have a motive yet," Tony said.

Mahogany added two question marks to the lines connecting Mike and Guy to Thad.

"Oh, how about the freak heaters?" Evelina pulled the flier from her purse and handed it to Mahogany.

Mahogany took it and wrote on the board, 'End Halloween.' She drew a line to the victims and added, 'freak haters,' beside it.

"Then there are all the strange clues like the photographs in Thad's room and the letters addressed to Mike and Neema," Mahogany said. She added a section for clues and wrote what they knew.

"There was the woman. You should add her too." Guy had floated back into the living room.

"What woman?" Mahogany asked as Guy headed towards the kitchen, disappearing into the refrigerator.

"The woman who came over several times and argued with Mike. I didn't catch what the argument was about, but she was really mad." His muffled voice was barely audible from inside the refrigerator.

"You didn't think to tell me this sooner?" Mahogany added the mysterious woman to the board. "Can you give me a description of the woman?"

"Nope. Never saw her, but I heard her yelling and threatening Mike." Guy paused. "Tony's got good taste in food. You should see what he has in here."

"Is she talking to the ghost?" Tony asked Evelina, his eyes wide.

"I think so," Evelina said, glancing around the room as if she might spy Guy's spectral form.

"There was some unseen woman who came to the brownstone and argued with Magic Mike before the murders." Mahogany stepped back and joined Tony and Evelina on the couch. They studied the board and munched chips with guacamole, pondering all they knew and didn't know. Perhaps solving the murder with Tony and Evelina wouldn't be so bad after all.

"What's our next move?" Tony asked.

"We need to go to the End Halloween gathering tomorrow." Evelina wagged a finger at the flier resting against the blackboard. Her bow-shaped mouth turned down at the corners.

"I'm in. I have the day off," Tony said.

"Stupid work. I'll try to get the last part of my shift covered," Evelina added.

Guy rematerialized through the refrigerator. "Mahogany, you will never guess what this guy has in his study."

Mahogany sighed. The sooner they solved this, the sooner she could get rid of her annoying ghost.

Chapter 16

After leaving Tony and the newly minted murder wall, Mahogany headed back to the Haughty Hemlock. As she walked through the door, Neema put her to work dusting the shop's jar-lined shelves. While she rid the place of dust, Neema helped a customer, and Guy belted show tunes from a musical unfamiliar to Mahogany. At least, she thought it was a musical.

"I'm just so happy I found you," the woman of about forty gushed as Neema placed her purchases in a paper boutique bag. "Ever since the flight, my stomach hasn't been the same. I've learned my lesson—never order fish on an airplane."

"The tummy tea and the mint drops should do the trick," Neema said, smiling politely. She pushed the bag across the glass display counter. "Please come see us again if you need anything else."

The woman took the bag and thanked Neema. Mahogany watched her leave from the corner of her eye. The woman's attire screamed 1950s office chic. She wore a light pink silk mock turtleneck fashioned with pearl buttons up the back. Her gray tea-length pencil skirt hugged her as she shuffled toward the door. Her pointy stilettos clicked over the polished tiles—glints of sequins twinkled as she walked.

"What was wrong with her?" Mahogany nodded to the closing door after the woman.

"She seems to have picked up something on her way into town," Neema said, replacing the glass jars she'd used to fill the women's request. "You know how plane travel can be. Everyone trapped together at 35,000 feet, breathing the same recycled air."

Mahogany glared at Neema, her feather duster poised over the next jar on the shelf. "I wouldn't have a clue," she said.

She and Neema hadn't left Pandemonium since they'd arrived twenty years ago. Sure, there had been day trips to the beach, hikes in the woods surrounding the town, and cider tasting at a nearby mill house. Anything far from home had been out of the question. When Mahogany had brought up going away to college, Neema had shut her down, disallowing her to pursue higher education outside of Pandemonium. This relegated Mahogany to online courses and lectures at the local library. After a year, she'd given up her dreams of leaving Pandemonium and living a semi-normal life most humans took for granted.

"Finish up in here, and then you can dust the living room," Neema said over her shoulder, ignoring Mahogany's comment.

"Yes, ma'am," Mahogany said under her breath.

Thirty minutes later, Mahogany wiped away a week's worth of dust from the coffee table, her gaze returning over and over to the writing desk. She had persuaded Guy to remain in the store while she worked. Thankfully, the distance wasn't enough for the spiritual bungee to activate. Mahogany relished the much-needed peace from Guy's catalog of off-Broadway tunes.

She moved from the coffee table to the end table nearest the desk and gave it a cursory swipe with the duster before moving to the antique writing desk. Mahogany flitted the feathers, sending dust into the air where it settled once again on the dark, cherry wood.

She peered through the doorway into the kitchen and listened. Neema's smoky voice assured someone her hair tonic would leave their locks luxurious and manageable.

Mahogany turned her attention back to the desk. Stacked atop one another were two sets of drawers, separated by a miniature cupboard at the center of the desk. The drawers were just wide enough to fit an envelope comfortably. A smooth leather-covered writing area opened over a large drawer filled with odds and ends.

Focused on the envelope-sized drawer on the right side, Mahogany tugged at the round brass knob, hoping it would slide open. It didn't budge. She searched the other drawers for something to pick the lock and found a small screwdriver intended for eyeglasses.

She slid the screwdriver into the lock and swiveled it around as she'd seen on television, to no avail. With a sigh, Mahogany stood, making a mental note to learn the art of lock picking.

"What are you doing?"

Mahogany nearly jumped out of her skin, a small yelp escaping her. She turned to see Neema standing in the living room doorway.

"Gods, you startled me." Mahogany set the screwdriver down on the desk.

Neema held up her foot. Instead of her usual heels, soft-soled tennis shoes clad her feet. "My new heels gave me horrible blisters, so I'm sporting these ugly things until they either heal or my foot falls off."

"Oh," Mahogany managed, her heart returning to its regular rhythm. "You wouldn't have a small notebook I could use? If I'm going to solve the murders, I need to take notes like a real detective."

Neema scowled. "I think you should leave it to the police, but if you insist, try the little cupboard." Neema waved a hand at the center of the desk. "There might be a few in there."

Mahogany slid the large drawer closed and opened the minuscule door. "Thanks," she said, grabbing a notebook without looking.

"If you're finished cleaning in here, you have company waiting outside."

"Company?"

Neema smiled. "Evelina and that handsome boy who's been buying all of your scented shaving soaps," she said with a wink.

Mahogany blushed and tossed the duster in the laundry room before heading outside to meet Tony and Evelina. She strode past Guy, hoping he hadn't noticed her, his caterwauling going full tilt.

"Were you able to get into the desk?" Evelina asked as soon as Mahogany exited the store. "Are there more letters?"

Mahogany shook her head and glanced over her shoulder, ensuring Neema wasn't in earshot.

"It's locked, and I don't know how to pick it."

"How about you, secret message guy," Evelina said, turning to Tony. "Do you know how to pick locks?"

Tony shook his head. "No, but I'd be happy to learn."

From across the street, Mahogany noticed a scaly hand holding back the corner of a thick black curtain of Humbaba, Pandemonium's statuary shop. A pale face hid in the shadows. Mahogany locked eyes with the hidden figure, and the hand dropped the drapery, cutting off all view.

"Interesting," Mahogany muttered. She started across the street to Humbaba. She made it to the double yellow line before the invisible tether ripped Guy from his perch on one of Haughty Hemlock's glass display counters. The force flung him through the door and into the street behind Mahogany. He was then dragged through a passing garbage truck.

"What's interesting?" Evelina said, trotting to catch up with Mahogany, trailed by Tony.

Guy's spirit rippled like Jello on the back of a horse-drawn buggy traveling over cobblestones and came to a halt next to Mahogany.

"Could you please warn me when you're about to enter the bungee zone?" Guy said, his voice warbling.

"No," Mahogany answered. She strode up to Humbaba's tinted glass door and yanked it open. A bell over the door tinkled.

"I know you've been watching us," Mahogany said into the dim interior. Shadowy stone figures of dragons, gnomes playing guitars, and hissing cats cluttered thick wooden shelves.

"What is this place?" Guy peered around and spotted a group of stone gnomes playing golf. "Oh! Garden art. How fun." He drifted over to better look at a collection of giant ladybugs in various poses.

Something scraped across the worn wooden floor to Mahogany's left. She turned in time to see a lock of flaming red hair disappear behind one of the heavy shelving units.

"Stheno? Euryale?" Mahogany called after the figure.

The Gorgon sisters were some of Pandemonium's oldest residents. Unlike their sister Medusa, who met her fate at the hands of Perseus, Stheno and Euryale escaped death, but not persecution.

After Poseidon had taken the beautiful Medusa to Athena's temple and had his way with her, the enraged goddess transformed the sisters into monsters. Like most men, Poseidon had sidestepped his sister's wrath and continued his easy, consequence-free life, deflowering maidens whenever it suited him. In search of a safe place to live, Stheno and Euryale had helped settle Pandemonium. They vowed to welcome any persecuted magical Folk and help them find peace within the town's borders.

"I'm waiting." Mahogany tapped her foot as she gazed around the ill-lit space.

"What do you want to know?" hissed a voice from the shadows that seemed to come from everywhere.

Mahogany suppressed a shiver. "I want to know if you saw anything unusual across the street in the last few days?" Her shoulders relaxed when her voice came out strong and confident, belying her apprehension at having marched into a den of snakes.

Outside, Evelina rapped on Humbaba's glass door. Mahogany glanced over her shoulder and gave Evelina a thumbs up. Evelina nodded, but remained outside with Tony. Their brows wrinkled in curiosity.

"Can you be more specific? This is Pandemonium. Everything is unusual here," came the voice.

Mahogany rolled her eyes. "Anything having to do with the murdered wizard or Neema?"

"And me," Guy said. "Why do you keep forgetting me?"

"There may have been something," hissed the voice.

"I'm listening," Mahogany said.

Stheno emerged from the shadows. Her curly, flame-colored hair coiled about her head like serpents ready to strike. Over Stheno's shoulder, Mahogany glimpsed the Gorgon's younger sister. Euryale's scaly visage peeked around her sister before vanishing into the darkness again. The sight of Euryale's ichthyosis-plagued skin gave Mahogany a start, but she hid her surprise.

"A week ago, a fat wizard came to see Neema. They argued, and right before he left, Neema slapped him across the face," Stheno said. "Then the wizard's picture showed up in the paper, only now he was no longer among the living."

"You're positive it was the same wizard," Mahogany asked.

Stheno glared at Mahogany. "Do not question me, girl. You know what we are capable of."

Mahogany nodded; her mouth dry. "Of course. Apologies. I didn't mean any disrespect. I'm just searching for the truth."

Stheno held Mahogany's gaze for an uncomfortable beat before nodding. "Yes, I imagine so. I would, too, if I had a ghost trailing after me."

Guy and Mahogany stared at Stheno, their jaws agape.

"Can she see me?" Guy said to Mahogany. "Can you see me?" He turned to the statuesque Gorgon.

"I see much," Stheno said. She turned to gaze in Guy's direction, but her eyes didn't lock on his precise location. "When you've lived for thousands of years, seeing through worlds becomes easy." Stheno swiveled her head back toward Mahogany. Her neck and shoulders following the movement like the rectilinear locomotion of a snake. "One day, you will see too." Stheno peered at Evelina and Tony, waiting on the sidewalk. "You should go."

Mahogany stared at the Gorgon, her mind reeling. She prised her eyes from Stheno's imposing figure and nodded. "Thank you for your help. May I come and see you again?"

Stheno nodded and disappeared into the shadows.

"Wow, you're really taking to this. Breaking into Thad's room boosted your confidence. You were great in there," Guy said, nodding with appreciation.

"Who in the world was that?" Tony asked. He scowled at Humbaba's storefront.

"Gorgons." Evelina rubbed her bare arms despite the evening's warmth.

"Nosy neighbors," Mahogany said. "They saw Magic Mike come by the Haughty Hemlock before the murders."

"What for?" Tony asked.

Mahogany frowned, her gaze falling on Neema as she closed the apothecary for the day. "To see Neema."

Chapter 17

The next afternoon, Mahogany, Evelina, Tony, and Guy stood in front of a modest two-story Victorian. A sign impaled the pristine lawn read:

End Halloween! Meeting at Noon.

A similar, yet smaller sign with an arrow pointed to the side of the house where a wooden gate stood open. The smoky scent of fire-cook meats filled the air, making Mahogany's stomach tighten.

"What do you think Magic Mike wanted with Neema?" Evelina asked, casting a wary eye on the house.

Mahogany thought about the photo of Neema and Mike in their teens, but said nothing. Guy scowled at her as if reading her thoughts. Fate had cleaved them together only five days ago, and already he could see past her mask. Guy's astute ability for observation irritated Mahogany, and she ignored his insistent frown, turning to Tony and Evelina.

"Guy mentioned a binding spell he and Mike were working on when they were murdered. Maybe they needed special herbs from the apothecary?"

She reached up and patted her shoulder, expecting to find Bazgul, but found the space unoccupied. A small empty spot opened in her chest. She'd forgotten she'd told Bazgul to say home. If these people hated Pandemonium's 'freaks,' they would lose their minds over a giant pet spider.

"In similar news, I may have made some headway with the letters," Tony said.

"That's great," Mahogany said. Warmth fluttered in her chest at the thought of him researching late into the night. Bob curled into the lap of a freshly showered, bare-chested Tony.

"My uncle's library has some outstanding books on encoding magical messages," Tony said. He smiled down at Mahogany. "I'm close to finding the answer. Shall we?" He held his hand out, motioning for Mahogany and Evelina to go first.

Guy snorted. "Such a gentleman."

"You're just jealous," Mahogany said and started toward the gate.

"What?" Tony asked.

"Nothing," Mahogany said. A few random couples carrying casserole dishes with tea towels draped over them entered the backyard ahead of them.

"Should we have brought refreshments?" A worried frown brought Evelina's eyebrows together. "I can run back to Hot Brews and grab some scones or brownies."

Mahogany entered the manicured backyard and gazed about the area. Pristine grass stretched from an impeccable fenceline to a flawless side garden. Picture-perfect hydrangeas, their blooms like sapphires, shimmered in the afternoon sun.

The landscaping screamed of kobold handiwork. The blue-skinned household sprites loved gardening, especially tending blue flowers like hydrangeas. Mahogany snorted at the irony of a home set against Folk employing them as gardeners.

A man in a pale yellow polo shirt and khaki dockers flipped various burgers at a stainless steel, built-in barbecue. A shelter of snappy red bricks encased the large outdoor cookery nestled under an arbor, spilling over with purple and white wisteria blooms. Next to the barbecue stood a glossy granite counter piled high with food. A mountain of hamburger buns, a year's worth of condiments, bowls of chips, platters of cookies, and vats of potato salad and coleslaw waited in the warming sun. A crowd of around fifty people attired in various pastel floral prints, stripes, and polka dots milled about the yard. Several middle-aged white women held wine glasses; the yellow liquid chilled with a single ice cube.

"Definitely not," Mahogany said.

"Oh, my, gods." Evelina stifled a giggle against her cupped hand. "It's like a Caucasian heaven."

"Can confirm," Tony said. "Someone put raisins in the potato salad."

"Monsters," Mahogany said, making a face.

"Welcome!" the man in the yellow polo said. He gave a jaunty wave from the grill with the heavy metal spatula.

Mahogany, Tony, and Evelina raised their hands and gave a small wave in return.

"Oh, good! The more, the merrier." A woman wearing a yellow jumpsuit that matched the man's shirt at the grill approached them.

Her platinum blond hair was in a neat bun at the back of her head. Tendrils of hair curled in perfect spirals kissed her neck. "New faces! How lovely. Please, tell me your names." She leaned in towards Tony, her eyes blinking expectantly.

"I'm Tony Applegate. This is Evelina." He stopped and peered at Evelina.

"Moore. Evelina Moore," Evelina said, finishing Tony's sentence.

"Mahogany," Mahogany said, her voice flat.

Tony and the blond woman turned to Mahogany, waiting for her to finish.

"Just Mahogany," she said.

"Her parents were fans of Cher," Evelina said, squeezing Mahogany's hand.

"Well, that's interesting." Something cold crept into the blond woman's eyes, and her gaze lingered on Mahogany's pink hair. "Have you lived in Pandemonium long?" she asked. Her thin lips curled up in a practiced smile that lingered beneath her eyes but didn't touch them.

"Most of my life," Mahogany said. Beside her, Guy's semi-solid form flickered. Mahogany side-eyed him.

Evelina nodded. "Born here."

The woman turned her plastic smile and vapid stare to Tony. "Just a few months," he said.

"Marvelous!" the woman said. "I'm Nancy Roberts. Head of the committee to revamp Pandemonium. You know, make it more family-friendly." Again, her gaze lingered on Mahogany's hair.

A young man, wearing black slacks and a white button-up shirt approached them. He carried a tray heavy with glasses half-filled with various wines. Nancy stopped him with a much too familiar hand on his chest. Her red nails glinted like blood against the pale of his shirt.

Evelina raised a shapely eyebrow, and Tony coughed.

"Would you like something to drink?" Nancy's hand lingered on the server's well-built chest. One of her red lacquered nails slipped under a button on his shirt.

"No, we're good," Mahogany said. She grabbed Evelina and Tony's arms and steered them away from Nancy.

"I have to work later." Tony gave an apologetic smile as Mahogany towed him away.

"That was strange, right?" Mahogany said once they had placed some distance between themselves and Nancy.

"I've stepped into suburban hell," Evelina said. "These people are the 'freaks.' They want to get rid of what makes Pandemonium great." She blew out a long breath. "I'm getting angry."

"Down, girl." Mahogany nodded toward a small stone patio raised higher than the rest of the yard. Nancy had moved to take center stage and clapped to get everyone's attention.

"Thank you all for coming today. Keith and I appreciate it." The man at the grill saluted with his spatula.

Next to Mahogany, Guy flickered again.

"What's wrong with you?" Mahogany leaned over and whispered.

"I recognize that voice."

"What's going on?" Tony whispered back, tilting his head toward Mahogany.

"From where?" Mahogany asked.

"Who's where?" Evelina joined in.

"The woman who came to the brownstone and argued with Mike before our murderers." Guy's flickering quieted. "I wasn't sure at first, but that's her all right."

"Now that is interesting." Mahogany turned her attention back to Nancy. "Guy says she's the woman who argued with Mike at the brownstone." She lifted her chin at Nancy.

Evelina and Tony refocused their attention on the bottle blond. Evelina made a tiny noise in the back of her throat while Tony crossed his arms and watched Nancy's every move like a bird of prey watching a mouse.

"If you're like me, you moved here to leave the bustle of the city behind. To raise your kids in a safe town with top-notch schools," Nancy addressed the crowd.

Those gathered nodded. Mummers of agreement floated through the smoky, meat-scented air. "Pandemonium could be the perfect place if it weren't for the strange elements polluting the area."

More nods and mutters of agreement followed Nancy's statement.

"Scaly women selling demonic lawn ornaments. Crime rates are off the charts. People walking around in elf and fairy costumes all year long, drunken brawls at that skeevy pub with the ridiculous name, and now murder!" Nancy raised her fist that wasn't clutching her ice cube chilled chardonnay and pumped it in the air.

The crowd cheered and bellowed. It struck Mahogany how much the pastel-clad suburbanites resembled a pitchfork-wielding mob—the type of mob Pandemonium's founders had fled.

Mahogany, Tony, and Evelina stood huddled together, the only people in attendance not frothing at the mouth.

"Do you know how that man died?" Nancy eyed the rapt crowd, pausing for effect. "Someone stabbed him with a jeweled dagger. What kind of person kills someone with an antique knife?" She paused again, allowing her rhetorical question to spin in the crowd's collective brain. "A freak, that's who." Nancy pulled her shoulders back and gave the group a smug smile.

"Um, excuse me." Evelina waved her hand in the air. Her cheeks flushed with emotion.

Mahogany and Tony peered at the Fae; their eyes wide.

"Excuse me, Ms. Roberts." Evelina gave a little jump.

Nancy raised a dark eyebrow and scowled at the pretty, natural blond. "I'm not taking questions."

"Perfect, because I don't have a question. It's more of a correction," Evelina said. "I have it on good authority Pandemonium's crime rate is the lowest it's been in a decade."

"How would you know?" Nancy's plastic mask barely concealed her rage bubbling beneath the surface. Clearly, she didn't like people contradicting her.

"I work at Hot Brews. The officers come in and brag about how safe Pandemonium is," Evelina said, her tone challenging.

"Didn't you say you've lived here your whole life?" Nancy questioned, her Botox smooth forehead twitched, but her eyebrows didn't budge.

"That's right." Evelina nodded. She folded her arms over her chest in defiance, ready for a fight.

"A local?" A man in a powder blue fedora and unironic matching miniature tie said.

"Do you see? These are the lies and deceits we need to do away with. We need to eliminate this destructive element to keep our families safe. Halloween Town must end!" Nancy screeched. Several sips worth of wine sloshed over the rim of her glass in her exuberance.

The crowd flew into a frenzy, jeering and yelling obscenities.

Nancy smoothed her butter-colored jumpsuit and snapped her fingers several times. A short, round woman scampered in from the side of the yard, holding a clipboard stacked with papers.

"Sylvia Stout, the secretary of the End Halloween Committee, will come around with a petition for you to sign." Nancy waved to Sylvia to collect signatures. "If we are going to make genuine change, we need to get good people on the town council. People sympathetic to our plight."

"I only meant people shouldn't get so worked up," Evelina muttered through gritted teeth.

"It's okay." Mahogany squeezed Evelina's hand. "Next time, refrain from calling out a murder suspect."

Evelina blanched and gave a meek nod. "Right. That was pretty stupid."

"Okay, gang. Besides Guy placing Nancy at the brownstone before the murders, does he recognize anyone else?" Tony glanced around the crowd.

"I recognize her," Evelina pointed to Sylvia Stout.

Mahogany grabbed Evelina's outstretched arm and pushed it down.

"Sorry. I did it again, didn't I?" Evelina blushed.

"Her?" Mahogany frowned in the direction Evelina had pointed. "The End Halloween secretary?"

"Yeah, she was the woman with Brian O'Malley in Tipsy's yesterday," Evelina said. "The woman with the black hat."

Understanding dawned on Mahogany's face, and she slapped Evelina on the arm. "The cobbler's booty call."

"Do you think Nancy knows she slums with the locals?" Guy asked.

"Not a chance," Mahogany replied, shaking her head.

"We should split up and mingle," Tony said. "See what we dig up. Maybe Jeff is around here somewhere."

"I'll go with Guy. Tony, you stick with Evelina, just in case someone decides to," Mahogany paused, studying the group of budding fascists, "get out of order. Also, keep an eye out for any festering demon bites."

"Festering what?" Tony said, his expression perplexed.

"I'm with him," Evelina said, hitching a thumb at Tony. "Did Bazgul bite someone?"

"He jumped at the murderer when we were at the brownstone," Mahogany said. "He may have bitten them. Bazgul isn't sure. He closed his eyes." Mahogany remembered Bazgul's mood after they'd returned home, and how defensive he'd become. Had she been too hard on him? Her hand went to her necklace and rubbed the pentagram, trying to ignore the growing pit in her stomach.

"You were there with the murderer?" Evelina leaned away; her face stricken. "You didn't mention that."

Tony's golden skin shed some of its glow. "You never said the murderer knew who you were. This changes everything. You could be in danger."

Mahogany shrugged off their concern, her pink curls bobbing. "Everything happened so fast, I doubt they got a good look at me. Let's see what clues we can find and get out of here." She started toward Sylvia Stout, leaving Evelina and Tony staring after her, their expressions incredulous.

Chapter 18

Mahogany crossed the yard and approached the other woman. "Sylvia? Hi, I'm Mahogany." She offered her hand to the other woman.

Sylvia's small eyes studied Mahogany's outstretched hand, but made no move to take it.

"All right then." Mahogany lowered her hand, hooking her thumb into a belt loop of her jeans. "How did you get involved with this whole End Halloween endeavor?" Mahogany made a sweeping motion to the crowd in Nancy's backyard.

Sylvia pressed the clipboard to her chest and folded her plump arms over it as if it were a child in need of protection. "Nancy is the mastermind behind the project. Her son attends the local public high school, but she wants to get him into the private school instead. The discriminatory administration denied his application."

It was Mahogany's turn to stare blankly at Sylvia. "Hippolyte is a private girls' school," she said.

Hippolyte's School for Girls had been a fixture in Pandemonium since the town's inception. Started and overseen by displaced Amazonian warriors, Hippolyte boasted an outstanding equestrian program. Their archery coaches had churned out more Olympic medalists than any other.

"It's discrimination," Sylvia said, blinking rapidly.

"Is it, though?" Mahogany asked. "There has to be more to this End Halloween thing than Nancy's son getting rejected from the girl's boarding school."

Sylvia's gaze lingered on Mahogany's pink kinky hair. "Of course there's more to it. His rejection from Hippolyte was the breaking point."

"Does the committee meet regularly?" she asked, trying to find a delicate way to ask where she and Nancy might have been when Guy and Magic Mike had been killed.

"Yes," Sylvia answered slowly. "We try to meet once a week, but we do most of our work by phone. Are you interested in signing the petition for a special election? If not, the conversation is over."

Okay, so delicate wasn't the right approach. Mahogany squared her shoulders and plunged in. "Where were you when the murder went down the other night?"

Behind her, Guy folded his arm over his chest and narrowed his gaze at Sylvia. "That's right, Mahogany. Let her have it."

"You're joking?" Sylvia snorted but shook her head when it was clear Mahogany was serious. "I was with Nancy planning this meeting," Sylvia said. While her voice exuded confidence, she blushed from the collar of her lavender blouse to the roots of her red hair.

Mahogany smirked. "If I were to go over and ask Nancy where you were, would she corroborate your story?"

"Of course she would." Sylvia nearly spat the words.

"All right," Mahogany said and started toward Nancy, who stood next to her favorite server, downing another sweaty glass of chardonnay.

"Wait," Sylvia said, her eyes wide. A thin film of sweat beaded her thick upper lip.

"Got her," Guy said.

Mahogany turned back to Sylvia, an eyebrow raised inquisitively.

"I wasn't with her. I was with," Sylvia peered around to make sure no one listened to their conversation, "Brian O'Malley."

"The town cobbler?" Mahogany said, an eyebrow arching high on her forehead. It turns out their afternoon romp at Tipsy's was a regular thing.

"Keep your voice down." She glanced around like a plumber sifting through a customer's panty drawer. "We were in a private room at Tipsy O'Lush's getting dinner."

"Let me get this straight," Mahogany said. "You were out with the town cobbler, a local, in a private room at Tipsy's, the den of inequity?"

Sylvia nodded, her blush darkening. "Nancy would kick me off the End Halloween Committee if she knew."

"If I knew what?" Nancy said. Her tidy bun had come loose. She swayed on her long, thin legs from what Mahogany concluded was chardonnay poisoning.

The blush drained from Sylvia's pudgy neck and round cheeks as if she were the victim of a Vampire attack. "Oh, um, I, uh," Sylvia stammered.

Nancy placed her hands on her hips and glared at Sylvia, jettisoning the rest of her wine into the grass. "I'm waiting."

Sylvia's shoulders slumped, and she closed her beady eyes. "I've been seeing Brian O'Malley."

Nancy recoiled as if slapped. "The cobbler, again? You told me you'd finished with him." The words dripped from Nancy's lips like venom from a cobra's fangs. "First, Jeff is a no-show, and then you betray me."

Sylvia opened her eyes and met Nancy's gaze. The shorter woman's eyes brimmed with tears. "I love him. He's just so beautiful. Those muscles. His piercing blue eyes. The red hair. He's my kryptonite." Sylvia prised her gaze from Nancy's enraged glare. She raked her glare over the yard before landing on the handsome buff server Nancy had sexually harassed.

Nancy turned to follow Sylvia's gaze and sputtered. "How dare you?"

From his station at the grill, Keith, Nancy's husband also followed Sylvia's eye line. His meek, plastic face flushed at the realization of what Sylvia implied.

"You're off the committee! How could I have ever trusted you?" Nancy collapsed in a nearby lawn chair and began sobbing.

Tony appeared and took Mahogany's hand, breaking her trance. She shook her head at the slow-motion, drunken, white woman train wreck occurring before her eyes.

She smiled and allowed him to lead her from the party.

"That was bananas," Evelina said. In her arms, she held a bowl filled halfway with potato chips. Balanced atop the chips was a paper plate containing three steaming veggie burgers, complete with buns and all the fixings.

"No, that's bananas," Mahogany said, pointing to the stolen food.

Evelina puffed out her chest. "I'll have you know this is not only our lunch, but it allowed me to interview the hot-stuff server."

"I wondered where you'd gone. What did the server say?" Tony asked.

"Well, his name is Hank Williams," Evelina began.

"Like Hank Williams, the country singer?" Mahogany interjected. A smirk played across her full lips.

"His mom's a big fan," Evelina said. "He just graduated from high school, and he's doing yard work around the neighborhood to save for this fall when he goes off to college in Eugene."

"Just graduated high school?" A look of disgust twisted Mahogany's features. Evelina nodded, her expression mimicking Mahogany's. "Isn't it illegal to have minors serve alcohol?"

"Gross," Tony said. "Nancy's old enough to be his mom."

"Oh, that's not the half of it. Nancy pays him extra if he works with his shirt off," Evelina added, taking a large bite from a burger.

Mahogany and Tony both grimaced.

"Apparently, Nancy has a slew of newly graduated high school boys working for her. Some of which would do almost anything to make her happy."

"Like murder?" Mahogany said, raising an eyebrow.

"Perhaps. Hank mentioned that there is one special boy who Nancy keeps on the down-low." Evelina took another bite of her burger.

"Who?" Tony asked.

"Hank wasn't sure."

"It's a good lead," Tony said. "Let's head back to my place to update the murder wall, check out the letters, and eat before it gets cold." He eyed the burgers hungrily.

"That's stealing," Mahogany said, nodding to the bowl as they headed to their respective vehicles.

"I prefer unauthorized borrowing, thank you very much," Evelina said. "I doubt they'll miss it."

"We need to confirm Sylvia's story," Mahogany said. "If she was with the cobbler, she's off the suspect list."

"Oh, I love shoe shopping," Evelina said. "Nancy mentioned watching a movie with her family, but when I asked her husband what he was doing the night of the murders, he said he and his son were home alone. No wife."

"She was probably with the hunky server," Tony said. "What about MIA Jeff? Karrie said he'd be here."

"Nancy mentioned he was a no-show. She seemed upset about it." Mahogany said.

"No last name Mahogany. What brings you here on this fine summer day?"

Startled, Mahogany turned. Detective Teresa Sawyer strode over the immaculate sidewalk toward them, her New Balance sneakers nary making a sound.

"Hello, Detective. Just enjoying a bit of barbecue." Mahogany's heart danced the mambo against her ribs.

"I just finished chatting with Karrie Samuels. She mentioned three private detectives came and spoke with her about the murders at the brownstone. You wouldn't know anything about that?" The detective studied them with a keen eye.

Evelina made a squeaking noise in her throat.

"I don't know what you mean?" Mahogany said, silently cursing Evelina for telling Karrie they were investigators.

"She described the three of you as if you were standing in front of her. Quite a feat of mental gymnastics for someone three sheets to the wind. You must have made a lasting impression."

Mahogany, Tony, and Evelina stared at the detective, but remained silent.

"You wouldn't mind showing me your investigator's license?"

"We're sorry," Evelina blurted, her face the color of beets. "It just came out. It won't happen again."

"You're right. It won't. Now get out of here with that stolen food before I arrest you for criminal impersonation."

Chapter 19

T ony jogged up the cement walkway to his front door and paused before slipping the key into the lock.

"What's the matter?" Mahogany asked. She joined him on the narrow front porch, followed by Evelina. The porch's shade was several degrees cooler than the sun, and she welcomed the reprieve.

"It's open," he said, not taking his eyes off the front door.

"Did you forget to lock it?" Evelina shot Mahogany a concerned look. Mahogany's scalp prickled, telling her she already knew the answer to the question.

"Not a chance," Tony said. "I grew up in San Francisco. I lock the door on autopilot."

Tony slowly pushed the door with the tip of his shoe. Mahogany stopped him, placing a hand on his arm. "Wait. Guy, can you check to see if it's safe? Someone might still be in there."

Guy nodded and vanished into the house, and Mahogany closed her eyes, summoning Bazgul. Much to her concern, Bazgul didn't arrive immediately. Nearly a minute later, a red-brown haze lazily appeared before solidifying into a tarantula. Bazgul perched on Mahogany's shoulder and took a defensive posture. Ready to sink his mandibles into anything that threatened his master and her friends. Well, Evelina, at least. Tony might be on his own.

A few minutes later, Guy reappeared. "All clear. It looks like they broke in through the sliding glass door from the backyard. They trashed the place." He shook his head. "It looks like the brownstone after my murder."

Mahogany nodded, her heart sinking. "They're gone but brace yourself. Guy says whoever broke in left a mess."

The intruder or intruders had ransacked the cozy home. Books were thrown from their shelves and lay in heaps. Broken glass littered the kitchen floor and countertops. A spiderweb of cracks distorted the images of the framed Led Zeppelin poster hanging over the fireplace. The couch cushions lay in ruins, sliced open beyond repair.

"Do you think the murderer did this?" Evelina asked. She clutched the sizable yellow chip bowl defensively to her chest.

"No doubt in my mind," Mahogany said.

"Bob," Tony said, his voice giving a slight shake. "Bob, here, boy."

After a pause that hung in the air with heart-wrenching uncertainty, Bob emerged from a bedroom. He trotted up and wove himself around Tony's legs, purring like a jackhammer. Tony bent to pick up the large black cat. "Thank goodness they didn't hurt you." He buried his face in Bob's fur.

"Your eight-legged friends are in one piece too," Evelina said, nodding to the untouched terrariums.

"Tony, I'm so sorry," Mahogany said. "This is all my fault. If I hadn't let you and Evelina investigate, this wouldn't have happened." She surveyed the mess, guilt tightening her throat.

"Don't be ridiculous. I understood what I was getting myself into. We're investigating murders. Plus, this tells us something significant," Tony said.

"What's that?" Mahogany asked. Her gaze roved over the destroyed house. How on earth could this be a good thing?

"Now we know the murderer is still in town, and they know we're on to them." Tony scratched Bob behind the ears before setting him on the couch. The large black cat sat primly and blinked at his owner with large green eyes.

On her shoulder, Bazgul relaxed. "Does it look like anything's missing?" Mahogany asked.

Tony peered around the once-tidy house. It looked as if a tornado had touched down. "I'm not sure." A tinge of hopelessness colored his tone.

Evelina walked over to the coffee table and lifted one side. A slew of broken and misplaced objects cascaded onto the floor. Bob jumped into the air and landed on the other side of the couch, hightailing it down the hallway. Evelina set the bowl with their lunch on the now unencumbered surface and said, "Neither of you is good to me on an empty stomach. Let's eat and then start cleaning."

Mahogany and Tony nodded. They flipped over the ruined couch cushions, shoved them back into place as best they could, and dug into their veggie burgers. Evelina coaxed Bob from his hiding place with the promise of treats. Mahogany shared her lunch with Bazgul, who thankfully remained in his dry, non-slimy spider shape.

"You know," Mahogany said around a mouthful of burger. "Stolen burgers taste better than the ones you pay for." However vanilla the End Halloween party might have been, Kenneth Roberts sure knew how to barbecue.

"If this is good, wait until you taste the stolen candy." Evelina reached into her purse and pulled out a handful of miniature-sized candy bars. "They had a bowl of the stuff with the food."

"They had trick-or-treat-sized candy at an End Halloween barbecue?" Mahogany rolled her eyes. "Will the irony ever cease?"

"I can't believe the intruder ruined the murder board," Tony said. He stared at the rolling chalkboard. Whoever had broken in had smashed the slate and erased their notes.

"Here, have a Milk Dud," Evelina said, offering him a small yellow box.

"Thanks," Tony said, taking the candy. His lower lip protruded in a pout.

Evelina glanced around the living room and kitchen. "Maybe we should call the police. You could be in danger."

Tony shrugged. "I'll be fine. Getting the police involved will be more trouble than it's worth. I've experienced several break-ins in the Bay Area, and the police didn't catch the intruder or recover anything they took. No. We'll clean up and move on."

Evelina glanced at the sliding glass door—the ransacker's entry point. "Doesn't your uncle have protection spells on the house?"

"He did, but they need refreshing every few weeks. It's been too long for them to be effective." Tony shrugged and pointed to himself. "Human, remember?"

Evelina approached the back slider. "This looks forced." Evelina squinted at the bent latch on the door.

"Do you mean a human broke in?" Mahogany asked. A person possessing magic would have used a spell to enter an unprotected home.

Mahogany joined Evelina and glanced into the yard. It would have been easy for anyone to walk in from the street. "They could have been Folk who didn't use their magic intentionally to throw us off."

"That does it," Evelina said. "I'm calling my aunt. She is fantastic at locking spells. She'll have this place sorted so no one, human or magical, will break in again." Evelina grabbed her phone and dialed. "Aunt Cecilia, I need a favor." She wandered into the kitchen, carefully stepping around the broken glass as she proceeded.

"Okay, let's get started." Mahogany hopped to her feet. "Where do you keep your cleaning supplies?"

Tony pointed toward the kitchen. "The cupboard next to the fridge."

Mahogany opened the pantry and retrieved several trash bags and a dust broom. "We'll get all the big items and then vacuum."

"Right," Evelina said. "My aunt will be over this evening and sort everything out." She grabbed a trash bag from Mahogany. "I'll start in the living room."

"I'll work in the kitchen," Mahogany said.

Several hours later, Mahogany placed the last book on the shelf near the front door. She glanced over her shoulder at Evelina and Tony in the living room and asked, "Have either of you seen anything suspicious recently? Strange cars? Anyone out-of-place watching you?"

"Define suspicious," Evelina said, rolling her eyes. "Everything that takes place in Pandemonium is suspicious."

"You know what I mean," Mahogany said. "Being followed. Strange phone calls, that sort of thing."

Both Tony and Evelina shook their heads.

Mahogany frowned. "Me neither. Whoever did this has to be watching us but is staying on the down-low." She thought back to all the photos of her in Thad's hotel room. She'd never noticed him or his camera, and he'd been creeping around for weeks.

"It could have been Thad. We know he's sneaky," Mahogany offered.

"Good point," Tony said.

"Maybe Nancy Roberts's special someone that Hank Williams mentioned did this. While we were at the party, she got her boy toy to break in to scare us off the case," Evelina said. She brushed a sweaty lock of golden hair from her face and sighed. "All right, that's the living room finished."

"Perhaps. But we can't discount Jeff Samuels, either. He didn't show up at the barbecue this afternoon. He could have easily broken in here," Tony said. "The kitchen's back to. Well, as normal as it can be. I'll have to go shopping again." He peered around the once well-stocked space. Two large trash bags sat at his feet, filled with most of the food he bought on his last shopping trip. "I don't understand why anyone would come in and wreck my shopping. It's so unnecessary."

"Guy said this looked like the brownstone after the murders, but I disagree. It's worse," Mahogany said.

"What do you mean?" Evelina asked.

"Both have this undercurrent of rage, but this ransacking feels more personal," Mahogany said.

"More personal than being murdered?" Evelina asked, raising an eyebrow.

Beside her, Guy snorted.

"I mean spoiling food, the unnecessary evisceration of the couch, nearly breaking Oleander. It's different." Mahogany gave the wooden owl a loving squeeze and placed him on the shelf.

"Oleander!" Tony leaped over the garbage bags and took Oleander into his hands. "Hey there, buddy. Did you see anything? Did you see the ransacker?"

The air buzzed around Oleander, making Mahogany's ears itch.

"Thanks anyway." Tony placed the wooden owl housing the spirit of his uncle's familiar back on the bookshelf. "They wore a black hoodie. He didn't see their face."

Mahogany and Guy glanced at each other. "That's what the murder wore when I ran into them at the brownstone."

"What this reminds me of is a police raid," Evelina said. "We've all seen them on TV. Someone gets a RICO charge, and the cops go nuts on their house, slicing mattresses, breaking toilets, tearing apart books, etcetera, etcetera.

"Oh, no!" Tony turned and raced down the hallway.

Mahogany and Evelina exchanged a startled glance.

Tony reemerged from the hall. "They took them."

"Took what," Mahogany said, moving into the living room.

Tony's deep-set eyes met Mahogany's. The emotion held there made her heart beat faster. "The letters," Tony said. "They're gone."

"I can't believe we forgot about the letters. That was the whole reason we came back here." Evelina threw her hand into the air and flopped onto the sagging couch.

"Are you sure they're gone, and we didn't accidentally clean them up?" Mahogany said, her stomach sinking. They needed those letters. What if they held the key to this whole murder mystery?

"Positive. I left them in the bedroom this morning," Tony said. "In my uncle's study, I found a book on magical ciphers and masking inks. I was sure the answer would be in here."

"We could try stealing another letter from Thad's room," Evelina suggested, but her voice didn't carry its usually optimistic lilt.

"I need a drink," Tony said. "Either of you want to join me?" He walked around the counter and into the kitchen, pulled open a cupboard, and filled Bob's food dish with fresh kitty kibble. "At least they took pity on you, Bob."

"I can't," Mahogany said, checking her phone. "I told Neema I'd help her in the store this evening."

"I'll go," Evelina said. "I start work early tomorrow morning, so I can't stay out too late." She grabbed her purse and headed for the door.

Mahogany suppressed a burp of irritation as Tony grabbed his car keys and joined Evelina near the door. She held out her hand, and Bazgul, who ogled Bob as he ate, crawled into her palm.

Chapter 20

M ahogany maneuvered her Vespa into the parking space at the back of Haughty Hemlock and entered the kitchen. She set Bazgul on his cat tree before grabbing a few treats of freeze-dried mealworms, which he gobbled up.

"Oh, good. You're back," Neema said, popping into the kitchen to start the kettle for tea. "Would you mind watching the store while I get a fresh cup and hit the powder room?"

"Sure," Mahogany said, smiling. Neema was in her early fifties and still couldn't use the word bathroom. Any semblance of what she did in the small, windowless room that kept her secrets was off-limits.

Mahogany and Guy headed into the apothecary while Neema danced upstairs to relieve herself. The store door opened, and Cheryl, their postal carrier, rushed in. She nodded to Mahogany and dropped off a stack of letters fastened to a small package by a rubber band before dashing back outside.

"Thanks, Cheryl," Mahogany said. Cheryl waved through the window as she quick-stepped to her next delivery. Mahogany thumbed through the letters. Most were supplier invoices. The package was from one of their distributors.

"That's better," Neema said, returning to the store, holding a steaming cup of tea. "Anything good?" She nodded to the stack of mail.

"Nope. Just bills and junk mail," Mahogany said, handing the pile to Neema.

"The trash needs taking out," Neema said as she sifted through the mail.

"No problem." Mahogany gathered the sheer plastic bag from the wastebasket behind the counter. As her fingers gripped the door's brass handle, someone pushed it open, almost hitting her.

"I'm so sorry," said a tall woman, her auburn hair coiffed into a vintage bob. Mahogany recognized the woman from the day before.

"That's all right," Mahogany said, taking the door from the woman and holding it open. "How's your stomach?"

"My stomach?" The woman frowned.

"You bought tea for your stomach yesterday. Something about the plane food bothering you," Mahogany said.

"Yes, of course. I rarely share my health issues with strangers. My stomach is much better. Your, um, employer's tea did the trick. I'm here for more in case my issue crops up again." The woman held her hand to the side of her mouth when she said 'issue' as if it were a euphemism for explosive diarrhea.

"Neema makes the best teas in the state." Mahogany held up the trash bag. "If you'd excuse me." She mimicked the woman's gesture and whispered, "Duty calls."

The woman gave a high-pitched giggle and swept past Mahogany into the store. Mahogany stepped onto the sidewalk and let the door fall shut behind her. She rounded the side of the building to the alley and tossed the trash bag into the dumpster. As she turned, Cheryl waved to her from across the street, an envelope in her hand.

Mahogany jogged to meet her—boot heels tapping on the smooth asphalt, and her pentagram necklace bouncing around her neck.

"This one got mis-sorted," Cheryl said, handing over the envelope.

Mahogany took the letter, thanking Cheryl. She glanced at the piece of mail, her heart skipping a beat—Thaddeus Spike's neat block lettering graced the front.

She peered over her shoulder towards Haughty Hemlock, ensuring Neema wasn't checking up on her. Mahogany stuffed the letter into the back pocket of her jeans. She couldn't believe her luck—just as the investigation had tanked with the break-in at Tony's, the post office had hand-delivered a new lead. In high spirits, Mahogany skipped across the street, unaware of the scaly hand holding back the black curtain in Humbaba's window.

Guy stood in front of the apothecary, eyeing the slow-moving traffic warily. "Love letter?" Guy said, his voice teasing, hands on hips.

"It's from Thaddeus Spike to Neema," Mahogany whispered, heading for the Hemlock's door.

Guy squealed like a fifteen-year-old girl who'd come face to face with her celebrity heartthrob. "What are the chances?"

"Low, but not impossible," Mahogany said. Before she could open the Hemlock's door, Neema pushed it open and held it for the woman with the digestive 'issue.'

"Thank you so much, Ivy. Please come again if you need anything," Neema said.

"Absolutely!" Ivy said, her bob swishing. "Before I head home, I'll stop by and pick up presents for my family."

"We look forward to seeing you again."

Neema turned to Mahogany. "You were gone awhile."

"I ran into Tony and Evelina." Mahogany waved vaguely to the other side of the street.

"They didn't go into Humbaba, did they?" Neema gave a slight shiver. "Those women give me the creeps. I don't understand how they stay in business."

"Never underestimate the tunnel and bridge crowd. Tourists will buy anything," Mahogany said, following Neema inside the apothecary.

"About that Tony," Neema said, changing the subject.

"What about him?" Mahogany asked, a cautious eyebrow raised.

"He's super cute. And those eyes. Is he part Asian?

"Japanese," Mahogany said, feigning interest in Tony's eyes. It was a subject she'd spent long hours musing over; their shape, the way the light caught their gold-green color, the feeling she got when they found hers.

"What's the deal with him and Evelina?" Neema asked.

"Um, as far as I know, they're just friends," Mahogany said. At least, she hoped they were just friends.

"And you two? Is there anything more than friendship with him?"

Mahogany gave a short laugh and waved away the notion of her and Tony. She would rather an angry mob boil her in oil on the Witches' Sabbath than admit to Neema she had a crush on Tony. "We're just friends."

"That's too bad. I had hoped he was a catch." Neema picked up a sheet of paper from the counter. "Gather these for me. We have an order to fill. I have to run out and grab a few things we don't have. You'll have to watch the store." Neema headed into the house, leaving Mahogany on her own.

"When are you going to admit you've got the hots for Tony?" Guy asked.

"Mind your business," Mahogany said, looking over the list of items.

"Let me tell you. Life is short. Super short. Don't waste it being afraid." As Guy spoke, he stared out the Hemlock's large plate-glass windows. Karrie Samuels stood on the sidewalk in front of the apothecary, blotting her eyes with a soggy tissue. She looked as if she hadn't stopped crying since the last time Mahogany had seen her.

Mahogany watched Karrie struggle to wipe her nose with the disintegrating tissue. Sighing, she swept away a crumb of apprehension at engaging the dreary young woman and got her feet moving. She opened the heavy front door and peered out. "Karrie, would you like a cup of tea?" she asked.

Karrie shoved the crumbling tissue into her pocket. The way the fabric bulged, Mahogany could tell it wasn't alone. "Tea?" Karrie sniffled and her eyes filled with fresh tears. "That's the nicest thing anyone's said to me since..." Sobs overtook her and she couldn't finish her sentence.

Mahogany resisted the urge to scurry back into the store and pretend she hadn't spoken to the puffy-eyed young woman. Instead, she held the door wide and stepped aside for Karrie to enter.

"What are you doing?" Guy floated next to Karrie, his semi-solid body flashing. "This isn't what I meant when I said life is short. I meant to ask Tony out, not bother Karrie. She's told you everything she knows."

"The kettle's hot. I'll just be a second." Mahogany left Karrie in the Hemlock, who stared wide-eyed around the multitude of glass jars filled with herbs from around the world. Mahogany returned a minute later and offered a steaming mug to Karrie.

"What's in it?" Karrie sniffed the mug's contents and made an encouraging face. "It smells nice. Lemony."

"It's lemon balm, St. John's Wort, and a little red rooibos. It's a calming blend."

Karrie took a tentative sip and smiled. "Thank you." She gazed around the apothecary. "This place is neat. I've never been in before. Jeff would disapprove."

"Speaking of Jeff," Mahogany said, plunging in. "I went to the End Halloween meeting today, but he wasn't there. Nancy seemed pretty upset he didn't show." Mahogany scowled, remembering Nancy, the creepy predator of teen boys.

Karrie had wandered over to a rack of posters depicting images and Latin names of various herbs and mushrooms. "I haven't seen him since Wednesday morning. He came home in a huff, shoved some clothes into a bag, and left."

"What time did he come home?" Mahogany asked.

"About three in the morning." Karrie took a sip of her steaming tea and swiped at her eyes with the back of her hand. "He made a ruckus when he got home and woke me up. Guy and I were supposed to meet later in the day and have a picnic." She sniffled and closed her eyes, sending tears streaming down her damp cheeks.

Mahogany thought back to the night of the murders. Shortly before she'd entered the brownstone, the town clock had struck two. That left plenty of time for Jeff to stab Mike and bludgeon Guy before trying the same on her with the fireplace poker. A bitter taste flooded her mouth. The timeline didn't bode well for Jeff Samuels.

"Does Jeff usually disappear for days at a time?" Mahogany asked, raising an eyebrow.

Karrie shook her head. "Maybe once in a while, but not like this. I'm sorry I lied, but I expected him to be back by now." She stared at the posters, her eyes swimming behind pools of tears. "What if he killed Guy and Mike? What if he's on the run?"

"Are you sure you don't know where he might be?" Mahogany repositioned herself, forcing Karrie to look at her.

Karrie took a deep breath and let it out in a rush. "Well, maybe." Her voice hitched. "If he hurt Guy and his friend, I don't think I could bear it."

Empathy, an emotion Mahogany wasn't used to, squeezed her throat and made her eyes prickle. If Karrie's older brother had murdered her boyfriend, what would that knowledge do this fragile girl? Mahogany hated to think.

"Let me help clear his name," Mahogany said. "The sooner I talk to him, the better."

Karrie nodded and sighed. "We have a family cabin out by the beach. He might be there."

Excitement radiated through Mahogany. "I need the address, Karrie. This is very important." She went to the counter, grabbed a sticky note and pen, and looked at Karrie expectantly.

Chapter 21

Mahogany and Karrie chatted until she finished her tea. Before Karrie left, Mahogany supplied her with a handful of fresh tissues.

"You know, Karrie's quite likable," Mahogany said, locking the front door and flipping the sign from open to closed.

"Don't sound so surprised," Guy said, scowling.

"I can't help it. I figured there was something wrong with her since she was interested in you." A sly smile played across Mahogany's lips.

"Ha, ha," Guy said, a touch of mirth dancing in his blue eyes.

Mahogany let the smirk slip from her lips, where it shattered on the polished tile floor. "I hope Jeff didn't kill you, for her sake."

Guy's spectral form flickered, and he let loose a yell that rattled Mahogany's insides. "I hate this. It's frustrating beyond measure not being able to communicate with anyone. Invisibility is the worst. If only I could talk to her."

"Hey, I'm somebody," Mahogany said wryly, then sighed. "I know I'm a sorry substitute for Karrie, but I'm doing my best here." She pulled out her phone and texted Tony: *Intercepted a new Thaddeus letter.* "Besides," she continued, "this new letter might provide some answers." She put the Post-it note with the Samuels family cabin address in her back pocket with Thad's letter. "We'll check out the cabin tomorrow. Hopefully, Jeff will be there."

A second later, her phone buzzed with Tony's reply: *Get over here now!*

Butterflies bumped and fluttered in Mahogany's stomach, and she headed to her Vespa. As she passed the cat tree, Bazgul leaped onto her back.

"Get over here now," Guy trilled. "Aren't you going to text Evelina?" He took a seat behind Mahogany on the scooter.

"Maybe when I get there," Mahogany said, starting the scooter.

Mahogany maneuvered the Vespa through the evening traffic and arrived at Tony's a few minutes later. As she walked up the path, a tall, lith blond woman passed her.

"Good evening, Miss Mahogany," said the woman and inclined her head in greeting. She wore a long skirt that looked to be made of a collection of brightly colored scarves sewn together that swished and coiled about her legs as she walked. Two large earrings dangled from her lobes, glinting in her fair hair.

"Hi Cecelia," Mahogany said. "It's great that you could come over so fast."

"Anything for Evelina," Cecelia said. "She's my favorite niece." A playful smile lifted the corners of her mouth, crinkling her eyes.

As far as Mahogany could remember, Evelina was Cecelia's only niece.

Cecelia glanced over her shoulder at Tony's house. "It's locked up tighter than a frog's butt in water."

Mahogany searched her brain for a response, but Cecelia nodded again and strolled down the walk, her feet making no sound as she went.

Shrugging, Mahogany started up the walk once more when the door flew open. Evelina stood, backlit on the threshold.

"Another letter? What are the odds?" She rushed out the door and slipped her arm through Mahogany's, pulling her onto the porch. Tony met them at the door, beaming. "Ladies," he said and ushered them into the house with a wave of his hand. "Cecelia's charm allows people entry only after I've invited them in."

"Clever," Mahogany said, her jaw clenched. "When did you get here?" she asked Evelina. A tightness cinched around her chest, and she found it hard to breathe.

"Oh, I never left," Evelina said. "We went for beers, which turned into pizza, and then we rebuilt the murder wall."

So much for a super early evening for Evelina, Mahogany thought sourly.

"What do you think?" Tony smiled. He spread his arms wide at one of the living room walls. His energy intoxicated Mahogany, and the tightness in her chest faded. "We've upgraded."

Mahogany approached the new murder wall. The suspects were color-coded and arranged in neat rows with the motives and connections labeled beneath their names. A town map listed the significant points of interest. Far to one side hung a tight cluster of clues, their significance listed on colorful scraps of paper.

"It's beautiful," Mahogany said, and she meant it. A pang of jealousy crept into her throat. While she was stuck at the Hemlock watching a red-eyed Karrie Samuels slurp tea, these two have been here shoulder to shoulder, all afternoon, alone. She bit her tongue to keep from saying something she couldn't unsay.

"Do you have the letter?" Tony asked. He held out a beer to Mahogany. Beads of moisture trickled down the bottle's dark sides.

She took the beer with a thankful nod and drank deeply to hide her irritation. "Got any pizza left?"

Evelina skipped into the kitchen and returned with a plate. Two large pieces of pizza sat at the ready. "I ordered something vegetarian in case you came back."

"Thanks for remembering." Mahogany wished Evelina wasn't so kind. It would be much easier to hate her for getting so much alone time with Tony.

"She's the nicest bitch I've never met," Guy said, reading Mahogany's thoughts.

Mahogany set the beer on the kitchen counter and handed the folded envelope to Tony.

He reached for the letter, his finger brushing against hers, sending a jolt of lightning through her arm. The invisible fishing hook pierced her sternum again, making her hands shake.

Evelina set the plate of pizza next to Mahogany's beer. "Can I get you anything else?"

Mahogany shook her head, loathing that Evelina acted as if she lived here.

"Wait. What's this?" Tony asked, pealing the note with the address off the envelope.

"Karrie Samuels and I had a cup of tea, and she gave me that little gem. It's her family's cabin out by the beach. She thinks Jeff might be there," Mahogany said, and took a bit of pizza. Her stomach gave a grateful growl, and she realized she hadn't eaten since their lunch of stolen burgers.

"That's fantastic!" Evelina crowed and gave a little jump of pleasure. "Oh, but wait." Her face fell. "I can't go tomorrow. I have to work. Eric is threatening retaliation if I miss any more hours."

"Mahogany and I can go," Tony said. "I mean," he hesitated, "if that's all right with you?" He peered at Mahogany. Was that hopefulness in his gold-green eyes?

A flush warmed Mahogany's face, and she nodded. "You can pick me up tomorrow morning," she said. A thrill of excitement plunged through her stomach. A hot lead and a drive with a hotty. What could be better?

"Fantastic," Tony said, pocketing the address. He picked up a dusty, faded tome from the coffee table with the letter in hand. "My research has turned up several types of magically encoded messages and how to reveal what's written." Tony flipped through the book. The musty scent of old paper drifted through the room. "Moonlight works for letters written between lovers. Minotaur urine reacts with messages written in magical blood. Mermaid tears work on ocean water, and letters written with a phoenix feather react to firelight." Tony ran his finger down the page as he read.

"Cool and gross," Evelina said. "Now, we just need to figure out which solution to use."

"I say we start with the least invasive," Mahogany said, wrinkling her nose. "We don't want to cover the thing in bull urine if it doesn't work."

"Excellent point," Evelina said. She pulled back the curtain on the kitchen window over the sink. "The moon's out now. Let's try."

Tony joined Evelina at the window. "Mahogany, would you mind getting the light?" He walked to a standing lamp in the living room and switched it off.

Mahogany flipped the kitchen wall switch and bathed the room in the silver moonlight. Mahogany joined Evelina and Tony at the kitchen window, and together they peered at the blank page as the waning moon shone upon it.

"How long should it take?" Evelina asked after nearly a minute had passed.

"I'm not sure. My uncle's book isn't that detailed," Tony said, lowering the letter.

"Something should have happened by now," Mahogany said, thinking of all the spells Neema had performed using the moon. "At least we know Thaddeus and Neema aren't lovers. Let's try another from the list."

"Firelight is the driest of the three left," Tony offered.

"We need a candle unless you want to start a fire." Mahogany said, glancing at the fireplace. She returned to her plate and took another grateful bite of her cold pizza.

Tony eyed the fireplace doubtfully. "There are some candles in the study." He disappeared down the hall and returned with a long taper standing in a brass candleholder. From his pocket, he retrieved a silver Zippo.

"Set it up over here," Evelina said, patting the kitchen counter.

Tony did as requested and lit the candle. The firelight cast a warm glow through the paper, and they held their breath, waiting. Just when they were about to move on to one of the wet alternatives listed in the book, faint writing appeared on the page.

"It's working," Evelina said, clapping her hand. "Phoenix feather for the win!"

Thad's heavy block lettering darkened until they could decipher the entire message:

YOU ARE IN DANGER. COVER BLOWN. WE COULD BE NEXT.

"Cryptic much?" Evelina said, the excitement fading from her eyes.

"What cover?" Mahogany said, plucking the letter from Tony's fingers. "Blown by whom?"

"She must be hiding from something," Tony offered. He turned to Mahogany, his forehead crinkled in an unspoken question.

Mahogany's thoughts raced. "We came to Pandemonium about twenty years ago. That's a long time to hide." Did this have something to do with the scandal all those years ago in Boston? Was Neema hiding from someone or something? Is that why she changed her name and moved across the country?

"When are you going to tell them about the photo and the mysterious death of Aurora Kingsley? Don't you think it's important that Neema and Mike know each other?" Guy asked.

Mahogany turned toward the murder wall, ignoring Guy.

"Thad had a lot of photos in his room of Neema," Evelina said, her brow furrowed. "If he's the murderer, she might be his next target."

"But why warn her?" Tony asked. "This seems like a heads-up. Not a threat. Maybe the person who murdered Guy and Magic Mike is after them, too."

The frown on Evelina's face deepened. "But why?"

Tony frowned at Mahogany. "We need to talk to Neema."

Mahogany had to agree, but the thought of confronting Neema made her palms sweat and her mouth go dry. They should speak with Neema, but she hesitated. The years of lies, the abduction, and the denial of knowing her family had hardened her heart to the fate of Neema. Even if it meant potential harm coming to herself, she knew she was being irrational, but she couldn't help herself. Maybe she wanted something bad to happen to Neema. The thought sent a chill up her spine.

Mahogany shook her head, sending her pink curls swaying. "I agree," she said, sighing. "But she's not home. She went out to gather some supplies for an order. We could try in the morning before we go searching for Jeff."

Chapter 22

Mahogany woke early the following morning and found Neema hadn't come home. A seed of worry planted itself in her chest, and she checked her phone. Neema had texted late in the night: *ran into an old friend. be home tomorrow.*

To say that Neema staying out all night was odd would be lying. Neema had never spent the night away before. What the hell was going on?

She focused enough to get herself ready before Tony arrived.

Half an hour later, he knocked on the back kitchen door. Mahogany pulled it open, willing the butterflies bumping in her stomach to chill.

"I stopped by Hot Brews on my way," Tony said, holding out a white to-go cup adorned with a silhouette of a witch flying past a full moon. "Chai, whole milk."

"Thanks." Mahogany took a grateful gulp. "This is perfect."

Tony smiled and took a step back as Mahogany crossed the threshold. Bazgul leaped onto her shoulder as she passed his cat tree.

Nervous jitters buzzed through Mahogany at the thought of being alone with Tony for the hour-long drive to and from the beach. A slight sweat glazed her underarms.

He opened the passenger door, and Mahogany and Bazgul slid into the seat. "Thank you," she said, wracking her brain for the last time anyone had opened a car door for her and came up empty.

Tony replied with his stunning smile that crinkled his rectangular eyes and headed around the car.

"Smooth," Guy said as he passed through the back passenger door and settled on the bench seat.

Mahogany ignored him. "Do you know where we're going?" she asked as Tony hopped behind the wheel and started the engine.

"Yep, already plugged into the GPS." Tony backed out onto the street and headed toward Old Beach Road.

"What exactly are we going to do once we get out there?" Mahogany asked. She peered out the window, all too aware of how close Tony's arm was to hers.

"Stake out the house. I've brought snacks." Tony smiled, his eyes twinkling.

"He opens doors, brings your favorite drink, and provides snacks. What's not to love?" Guy said from the back seat. "He brought kettle chips and Milk Duds. If you don't want to date him, I will."

Mahogany returned Tony's smile, her heart hammering against her ribs. "You are a true crime junkie," she said before glancing into the back seat. "Guy, quit snooping around Tony's car."

Guy stuck his tongue out at her and settled back against the seat.

"It's been a secret dream of mine to become a private investigator," Tony said. "Wow. I've never told anyone that before."

"Why not?"

"Well, my mom is a cop, and she hates PIs. Much like our Detective Sawyer." Tony guided the car through the gently curving road toward the beach. Behind them, Pandemonium fell away, giving room for thick groves of pines growing on either side of the blacktop.

The thick forest had once produced a magical field that deterred humans from venturing into the town. Over the years, humans had become less superstitious. They'd attributed the foreboding vibe coming from the woods to their imaginations. Nothing that science couldn't explain. For nearly a century, the spell had kept Pandemonium invisible to humans passing by. Now they flocked to the area, thinning the woods to make room for larger and larger houses. The Guild of Myth and Magic had helped the Pandemonium city government pass laws preventing new construction in the woods surrounding the town. However, with the human interest in town committees, it was only a matter of time before they challenged the ordinances.

"Well, I don't know if our fine detective hates PIs or people who pretend to be them. How was growing up with a cop for a mom?" Mahogany asked.

"She's pretty cool now that I'm an adult, but as a teenager, well, you can imagine. Super strict. My brother and I couldn't do anything: no sleepovers, no trick-or-treating, background checks on our friends and their parents."

Mahogany could do more than imagine. She had experienced a very similar childhood. Neema hadn't let her do anything most kids got to do.

"A couple of years back, she made detective with the San Francisco Police Department, but by then, I'd moved out." Tony let the sentence dangle and Mahogany waited for him to say more. When he spoke again, he changed the subject. "How about you? You mentioned growing up in Pandemonium." He glanced at her before returning his eyes to the road.

Mahogany gazed out the window. She hated talking about her childhood. "Yeah. Neema and I got here when I was about three."

"Where were you before that?"

"The Boston area." Or so she'd been told. Mahogany was never sure if Neema was spinning tales or telling the truth. However, the photo of Neema with Magic Mike as teens seemed to confirm the Boston story. Part of it at any rate.

"Is that where the rest of your family is?"

"Yep." Maybe, she thought.

"Do you ever see them?"

"Not exactly." Mahogany turned her attention back to Tony. "I'm surprised Evelina didn't mention it."

"About what?" Tony glanced between Mahogany and the road, a frown drawing his eyebrows together.

"About me. About how Neema and I came to Pandemonium." A light buzz rattled Mahogany's head, causing a nervous tingle to crawl over her scalp.

Tony shook his head. "What about it?"

Mahogany shrugged and gave a heavy sigh. "What do you know about changelings?"

He paused for a moment. "My dad told me and my brother stories of fairies taking human babies and then leaving one of theirs in its place. Sometimes the fairies used the stolen baby as a servant. Sometimes they raise the baby as a Fae." He glanced at Mahogany, confusion scrawled over his face.

"Neema says she saw me sitting in a random front yard and had to have me," Mahogany said, her voice hard.

Tony gawked at her, the car veering slightly to the shoulder before he corrected their course. "You're serious," He said. Out of the corner of her eye, Mahogany noticed his knuckles go white as he gripped the steering wheel. "Why would she do that?"

Mahogany shrugged. "The ways of Folk are a mystery," she said vaguely.

Tony was quiet for nearly a minute. The road slipped past the car—the trees blurring to streaks of green, coloring their periphery. The scent of pines tinged with salty ocean air as they neared the coast. "That's truly messed up, Mahogany. I'm so sorry." He reached over and grabbed Mahogany's free hand and squeezed it, but didn't let go. Her sexy garden dream flooded back in Technicolor vibrancy, making her skin tingle and her stomach knot.

"You have arrived at your destination," chimed the GPS, jarring Mahogany from her thoughts of starry nights and passionate kisses.

Tony released Mahogany's hand and steered the car into a small gravel lot. Across the road, a small contingent of trailers sat in a cleared patch along the highway nestled into the trees. The Samuels family cabin was less log and more double-wide. Parked outside one of the shabbier models was Jeff Samuel's battered black jeep.

"I don't want to stereotype, but that tracks," Mahogany said, peering across the road at the rusty trailer.

"Snob," Tony said, sending a playful glare in Mahogany's direction, a smirk on his full lips.

Mahogany gave a dry laugh, throwing her head back against the seat. "I don't want you to feel sorry for me about the whole changeling thing. I do that enough myself."

Tony turned to Mahogany, his face stricken. "I'm outraged, Mahogany. She kidnapped you from your family and then raised you as your abductor. That's horrible. Why haven't you left? Turned her in? Gone in search of your family?"

She took another sip of her chai, which had gone cold. "That all seems easy on the outside, but that's not how it works around here." She turned to face Tony and was startled by how steely his welcoming eyes had become. "In the magical world, they handle differently things. It's perfectly normal for a magical family to show up with kids that aren't theirs. It's how some families operate. In their eyes, Neema did nothing wrong. She's cared for me since I was a baby. She didn't make me a servant or mistreat me, but she won't let me leave either." Mahogany shrugged. "I've tried. I wanted to go to college, but without a birth certificate, it's hard to get around."

Tony gave a solemn nod, his gaze softening. "What I want to know is, do the murders have anything to do with Neema taking you all those years ago? I mean, the letter warning Neema to be careful that someone had blown her cover. What if one of your family members discovered what had happened and came looking for Neema and their missing baby?"

Mahogany had given the idea of her family searching for her lots of thought over the years. "It's unlikely," she said. "After the Fae leaves the changeling with the human family, it withers away and dies. They would have no reason to look for me. To them, their baby died over twenty years ago."

"Wait. Is Neema a Fae? Where did she get a Fae baby?"

Mahogany shook her head. "A Fae came to her for help, and the bargain they struck was her baby for a potion."

Tony turned in the driver's seat to face Mahogany. "That's some dark fairy tale stuff."

Mahogany shrugged, her pink curls bobbing. "Welcome to Pandemonium."

Her phone chimed with a text from Evelina: *The cops took Karrie Samuels in for questioning. They want Jeff.*

"Holy crap. The police are on to the Jeff lead," Mahogany said, pocketing her phone again.

"Then we don't have a lot of time," Tony said, frowning.

Movement across the road grabbed their attention, ending the conversation. One of the trailer doors flew open, and Jeff Samuels stumbled down the steep, weather-beaten wooden steps. He wore dirty jeans and an opened flannel shirt, revealing well-toned abs and chest.

"There he is," Mahogany said, and instinctively scooted down in her seat.

Tony did the same, and they gazed over the dashboard at the trailer.

"Wait. Who's that?" Tony asked, nodding to the open trailer door. A tawny arm appeared, covered in tattoos.

"Holy crap," Mahogany said.

A lithe leg followed the tattooed arm, bare to the thigh. Silver bells jiggled on a slim ankle.

"Layla?" Mahogany asked. She leaned forward to get a better look.

"Who's Layla?"

"She owns the reptile store in Pandemonium, Beast of Burden." Mahogany squinted at the tall, dark-skinned woman across the road.

"I didn't know Pandemonium had a reptile store."

"It's over by the museum." Mahogany reached for the door handle, and before she knew what she was doing, she stepped out of the car.

Chapter 23

"Hey, Layla." Mahogany stood on her tippy toes and waved her arms over her head.

Across the road, Layla turned and squinted. "Mahogany? What are you doing here?" she called. She hopped down the trailer's steps and passed a bewildered and somewhat panicked-looking Jeff.

Layla and Mahogany bonded years ago over Bazgul. While they weren't friends per se, they were on friendly terms. Mahogany frequented Beast of Burden to resupply Bazgul with his favorite treat of mealworms. Maybe Evelina was right about the younger generation of Folk not hating humans, Mahogany thought. Why hadn't she seen it before?

Mahogany trotted across the road. "I might ask you the same thing." She eyed the bare-chested Jeff, who had turned a lovely shade of crimson.

Layla nodded toward Jeff. "Just letting off a little steam." She winked and then leaned over and whispered in Mahogany's ear. "But just a little."

"No doubt." Mahogany glanced at Jeff again, her eyes narrowing.

Tony's shoes crunched over the gravel as he joined Mahogany. "Hi, I'm Tony." He held his hand out to Layla.

"You sure are." Layla's black eyes sparkled as she took Tony's hand. Her long, wavy black hair fell like a dark river over her shoulders.

"What the hell are these freaks doing here?" Jeff demanded. He puffed out his chest and sauntered over like a rooster defending his territory. His gaze fell on Bazgul, and his lip curled in a sneer.

Layla raised an eyebrow. "Freaks?"

"We're investigating a murder," Mahogany said.

Beside her, Guy cleared his throat.

"A set of murders," Mahogany added. "Can you tell us where you were from midnight till 4:00 on Tuesday morning?" Mahogany said, turning to Jeff.

"Investigating? You two aren't the cops," Jeff said, his sneer widening, baring his teeth in an animalistic warning. "I don't have to say anything to you about anything. Babe, let's go back inside."

"Don't you want to know who was murdered?" Tony asked.

"I do," Layla said. "We've been out here since Tuesday. Drove out at about 5:00 a.m."

"An older man who went by the nickname Magic Mike and a young man named Guy Miller. Are you sure about the time?" Mahogany said to Layla, her gaze lingering on Jeff.

"Positive," Layla said. "We were listening to the radio on the drive. There was a station break, and the DJ gave the time."

Jeff hooted with laughter. "That little twerp Guy is dead? That's hysterical."

Layla, Tony, and Mahogany glared at Jeff.

"He's lucky I'm dead," Guy said through clenched teeth.

Bazgul chattered on Mahogany's head.

"You've got that right, Bazgul. He's a total jerk," Guy said.

"What?" Jeff said, sobering. "It's not like you knew the freak. Why do you care if one of them dies?"

"Wow," Layla said, her eyebrows shooting up in surprise. "You're cute, but a complete ass." She turned to Mahogany and Tony. "This fool was with me Tuesday night. He stopped by the Beast of Burden and hung out while I closed. Then we headed over to Diabolical Delight for dessert. We fooled around a bit in his jeep for a couple of hours. Then he dropped me at my place so I could pack a bag, and he did the same at around 4:30 before heading here."

Tony and Mahogany glanced at each other.

"That goes along with what Karrie told us yesterday," Tony said.

"You talked to Karrie?" Jeff's cocksure posture dissolved into a near-seething rage. "You have no business talking to my sister." Jeff closed the distance between Tony and himself in a few quick strides and grabbed his shirt collar.

"For the love of Sheeba," Layla said. She slipped a smooth, dark hand onto Jeff's shoulder and whispered in his ear. A split second later, Jeff relaxed, his eyes filming over. He released Tony and backed away.

Layla sighed. "Sorry about that. He has an unhealthy relationship with his sister. If Jeff hadn't been with me when those poor people were murdered, he'd be at the top of my suspect list."

"What did you do to him?" Tony asked. He waved his hand in front of Jeff's face. Jeff just stared back, as if in a trance.

Layla shrugged. "Jinn magic. I can be persuasive when I need to be."

Mahogany smirked at Layla. As an unshackled Jinn, Layla's magical capabilities ranged far wider than persuasion. Mahogany wondered if Jeff knew what kind of fire he was playing with, where Layla was concerned. The stupid grin on Jeff's face told her he understood very little about a lot.

"You should get him back to town. The police are questioning Karrie about the murders," Mahogany said.

Layla nodded.

Tony and Mahogany had just gotten into the car when a dark blue Charger pulled up to the Samuels' trailer. Detective Teresa Sawyer stepped out of the vehicle, her gray New Balance crunching on the gravel. As she scanned the area, her gaze lingered on Tony's car.

"Crap!" Mahogany said, ducking behind the dashboard. Tony stared at her, his expression blank, and she grabbed his collar, pulling him down.

"What?"

"It's the detective," Mahogany whispered.

"Crap," Tony whispered back. "Why are we whispering?"

The proximity of Tony's face to hers sent Mahogany's brain into an uncontrolled free fall. His aftershave drifted into her nostrils—salty air and sunshine. Butterflies bumped and tangoed in her stomach.

"It seemed appropriate." She managed. Mahogany inched her gaze back over the dash and watched as the detective shook her head, turned toward Jeff's trailer, and knocked on the door.

Tony peaked through the windshield and watched the detective enter the trailer. "That's our cue." He started the engine and got the car moving.

"Does Jeff know Layla's a Jinn?" Tony asked as they drove back to Pandemonium.

"No way."

Bazgul sat on Mahogany's lap, munching away on mini candy bars. So far, he'd remained in his spider form. Mahogany petted him as he ate, grateful he hadn't slimed her lap with frog goo.

"What a hypocrite," Guy said from the back seat. "That lunatic threw every wrench possible into mine and Karrie's relationship, and here he is, spending a week with a genie." He kicked at an empty snack bag on the car's floor, and it tumbled into the air.

"You just moved something," Mahogany said, her voice filled with astonishment.

"I did!" Guy's voice rose two octaves higher than usual. "Maybe when I get mad enough, I can affect my environment."

Tony glanced over at Mahogany. "Are you talking to Guy?"

She nodded. "He's angry about Jeff and somehow moved a candy wrapper."

"That might come in handy," Tony said. He glanced in the rearview at the empty backseat. "Keep at it, Guy. Maybe we'll be able to converse one day."

Guy leaned between the seats and said, "This one's a keeper. You better make a move before he loses interest."

"That reminds me," Mahogany said, changing the subject. She turned in her seat, the seat belt cutting into her neck. "Did you understand Bazgul back when he called Jeff a douchebag?"

"I did," Guy said. He rubbed his chin. "That hasn't happened before. Wow! Today is full of firsts." He kicked at the wrapper again, but his foot passed through it.

Mahogany frowned and faced forward again. Guy's power was building—interacting with the physical world and now understanding Bazgul. She wasn't sure what it all meant.

With a sigh, Mahogany let the sight of the thick pine trees wash over her as they sped back to Pandemonium.

Chapter 24

E velina strode up the walk to Nancy Roberts's well-tended
house and rang the bell. Against her belly, she held the large
plastic bowl she'd taken from the End Halloween barbecue.

There was a soft scuffling sound from the other side of the door,
and a few moments later, Nancy flung it open. She stared down her
small, surgically sculpted nose at Evelina and pursed her lips.

"Why, if it isn't the police statistics expert," Nancy said, recogniz-
ing Evelina.

"Oh, you remember that," Evelina said, biting her lip. "Listen,
I'm sorry for calling you out like that in front of everyone. It wasn't
very chill." Evelina said, remembering the venom Nancy had flung
her way after she contradicted her. "Here." She held out the bowl, an
apologetic smile raising the corners of her mouth. "I need to return
this."

Nancy snatched the bowl and began closing the door without
another word when Evelina interrupted her.

Evelina flung her hand up, stopped the door from closing, and asked, "You wouldn't know someone named Magoris?"

Nancy peered at Evelina through the gap between the door frame and the door. "Should I?"

"He was staying in one of the brownstone apartments. You know the rentals across town? Mid-fifties? Paunchy? Long gray beard? Ring any bells?"

"Doesn't sound familiar," Nancy said and pressed on the door.

"Well," Evelina said, jamming her foot in the gap, halting the door from closing, "it's just that you match the description of a woman seen speaking to Magoris before he was murdered." Well, Evelina thought, maybe not a physical description. Guy had recognized her voice, which was enough for her.

Nancy glared at Evelina's foot, barring her from retreating into the house. "A witness?" she said, aiming her glare at Evelina. "Are you some sort of private investigator?"

Evelina smiled. "Something like that," she said, noncommittally. "This witness is sure it was you. He said you showed up and argued with Magoris. When he wouldn't give you what you wanted, you turned to threats."

The acidic expression souring Nancy's prim face relaxed slightly, and she returned Evelina's smile. "Your witness is mistaken. I have never been to the brownstone apartments. And I certainly have never met this Magic Mike person you're referring to."

Evelina's smile widened. "I never mentioned his nickname."

Nancy's eyes narrowed, and Evelina could see the gears in the older woman's mind grind with the effort of keeping her composure.

"Listen, you little twerp. I don't know who you think you are, but you can't just show up at my home and question me like a common criminal." Nancy kept her voice low, but her words dripped with rage. "I demand to know who's been defaming my good name."

A snort sounded from behind Evelina, and she turned. Sylvia Stout stood at the foot of the porch, a box filled with what appeared to be office supplies held against her heavy bosom.

"Your good name?" Sylvia mocked. "Don't make me laugh, Nancy. You're the worst of the worst."

Nancy leveled her dagger-like gaze at Sylvia. "I hope that's the last of it," she said, nodding to the over-filled box in Sylvia's arms.

"Not as much as I do. If I never have to set eyes on you again, it will be too soon, you nightmare of a hypocrite." Sylvia swung the box toward the porch and released it. It arched through the air, narrowly missing Evelina, and landed with a thud. The force jettisoned a stapler and several pens upon impact, scattering across the porch's stained wood.

"Watch it," Nancy snapped, throwing the door open and stomping onto the welcome mat.

Evelina stepped to the side and watched the two women square off like old west gunslingers at high noon.

"Make me, you cougar slag," Sylvie shot back, moving up the steps like a jungle panther stalking its prey.

"What did you call me, fatty," Nancy spat back. She rolled her bony shoulders and cracked her neck.

"I said you're an old, dried-up hag who grooms high school boys because you can't hack it with men your age." Sylvia advanced another step. Red splotches crept up her neck, blending with her rosy cheeks.

A groan escaped Nancy, and she reeled to the side, bringing up her right hand, and swung.

Sylvia dodged the blow with the prowess of a ballet dancer. As she dodged, Sylvia cocked her left shoulder back and brought around a left hook that caught Nancy in the cheekbone, sending her sprawling.

Evelina watched wide-eyed and wished she were anywhere but on Nancy's porch. Sylvia turned and glared at her, and Evelina held her hands in surrender.

Sylvia dropped her indignant glare back at Nancy and snorted again before turning on her heel and returning from whence she'd come.

Nancy groaned and held her face.

Once Evelina was sure Sylvia was gone, she dropped to her knee and gazed at Nancy. Blood gushed from her nose, and her puffy right eye was turning a lovely shade of black.

"Nancy?" came a male voice from inside the house.

Evelina gazed up and swallowed a bark of laughter that bubbled up her throat.

Hank Williams's shirtless figure stood in the open doorway—a lacy maid's apron covered his bare chest. He gazed down at Nancy and Evelina, his eyes narrowing.

"Breath a word to anyone," he said, his jaw muscles twitching.

"You can call me Vor," Evelina said, placing an arm around Nancy and helping her to her feet.

"Who?" Hank said, moving to Nancy's other side and supporting her with a muscular arm around her waist.

"Vor is the Icelandic goddess of hidden knowledge and wisdom," Evelina said. She maneuvered the whimpering Nancy through the doorway and into the house.

Hank started at her, his expression blank as he and Evelina crouched, placing Nancy on the sleek, gray sofa. "If you say so."

"Don't just stand there," Nancy spat. "Get a towel. I'm bleeding everywhere." She held her hands over her nose, which continued to stream blood.

This snapped Hank into action, and he disappeared into the kitchen and returned with a dish towel. He placed it gingerly against Nancy's gushing nose.

"Ice would be good, too," Evelina said, nodding to Nancy's swelling eye.

"Right," Hank said. He placed Nancy's hand on the towel and disappeared into the kitchen again.

"Nancy," Evelina said. She took a seat next to the injured woman. "This whole thing you've got going with the high school boys is not only illegal, it's downright creepy. You know as well as I do that it's only a matter of time before that shiny new detective discovers you were arguing with a murder victim before his untimely death. Then you know she'll find out about your boy toys."

Nancy glared at Evelina around the blood-soaked towel. "What exactly do you propose?"

"His name is Steve," Hank said. He approached slowly with a zip lock baggy filled with ice.

"How do you know that?" Nancy demanded, her face stricken.

"Steve, who?" Evelina asked, her gaze bouncing between the pair.

"Murphy," Nancy said after a moment. "Steve Murphy."

Evelina gaped. "The Lepre, er, I mean the local kid from Tipsy O'Lush?" Evelina said, catching herself. Getting into an argument with these two over the fact that Leprechauns were real wasn't something she had the mental capacity for.

Nancy snatched the ice from Hank and sat back on the couch. "Sylvia's right. I am a hypocrite." She sighed heavily. "I was with Steve the night Magic Mike was killed."

"He's like, sixteen," Evelina stood, her face distorted with disgust. "Isn't your son the same age?"

Nancy closed her eyes, offering no answer.

"I take your silence as a sign of guilt." Evelina rubbed her temples, trying to calm the rage that boiled there. She was all about being sex-positive, but she reserved that positivity for consenting adults. "Where did you and Steve meet?"

"In the basement of Tipsy's. We have a weekly arrangement," Nancy said without opening her eyes.

Evelina got to her feet, feeling much heavier than when she arrived. "You're the freak, Nancy. Not the Folk who made this town what it is. It's people like you who hide behind self-righteous indignation," she said, heading for the door. "If I were you, Hank, I'd cut my losses and stay far from this family and its dysfunction. Maybe think about investing in some therapy."

Tony pulled a piping hot glass casserole dish from the oven and set it on the kitchen counter to cool.

Mahogany's stomach rumbled as the scent of steamy tomato sauce, garlic, melted cheese, and spinach hit her nose. "That looks and smells amazing," she said. She took a sip of wine to hide her watering mouth when a heavy banging on the front door startled them both.

Frowning, Tony went to the door and came back with a red-faced Evelina.

"Good to know your aunt can wield a strong security spell," Mahogany said, smiling. Tony had to verbally ask her, Guy, and Bazgul in after they'd returned from the beach.

"I have more pressing news. You will never guess what happened today, she said breathlessly.

"Whoa," Mahogany said. "You look like you've run a marathon."

"Practically." Evelina dropped her purse onto the floor, the items inside clattering in protest. "I walked to Nancy's from work to return the bowl and ran the entire way here."

"You did what?" Tony slid his hands out of the potholders bearing a pentagram and a black cat and plopped them onto the counter next to the casserole dish. "She could be the murderer. What if she had attacked you?"

Evelina brushed away Tony's concern with a flick of her wrist. "I'm fine. Plus, I couldn't just sit around waiting for you two to get back. There are murders to solve."

Mahogany caught Tony's eye from across the kitchen and shrugged. "Isn't Nancy's place only a few blocks from here? You look like you've run miles."

"We Fae are not runners. We're more like gliders," Evelina said. "Did you make that?" She pointed to the steaming casserole dish.

"He did," Mahogany said, a smile gracing her lips.

Evelina waggled her eyebrows. "Cute, smart, and he cooks? It's a trifecta of awesome."

Tony cocked an eyebrow at them. "The guys in Pandemonium sure have set a low bar."

Guy's head emerged from the center of the steaming lasagna. "You're in for a treat," he said to Mahogany. "This has got to be the best lasagna I've never tasted."

"So low you could trip on it," Mahogany said, scowling at Guy hovering inside the casserole dish.

"Remember Ralph Evans?" Evelina nudged Mahogany in the ribs. "He was so in love with you." She frowned. "I see him at the cafe, like, all the time. He became a cop."

Mahogany groaned and rolled her eyes. She'd done her best to pretend she hadn't seen Ralph's moon-eyed stare locked on her, beckoning her to sit with him.

"Old Ralphie boy, huh?" Tony put his elbows on the counter and rested his head on his hands. "What did Ralphie do?" He blinked at Mahogany, his mouth curving in a smile.

"More like what he didn't do," Evelina said before brushing Ralph Evans away with a flick of her wrist. "Forget about Mahogany's doomed love life. I have news."

Tony pointed at Mahogany. "This conversation isn't over."

Mahogany's cheeks tingled with a blush—of all the subjects she wanted to talk with Tony about, Ralph Evans didn't even make the list. "Right." She swiveled on the bar stool and peered at Evelina. "What did you find out?"

Evelina kicked off her sandals and hopped on the stool next to Mahogany. Tony placed an empty wineglass in front of her. "Red or white?"

"Red, please." After Tony filled her glass, Evelina launched into her odd encounter with Nancy Roberts, Hank Williams, and Sylvia Stout.

As she spoke, Tony dished out plates of lasagna, including a small saucer for Bazgul. The demon spider chattered before digging in, sending flecks of cheese and sauce onto the counter.

When Evelina had finished, Mahogany and Tony stared at her, mouths agape, their minds reeling.

"This is delicious," Evelina said, pointing to her nearly demolished lasagna with her fork. "I need the recipe."

"Wow, I mean, sure, no problem, but wow," Tony said in reply to the recipe request and Evelina's surreal encounter.

"The woman who wants to drive away all the freaks from Pandemonium is not only a practicing pedophile but dipping her hook in the local pool?" Mahogany shook her head and took a large sip of wine. "And with a Leprechaun to top it off."

"The image of them in the basement is seared into my brain," Tony said, and shivered. "I've seen Steve bringing up stock to the bar. I never would have thought he was Nancy's type. Not that there's anything wrong with him, it's just..." he trailed off.

Evelina stifled a snort. "Steve's more Naruto, while Hank could give Adonis a run for his money."

"I don't think it's so much how they look," Mahogany said. "It's their age."

"It's like she never grew up," Evelina said around a huge bite of her dinner. "I mean, what grown woman bones a teenager on a dirty couch in the basement of a pub?"

Tony held up a hand. "Stop. I can't." He shook his head. "It's too much."

Mahogany frowned at her plate, her appetite taking a sudden dive. "We need to verify both Nancy's and Sylvia's alibis."

"Oh, we can cross Sylvia and Brian O'Malley off our list. I ran into the sexy cobbler at the cafe this morning, and the topic just came up." Evelina winked. "He and Sylvia were together all night. If you know what I mean."

"That still leaves Nancy and Steve," Tony said, looking green.

"Which means we need to go to Tipsy's," Evelina said, her eyes shining. "Oh!" she gasped. "I almost forgot. How did the beach go? Did you find Jeff?" Evelina hopped off the bar stool and took her empty plate to the dishwasher. "Did you get my text?"

"We did, and he's been with Layla all this time." Mahogany carried her unfinished dinner to the sink.

"Get out! Layla the Jinn? I thought she had better taste than that." Evelina frowned and shook her head. "So, he has a solid alibi. Darn it."

"Detective Sawyer showed up as we were leaving," Mahogany said, helping Evelina load the dishwasher.

"Oh no. What happened?"

"Nothing much, but she made a point of letting us know she saw us," Mahogany said, drying her hands on a dishtowel.

"What do you mean?" Evelina asked, popping the dishwasher shut.

"She means I got a ticket for not signaling as I came into Pandemonium," Tony said, covering the casserole dish with foil.

"But there's no turn coming into Pandemonium." Evelina frowned as she gave Bazgul a loving scratch. "It's a straight shot."

"Exactly," Mahogany, Tony, and Guy all said together.

"That's harassment." Evelina stomped her foot in frustration.

"It's a warning," Mahogany said, holding her hand out for Bazgul, who climbed onto her shoulder and nuzzled her cheek.

Chapter 25

M ahogany, Tony, Evelina, and Guy entered Tipsy O'Lush's. Friday night revelers packed the pub, sending a din of conversation and alcohol fumes into the enclosed space.

Tony approached the crowded bar and spoke with the tall Walsh brother tending it. A few moments later, he nodded and returned to where Mahogany and Evelina waited.

"Steve's working," Tony said, bouncing from foot to foot. A crease pulled his eyebrows together.

"What's wrong?" Evelina asked. "Do you need the little boy's room?"

Tony shook his head. "He's in the basement."

"The basement?" Mahogany said, her face scrunching into a mask of disgust. An image of a worn couch crusted with unknown bodily fluids materialized in her head.

She turned to Guy. "Are you sure you want your murder solved?"

Guy crossed his arms over his chest. "Wimp."

Mahogany turned to Tony and Evelina. "Guy's fine with being a ghost. He says we don't need to go to the basement and witness Steve and Nancy's love nest."

"Quit being such a virgin." Evelina grabbed Mahogany's arm and guided her through the crowd to the door leading to the basement at the back of the pub. She pulled open the basement door and descended, towing Mahogany behind her, followed by Tony and Guy.

The well-lit basement held the same dimensions as the pub above. The dry concrete floor met sturdy brick walls. Crates filled with bottles of wine and a dizzying array of hard liquor mingled with cases of beer and soda stacked into neat rows running the length of the room. The smell of stale beer and wine hung heavy in the air. A scraping sound traveled to them from deeper in the basement.

They followed the sound and discovered Steve, a short, chubby, red-headed kid of sixteen puffing over a keg as he maneuvered it into place alongside several others. A multitude of coiled nylon tubes ran from the various casks through the basement ceiling, connecting to the taps in the bar above. Steve's pale cheeks and forehead carried a light dusting of acne mingled with dark freckles, making his sixteen years seem more like fourteen.

Tony cleared his throat, making Steve jump and almost upend the keg.

"What are you doing down here?" Steve's pitchy voice died against the brick walls. "Employees only."

"Hi, Steve. I'm Mahogany, and these are my..." she hesitated, searching for the right word. "Associates, Tony and Evelina. We have a few questions for you." She kept her gaze trained on Steve, trying to push images of Nancy and this child from her head.

"Associates?" Steve asked, raking his small eyes suspiciously over the trio. "What type of questions?" He turned back to the keg and affixed to the taps snaking to the bar upstairs.

"We're making inquiries into the murders that happened last week. Do you know anything about that?" Evelina's violet eyes narrowed with suspicion.

"Uh, why would I know about that?" Steve asked. His voice filled with teenage reproach, reminding Mahogany of her adolescence. Steve didn't wait for an answer and began loading a hand truck with cases of beer and wine.

"Where were you last Tuesday?" Tony asked.

"Here," Steve paused his work and gazed at Tony, frowning. "Why would you need to know where I was?"

"Can anyone vouch for you?" Mahogany asked. Her gaze drifted around the basement. Most of the space was backstock. However, nestled in a narrow alcove in the far back corner sat a small CRT television perched on an overturned milk crate. Two video game controllers were hooked to a gaming console on the floor. Their cords meandered across the dusty concrete. Beyond that was a ratty couch. *The* ratty couch they had heard so much about.

"My uncles. Why?" A flash of fear rippled over Steve's pale face. "What did you hear?"

"What can you tell us about Nancy Roberts?" Evelina asked, stepping toward Steve, her hands on her hips.

"Nancy, who?" The words came out as a squeak rather than actual speech. He cleared his throat. "I don't know any Nancy?"

"Well, she sure seems to know you?" Mahogany said, her gaze running over Steve's chubby frame.

Steve's small eyes darted over the trio, genuine fear spiking in them. Steve squeaked again. "She's my friend's mom. Why would I be with her?"

Beside Mahogany, Evelina brightened, and she knew the Fae had discovered the infamous couch. "We know about you and Nancy, Steve. She confessed that the two of you have been having an affair."

"What?" Steve said, trying to sound confident and failing miserably. "That's ridiculous. She's super old. I mean, sure, she's hot, super hot, but super old."

"Let's try this a different way," Evelina said, crossing her hands over her chest. "If I were to test those couch cushions for yours and Nancy's DNA, I wouldn't find any?" She nodded to the couch in the back corner.

Mahogany and Tony snapped their attention to Evelina, their eyebrows raised. Pretending they were legit investigators was one thing, but pretending they were CSI was next level. A level Mahogany was pretty sure Sawyer wouldn't tolerate, but, in for a penny, in for a pound.

"Yeah," Mahogany said, doubling down on Evelina's bluff. "I bet Mama Walsh would love to hear about your extracurricular activities after closing. What do you think?" She addressed Evelina and Tony. "Mama Walsh has to be around the same age as Mrs. Roberts. They probably even go to the same PTA meetings."

"Please don't do that," Steve pleaded, his gaze darting between Mahogany and the ratty couch. "My mom can't find out. She'd lock me up and kill Nancy."

"I mean, that wouldn't be a disappointment," Tony said, stroking his chin. "Nancy's a creep. However, I would hate to see your mom go to prison."

"You're avoiding the question, Steve," Evelina said, taking another step toward the couch. She turned to Tony. "Get me some swabs and the black light. I want to tear this place apart."

Steve's pasty skin blanched, making his pimpled, freckled face glow in the basement's stark light. "All right! All right! We meet Tuesday evenings after closing, but she wasn't with me last week."

"Are you sure?" Evelina asked.

Steve nodded frantically, resembling a bobblehead. Mahogany feared his head might pop off his shoulders. "I tried calling her, but it went straight to voicemail. My uncles let me sit in on their poker game." Steve's gaze fell to the floor. "I lost my paycheck."

Mahogany gazed from Tony to Evelina. Their expressions matched the gears grinding in her head—if Nancy Roberts wasn't with the underaged Steve, why lie about it? What could be so awful that someone would knowingly lie about committing a felony? Could Nancy have actually murdered Magic and Guy?

"Did she ever mention a wizard named Mike? Magic Mike?" Mahogany asked. An image of Nancy and Steve on the couch popped into her head before she could stop it. A shiver ran through her, tightening her stomach. If they couldn't nail this woman for murder, they had to stop her from molesting any more of Pandemonium's youth.

"Magic Mike?" Steve shifted from foot to foot. The scent of nervous body odor slowly filled the space, emitting from the quickly spreading saucers of sweat under Steve's arms. "Yeah, once or twice."

"Concerning what?" Mahogany asked, her tone clipped.

"About getting her family's powers back." Steve's beady eyes darted between Mahogany, Tony, and Evelina.

"Powers? Her family was Folk?" Evelina shot a look at Mahogany, her eyes wide.

Steve wiped his forehead with the palm of his hand. "She's going to kill me. Please don't tell her I told you. It's a big secret, especially with the whole End Halloween thing."

Tony approached Steve and placed a hand on his shoulder. "We won't say anything. Just tell us what you know."

Steve sighed and nodded. "The Guild stripped her family's power a few generations ago for messing with resurrection magic."

"One of her ancestors tried to bring someone back from the dead?" A wave of goosebumps traveled over Mahogany's arms.

"He didn't try. He did it. Her great-great-grandfather brought his wife back after a carriage accident." The saucers of sweat under Steve's arms had reached his waist. "If you don't believe me, there's a family photo of the Roberts in the bar."

"Why did Nancy think Mike could help restore her powers?" Mahogany said, taking a step towards Steve and Tony. Mahogany remembered a sepia photo containing several creepy towheads in Tipsy O'Lush. She'd thought they looked familiar. The family resemblance to Nancy was uncanny when she thought about it.

"She'd heard he was a powerful wizard." Steve shook his head and moved away from Tony, who let his arm drop. "I tried to tell her that once the Guild removes magic, that's it. There's no getting it back, but she wouldn't listen. Nancy wholeheartedly believed Mike could help her, but when he sent her away, she'd threatened him." Steve's head sank, and his shoulders slumped.

"Threatened him how?" Tony asked.

"She told him he'd be sorry." Steve looked up at them with large, doleful eyes.

"That could be murdery," Mahogany said, eyeing Evelina and Tony.

"If anything else comes to mind, please call us." Evelina pulled a white business card from her purse and handed it to Steve.

He took the card and nodded.

"Nancy's not off the hook for the murders. Steve just pulled her alibi out from under her," Mahogany said as they returned to the pub.

Evelina frowned. "I really hoped we had finished with that horrid woman. But," she said, brightening, "Nancy might go to prison for murder, and I'm okay with that."

"Not to change the subject, but I am both impressed and alarmed. Collecting DNA?" Tony said to Evelina as they headed for the door.

"It just popped into my head," Evelina said. "He looked so gullible. I figured he wouldn't understand that we'd have no way of doing anything I threatened."

"What I want to know is when did you have business cards made?" Mahogany said.

"Uh, Mahogany," Guy said, getting her attention.

Mahogany followed Guy's gaze. Thaddeus sat nursing a pint at his usual table in the back of the pub.

"Look," Mahogany said, nodding in Thad's direction.

"Perfect," Tony said. "Shall we?"

Chapter 26

Mahogany led the way to where Thad sat and joined him without asking. He eyed Tony and Evelina with curiosity, but when his gaze fell on Mahogany, his eyes lit with understanding.

"You found me," Thad said, staring into Mahogany's dark brown eyes as if trying to send her a telepathic message.

"You knew we'd come and talk to you?" Mahogany asked.

"I've been waiting for you to return after breaking into my room." Thad sat back in his chair, his tall, lean frame imposing.

Evelina's lower lip pooched in a pout. "I thought we'd been stealthy."

Thad nodded. "If I hadn't placed a protection charm on the door, I might not have known."

Mahogany nodded. "Wizards are a suspicious bunch."

"And when someone's out to kill you, you get paranoid, too." Thad rubbed a weathered hand over his face.

"Who's trying to kill you?" Tony asked, placing his elbows on the table, his expression lined with concern.

Thad shook his head. "I wish I knew. Maybe I could have saved Magic Mike, and his young apprentice."

"Guy," Mahogany said. "His name is Guy."

"How do we know you didn't murder them?" Evelina asked. "You seem to have a stalker streak with all those photos in your room."

"Occupational hazard. I've been a photographer most of my life. Journalism mostly." He sighed. Sadness pulled at his gaunt features. "I was outside taking photos when Mike was murdered. I raced inside, but Mike was already gone."

"We didn't see any pictures in your room of the murder," Evelina said.

Thad gave a dry laugh that cracked like dry bones. "I dropped the camera when I ran inside."

"Why didn't you go back for it?" Tony asked.

"I was in shock and didn't notice I'd lost it until the next day. When I went back, it was gone." Thad's gaze implored them.

Mahogany shook her head, her pink curls swaying. "I looked through Mike's evidence box. We didn't find a camera."

"Wait, you got into the evidence locker?" Tony said, his face lighting in astonishment. "How?"

"We'll talk about it later," Evelina said, patting Tony's arm.

"Maybe it's in my evidence box," Guy said. "We didn't search there."

"True," Mahogany said, pursing her lips in thought. "The port-o-hole is still there. We could check."

Thad nodded. "If you find the camera, you'll find the murderer."

A commotion passed through the assembled patrons as the front door banged open. A slew of uniformed police officers stormed into the pub, followed by the plainclothes Detective Teresa Sawyer.

The detective, swarmed by the officers, strode over to Thad.

"Thaddeus Spike?" Detective Sawyer said, knowing the answer.

Thad nodded.

"I am arresting you on suspicion of murder." The detective nodded to one of the uniforms, and she moved to handcuff Thad and read him his rights as she led him away.

"Imagine my surprise at finding you three here," the detective said with a scowl. "I should arrest you for interfering with a police investigation."

"We're just visiting with an old friend," Tony said.

"You know Mr. Spike?" Detective Sawyer raised an eyebrow and crossed her arms over her chest.

"Neema knew him a long time ago," Mahogany said. "Why is he a suspect?"

Before Sawyer could answer, two more uniformed officers approached. Each carried boxes filled with camera equipment and stacks of black and white photos.

"We gathered these from the suspect's room," the first officer said.

Mahogany stood and stifled a gasp. The officer was none other than Ralph Evans. He offered Mahogany a slight smile, then turned back to the detective.

"Well, well," Sawyer said, peering into the box of photos. She pulled a latex glove from her pocket and picked up the top image. "I think we need to have a chat down at the station, Mahogany."

The detective held the photo up so Mahogany could see it. Thad had captured Mahogany sitting on her Vespa outside of the library.

"You wouldn't know anything about this, would you?" Sawer asked.

Mahogany gazed at the image, feigning shock and wishing she'd taken some drama in high school to help prepare for all the lying she was about to do. "Where did you find that?"

Sawyer sighed. "I think you know perfectly well where we found this." The detective dropped the photo back into the box.

"I don't know what you're insinuating," Mahogany said, a deep frown drawing her eyebrows together. Don't lay it on too thick, she told herself. "I didn't know anyone was taking pictures of me."

Tony moved next to Mahogany and placed his arm around her shoulders. "Easy there, detective. Mahogany is a victim," he said, nodding to the box of images.

"Yeah," Evelina said, joining them, wrapping her arm around Mahogany's waist. "How on earth was Mahogany supposed to know Thad was stalking her?"

Detective Sawyer gazed at the trio. Her eyes narrowed. "You three have poked your noses into this murder investigation since the beginning, and you're lucky you haven't ended up hurt or worse. I'm letting you go home for the evening Mahogany, but I want you down at the station in the morning. There are things we need to discuss." With that, Sawyer turned on her heel and strode out the door, the mob of uniforms following her.

"We need to get a look at Thad's camera," Evelina said

Mahogany nodded. "What we need is at the apothecary." And who we need, Mahogany thought.

Chapter 27

M ahogany burst into the Haughty Hemlock, followed by Tony and Evelina, startling Neema as she closed the shop.

"Oh, good. You're back. Where did you put the port-o-hole?" Mahogany asked as she dashed to the kitchen and rifled through a pile of mail on the table, searching for the envelope holding the magical scrap of fabric.

"I put it back in the envelope, as you should have. Twenty-three years, and I'm still cleaning up after you." Neema slipped a white envelope from one of the kitchen drawers and cleared her throat. Mahogany turned and snatched it from Neema.

"What's happened?" Neema checked the clock over the oven. "It's nearly 7:00."

"The police just arrested Thaddeus Spike on suspicion of murder. They picked him up while we were questioning him at Tipsy O'Lush's." Mahogany tore open the envelope and withdrew the port-o-hole. She swiped a section of the kitchen table clear of stray papers and slapped the black circle onto the polished wood. She reached her arm into the portal, where it disappeared from view, and felt around the dusty shelf for an evidence box.

"They've arrested Thad?" Neema blanched and grabbed hold of the table to steady herself. "There's no way he could have killed Mike. They were best friends once."

Mahogany's fingers fumbled along the metal shelving unit for a long second before her fingertips grazed the edge of a cardboard box. Her disembodied arm skimmed the box's lid until it found the handle. She grasped the handhold and pulled it through the port-o-hole. Tony grabbed the side of the box and helped Mahogany maneuver it onto the kitchen table. To their relief, Magoris's name appeared on the lid.

"Thad dropped his camera at the murder scene," Evelina said, scanning the box, excitement shining in her eyes. "But never mind that. How do you know Mike and Thad were friends?"

Neema cast a weary eye at Mahogany as she ran to the writing desk in the living room and returned with the spectare. She slid the blade along the red tape, sealing the lid, and yanked off the top. A black camera in a clear plastic bag sat on top of the other items collected from the crime scene. Detective Sawyer had labeled the baggie with her name and the date and time she placed the camera into evidence. It appeared the police had discovered the camera at the brownstone the day after the murders.

"We'll talk about Neema's lies after we deal with this," Mahogany said.

"What's the plan?" Tony asked, peering at the camera.

Mahogany cut open the evidence bag with the spectare and reached for the camera when Evelina stopped her. "Gloves."

Neema threw a set of dish gloves at Mahogany and moved to the large kitchen hutch, housing part of her spell collection. She ran a finger along the gold-labeled spines, searching for the one covering mirror incantations.

Mahogany shoved her hands into the gloves, pulled the camera from the evidence bag, and popped open the back. "There's no film." Mahogany stared into the empty camera, her stomach tightening.

"Now what?" Tony asked. "Without the film, how are we supposed to know if Thad's telling the truth?"

"Like this." Neema tossed a heavy tome onto the kitchen counter and tapped the front cover: *27 Ways to Make Mirrors Work for You.*

"Mirrors?" Tony questioned. "I don't get it."

Mahogany stared into the back of the old-fashioned camera. "You don't mean this mirror?" She pointed to a small, square mirror in the back of the device.

Neema leafed through the book until she found the right chapter. "That's exactly what I mean. It's an SLR, single lens reflex. The mirror reflects the images seen through the lens up through the eyepiece. There are spells in this book that will retrieve images from mirrors and other reflective surfaces."

"How do you know so much about cameras?" Tony asked, looking impressed.

Neema waved her hand dismissively. "Oh, you pick things up when you spend years around a shutterbug."

Tony nodded and moved to the counter and read the chapter's first paragraph to the room. "Mirrors and other reflective surfaces can record images witnessed within a single moon cycle. The process of retrieving images is a time-honored piece of magic any witch worth her salt needs to know."

Evelina frowned and skimmed the rest of the page over Tony's shoulder. "The spell can take at least two hours. What if someone notices the camera is gone before we're done?"

"That is a chance we'll have to take," Neema said. She flitted about the kitchen, gathering objects: a casserole dish, a pitcher filled with water, and various herbs.

"It's pretty late," Tony said. "I bet the police will interview Thad in the morning instead of tonight."

"They're going to have him sleep in a cell?" Evelina's eyes grew wide. "How awful."

Tony nodded. "Since he isn't local, he's a flight risk. If they hold him overnight, at least they know where he is."

"Good point," Mahogany said. "Yet, if he's the murderer, wouldn't he have left town already?"

Tony's gaze fell on Neema. "Not if he has unfinished business here."

"How do you know all this?" Neema said. "And what do you mean, unfinished business?"

"His mom is a detective in San Francisco," Mahogany said, watching Neema gather the tools for the spell. "Can I help?"

"Yes. Get some of the nice printer paper we use for glossy flyers. There's some in the writing desk," Neema said. "We're also going to need a small screwdriver. I'm not sure where one might be."

"Got it," Mahogany said, remembering the tiny screwdriver with which she tried to pick the lock on the desk drawer.

"What can we do?" Evelina asked, motioning to herself and Tony.

"Wine. I need wine and my fuzzy slippers. These blisters are killing me," Neema said. She opened a glass jar filled with a dark, viscous liquid and sniffed it, grimacing. "Mermaid tears are nauseating."

"Tony, the wine glasses are in the cupboard next to the fridge. The wine is on the rack," Evelina called over her shoulder as she scampered upstairs to grab Neema's slippers.

Tony nodded, gathered glasses for everyone, and popped the cork on a bottle of Shiraz.

Mahogany returned with a ream of photo paper and the screwdriver. Neema took the tiny silver tool, unscrewed the camera's mirror, and placed it in the glass casserole dish, pouring water from the pitcher over it. She then sprinkled the herbs and mermaid tears into the water. Grabbing the sides of the dish, she gently agitated the mixture. As the contents blended, a bluish mist rose from the surface. The scent of lilacs and something acidic filled the kitchen.

"Wow. I've never seen actual magic before," Tony said, offering a glass of wine to Neema. "Now I've seen it three times in one day."

"You just wait," Neema said. She took the glass and sipped the Shiraz. "What were the other two?"

Tony opened his mouth to answer, but Mahogany cut him off. "He means two. The port-o-hole and now this, right Tony?" She sent him a pregnant look, willing him to pick up her lead.

"Right, sorry. I'm overwhelmed." He rubbed the back of his head, embarrassment coloring his cheeks. "I have a stupid human raised in a non-magical household question," he said, changing the subject. "If this spell pulls images from mirrors, does that mean it won't work on Vampires?" Tony asked. "If a Vampire walks in front of a mirror, would this spell retrieve their image?"

"Sure, it'll work on a Vampire unless it's Ranger Ted over at the Stone Circle. I doubt he has a soul," Neema said.

Before settlers arrived in the New World, the continent's indigenous residents had created the stone circle. Over time, it became a gateway to the Otherworld. After Pandemonium's settlement by magical Folk, the citizens erected the monument as an homage to the town's sacred history. Now instead of serving as a gateway to the Otherworld, Folk use the circle as a portal between other safe-haven cities worldwide. It allows Folk safe travel without human detection.

"Ted's all right. He's only a jerk to you," Mahogany said, watching the smoking casserole dish with rapt attention.

"An actual Vampire? I was half kidding," Tony said. He took a thoughtful drink of his wine. "Does he bite people?"

"Only tourists," Neema said, "but he's discreet." She agitated the liquid until the purple mist dissipated.

"Now what?" Mahogany said, taking a grateful sip from her glass.

"We wait," Neema said. "We need to let the spell process the images. When it's ready, the mist will turn yellow."

Mahogany's phone buzzed in her backpack. She retrieved it and saw she'd missed a message from Priscilla Wembley, the librarian.

"Tony, are you sure they won't question Thad tonight?" Mahogany asked, retrieving her voicemail.

"Pretty sure," he gave a noncommittal shrug. "Questioning him now will kill her overtime budget. No, she'll wait until morning."

Mahogany hoped he was right. She pressed her ear to her phone and listened.

"Hi Mahogany, this is Priscilla at the library. The photo intrigued me, and I did a little more digging. I'll be here until about 9:30, closing up. If you come by, knock, and I'll let you in."

"I have to go," Mahogany said, checking the time. It was just after nine. If she hurried, she could make it to the library before Pricilla went home for the night. She deleted the voice message. A yawn threatened to overtake her, but she clenched her jaw, willing it away. She couldn't believe how much had happened in one day—Jeff and Layla, Sylvia punching Nancy, questioning Steve, Thad's arrest, breaking into the police evidence for a second time, casting a spell, and now a late-night field trip to the library. Mahogany longed for sleep. Yet, as she glanced around the kitchen, she knew this would be another all-nighter.

Neema and Tony stared at her, their eyebrows raised. "Now?" they asked in unison.

"Yes," Mahogany said. She fished the Vespa's keys from her bag. "I'll be back in half an hour."

Chapter 28

Priscilla's cherry-red Harley was the only vehicle in the library parking lot. Streetlamps washed the area in yellow light, and an eerie sense of déjà vu itched at the back of Mahogany's brain. She rolled her shoulders and headed for the library's smoky doors, pushing the tingling feeling away.

The doors whooshed opened as Mahogany approached, the library's cool air engulfing her. Quiet greeted her, it being too late for Pandemonium residents to gather library books. Yet, something unpleasant needled at the base of her skull. A fresh wave of déjà vu gripped Mahogany's chest and squeezed. Gooseflesh sprang along her arms and the back of her neck.

"Something's wrong," Guy said and his translucent form shimmered.

Mahogany couldn't argue. The thick atmosphere of evil permeated the library. The brownstone flashed into Mahogany's mind; Magic Mike lying in a pool of blood, Guy's life slipping away.

"I can feel him. The murderer is close." Guy's shimmering ratcheted, and Mahogany thought she could hear the wave of energy vibrating off of him. "We should leave. Get some backup."

Mahogany considered this, but shook her head. "That would take too long. What if Priscilla needs help now?" She moved deeper into the library on tiptoe.

"Priscilla? I got your call," Mahogany called into the empty library, but no response came.

Nestled among a sea of waist-high bookshelves, Mahogany spied the empty reference desk.

"Maybe she's in the restroom," Guy said, his tone betraying the hopeful message of his words.

Mahogany nodded, her eyes locked on the desk. "Yeah, maybe."

After crossing what felt like an equivalent length to the Sahara, Mahogany reached the reference desk. She gave the space another cursory glance, searching for the AWOL librarian.

"Priscilla," Mahogany called again. Not waiting for a reply, she peeked over the top of the large semicircle desk. On the left, neat stacks of books awaited processing. On the right sat Priscilla's computer monitor and keyboard. A manila envelope with Mahogany's name on it lay next to the mouse pad.

Mahogany reached over the top of the desk and grabbed the envelope when something caught her eye; the tip of one of Priscilla's black motorcycle boots peaked from behind her office chair.

"Priscilla?" Mahogany croaked through parched lips. Her heart raced, and blood rang in her ears. She slid around the desk on numb feet.

The librarian's boots inched into view as Mahogany rounded the desk, a chunky toe followed by crenelated soles. Black leather traveled up her shin until it met a pair of red leather motorcycle pants.

Priscilla lay on her side—her eyes open and blank, pupils stretched wide. A thin, foamy line of drool fell from her lips and pooled on the tile floor beneath her cheek.

Mahogany stared at the scene before her without seeing it. Tiny dots of darkness paraded in on her vision, restricting her view. Her knees wobbled as if pudding filled her legs instead of bone, and she gripped the desk to keep from falling.

Guy approached Priscilla and placed his hand through her chest. He looked up at Mahogany and shook his head with a sad finality.

"Do you think her death was natural?" Guy asked. "An allergic reaction? Stroke?"

Mahogany took several deep breaths until her vision cleared. She'd seen many dead wizards over the last six months, but she had expected to find them. Coming upon someone who'd left you a message just hours before was shocking.

She kneeled on the other side of Priscilla from Guy. The scent of licorice and peppermint drifted in the air around the body. "She smells like herbal tea. Do you see a cup?'

They searched the area and found an overturned mug under the desk. Guy stuck his head in the remnants of the cup's contents puddled next to its overturned lip. "Peppermint and licorice," he confirmed.

"Do you taste anything else?"

Guy shook his head. "I'm not a wortcunner. I know very little about plants."

Mahogany nodded gravely. "We need to get out of here and call the police. If I'm right, Priscilla has been poisoned." She stood and grabbed the envelope, the corner of which caught something just behind the computer monitor. Mahogany peered behind the sleek black screen and discovered a small rectangular box decorated in a Victorian floral print. Mahogany's stomach lurched.

"Oh, no."

"What?"

She picked up the box. "Licorice and peppermint."

"No good. This is not good at all." Guy's eyes grew wide. "That's one of Neema's tea blends. What if someone laced the tea with poison?" Guy said. "That would mean someone murdered Priscilla, too. What if it's the same person who killed Mike and me?" Guy stopped, panic rippling across his face. "What if Neema's responsible?"

If the brownstone murderer also poisoned Priscilla, that would mean Mahogany caused the librarian's death by involving her. If she hadn't brought the photo to the library and asked for help, Priscilla would still be alive. Mahogany shoved the envelope and the tea box into her backpack and headed for the door.

"Neema's not stupid enough to poison someone with her own tea," she said over her shoulder.

"Where are you going?" Guy hopped onto the Vespa behind Mahogany.

Mahogany pulled the scooter onto the road, but didn't answer.

Chapter 29

"Where are we?" Guy looked around the unpaved parking area. A few lights attached to telephone poles partially illuminated the area—their yellow glow pooling on gravel in large circles.

"You mentioned you wanted to visit the stones. Well, here we are." Mahogany gestured to a green and brown painted sign attached to the side of a tiny ranger station that read: Historic Archaeological Site.

"Okay," Guy said, stretching the word, "but why now? We've just found Priscilla, who may or may not have been murdered by Neema's tea. This is hardly the time to play tourist." He hopped off the back of the sunshine-yellow Vespa and stretched his back.

"What are you doing?" Mahogany raised an eyebrow at Guy's semi-solid form as she cut the Vespa's engine.

"Old habit." Guy bent and touched his toes. "I used to have a terrible back. Car accident in my teens. I haven't gotten used to the whole no pain thing." He shrugged. "So, if we're not here to visit the site, why are we here?"

A short, hairy man exited the ranger station and strode toward Mahogany on stout legs. "Park's closed," the ranger said, waving his hand at Mahogany to turn her scooter around and head the way she'd come.

"Hey, Ted." Mahogany pulled off her helmet and placed it on the Vespa's seat. "How are you this evening?" She straightened her sweater and fluffed her pink curls.

Ted came up short and squinted at Mahogany. "What are you doing here? Park's closed." He curled his lip, baring the tip of one white fang. The waning moonlight gleamed off the needle-sharp point.

"That's Ted, the Vampire?" Guy eyed the small hairy man who looked more like an angry Danny DeVito than Brad Pitt in *Interview with a Vampire*. "How in the world does he persuade people to let him bite them? His charisma is zero."

"He's a Vampire. If he wants to put on the charm, you can't say no," Mahogany said through the corner of her mouth. "Plus, drunk frat boys are pretty easy prey."

"Good thing for him," Guy muttered.

"Bazgul, come, please," Mahogany whispered. In a flash, Bazgul appeared on her shoulder. "I need to use the ranger station to look over something I don't want Neema to see."

Ted's gaze landed on Bazgul perched on Mahogany's shoulder, and a greedy glint glowed in his black eyes.

Mahogany smirked at Bazgul, who danced on her shoulder. "Oh, go on."

Bazgul chattered and leaped from Mahogany to Ted and landed on the Vampire's shirtfront with the grace of an Olympic gymnast.

Ted's perpetually sour expression relaxed a bit. "Neema? What's that old crone done now? Steal another baby?" He pulled a small baggy from his pocket and offered a banana chip to Bazgul. The demon spider snatched the chip and munched it with delight.

"Not as far as I know," Mahogany said. She waited for Ted to pass his judgment.

The short, gruff Vampire turned on his heel and started back to the ranger station, muttering to Bazgul the whole way.

"Come on," Mahogany said, and started after Ted.

"What's up with him and Bazgul?" Guy said, following Mahogany.

"Ted's intrigued with the idea of a demon attaching himself to a human. Bazgul and I have been coming here since I was little, and we made friends with Ted."

"There's no love lost on Neema. He seems to hate her."

"It's something we've bonded over," Mahogany said, entering the station.

The tiny ranger station contained a tall reception desk that bisected the room, separating the on-duty rangers from the visitors. On the tourists' side sat a wall mount stuffed with colorful fliers advertising local and nearby attractions. A small bookshelf held baskets filled with postcards, stickers, travel guides, and patches promoting the stone circle. Behind the desk sat a large radio connecting the station to other state parks. A scuffed door led to a restroom the size of a postage stamp.

Ted reached over the desk, grabbed a headlamp, and slipped it over his square head. "Would your friend like to make my rounds with me? Bazgul tells me Guy missed seeing the stones while he lived."

Bazgul chattered on Ted's shoulder and eyed Guy.

"You know about Guy?" Mahogany gaped at Ted.

"The dead know the dead." Ted gave a wry smile. "I can't see or hear him like you, but I know he's here. Plus, Bazgul filled me in."

Mahogany narrowed her eyes. The longer Guy stuck around, the more he and Bazgul could communicate. She wasn't sure what their connection was, but it was getting stronger.

Guy gave a solemn nod. "Rain check."

Bazgul chattered, and Ted nodded, heading for the door. He paused, his burly hand gripping the dented brass knob. "If you need anything, kid, just call for Bazgul."

"Thanks, Ted," Mahogany said.

"Anytime." With Bazgul riding his shoulder, Ted headed out to patrol the stones.

She counted to ten before opening the manila envelope. From inside, she retrieved the printout of the original photo from Magic Mike's evidence box. On the back of the page, written in Priscilla's looping cursive, noted: Lion Gate High School yearbook photo. Class of 1990. Photo by Thaddeus Spike. From left to right, Aurora Kingsley, Kassandra Frost, Magoris Idrus, and Dorcia Frost.

Mahogany stared hard at the photo, placing the names with the faces. So Neema's real name was Dorcia Frost. Mahogany compared Dorcia to Kassandra. Without the black X obscuring Kassandra's face, the family resemblance between the Frost girls was easy to see. They had the same rounded nose, the same widow's peak hairline, and were similar in height. These two had to be sisters.

The mysterious Neema had a family somewhere—a sister, at any rate. Mahogany tried to imagine Neema as a child, growing up with a sibling, fighting over the bathroom, and staying up late, talking about boys. What had made Neema travel across the country and change her name? What was she hiding from? Or better yet, who?

Mahogany set the printout on the counter and examined the envelope's other contents. Priscilla had also printed out a newspaper article. At first, Mahogany thought it was the same article the librarian had printed about the strange death of Aurora Kingsley. Instead, this article reported a car crash that killed a married couple—Kassandra Frost and James Woods.

Authorities had deemed the crash intentional. Someone had cut the brake lines, yet the police had no leads or suspects. Mahogany checked the date of the article: June 8, 1999. Almost twenty-two years ago to the day.

What if the same person who murdered Magic Mike and Guy had also murdered Kassandra and James Woods? If so, why wait two decades to come after everyone else? Was this what Neema had been hiding from? If so, where did Mahogany fit into all of it?

Guy, who had been reading over Mahogany's shoulder, cleared his throat. "You need to tell Tony and Evelina about the photo."

Mahogany nodded, the throat tight. "Time to head back and confront Neema about her secrets." She crammed the documents back into the envelope and headed for the door.

"Aren't you forgetting something?" Guy said, hands on hips, his face wore a disapproving expression.

"Am I?"

"Priscilla."

"Gods!" Stomach acid flared in Mahogany's throat. How could she have forgotten to call the police about Priscilla? "There's a pay phone outside. I'll call from there."

As Mahogany ended the call without giving her details to the officer on desk duty, she heard two sets of feet crunching over the gravel. Startled, she turned to see a vaguely familiar couple bedecked in cliché Goth attire of black lace, crepe, and satin. The first woman wore a well-tailored black suit that fit her trim figure perfectly. She'd topped her ensemble with a black cape lined in a blood-red fabric that caught the light spilling from the ranger station window. The second woman wore a long black dress dripping with lace trimmings. Black lipstick painted her thin lips.

Mahogany gasped. "Nancy? Nancy Roberts?" She shook her head. What would the rest of the End Halloween Committee say if they could see her now? The severe blonde bun, pastel sweater, and iced Chardonnay were long gone. The black choker around Nancy's pale neck conjured the memory of the sepia photograph of the blond family hanging in Tipsy O'Lush's. This version of Nancy standing before Mahogany looked like one of her ancestors had risen from the grave. The resemblance was uncanny.

The pair of women stopped short and stared at Mahogany, the seductive smile melting from Nancy's red lips. "I'm sorry. You've mistaken me for someone else." Nancy turned and started towing the unidentified woman into the darkness toward the circle.

"Drop the act, Nancy. I know it's you. You look just like your creepy family photo hanging in the pub." Mahogany called after the retreating figures. "I also know you weren't with Steve Murphy when Mike and Guy were murdered. Wanna change your story?"

She pulled her phone from her pocket and aimed it at the retreating couple.

Nancy rounded on Mahogany, her face twisted into a mask of rage when the flash on Mahogany's phone startled her. Nancy froze, blinking, her rage replaced with wide-eyed shock.

"Not my best work, but it will do," Mahogany said, tapping her phone's screen.

"You wouldn't dare," Nancy spat, her eyes shiny with fear.

"Oh," Mahogany said, "I would." She slipped the phone into her back pocket. "Now answer my question. Where were you?"

"She was with me," said the other woman. She stepped into a circle of light slipping through the ranger station window.

Mahogany stared, her mouth agape. The other woman was none other than her employer at the Pandemonium Museum, Agalia Sorrowsong.

Had the world gone mad? What in Hades was Agalia, the meanest witch in Pandemonium, doing on a secret rendezvous with Nancy Roberts, a creepy pedophile whose family had been stripped of magic?

"Close your mouth, Mahogany. You'll catch a moth," Agalia said, her voice bored.

"I'm sorry," Mahogany said, chuckling. "I thought you said you two were together."

"You heard correctly. Nancy and I were here when Mike met his demise." Agalia stood beside Nancy and placed a protective arm around the bond's corseted waist.

Mahogany took a step back, her mind reeling. "Nancy, I underestimated you. When your plan didn't work with Magic Mike, you moved on to someone with genuine power to change your situation." She pointed to Agalia. "She won't give you back your family's lost powers."

"No," Agalia stepped close to Mahogany, "but I can get her an audience with the Guild." Her voice carried a lethal edge like a well-honed dagger. "Now, about that photo."

"Tell her to keep away from underaged boys and to drop the petition for a special election. I want the End Halloween Committee disbanded, or I'll make posters with this pretty picture and stick them all over town," Mahogany said, lifting her chin at Nancy. "I bet Mr. Roberts would be very interested in your little outings."

Nancy's mouth opened, but Agalia silenced her with a raise of a jeweled hand. "You have my word that she will behave." On silent feet, she returned to Nancy's side and led her into the darkness.

Mahogany stared after the odd couple, her expression perplexed. This had to be one of the most eventful trips to the stone circle ever.

Guy gave a whoop, making Mahogany jump. "Well played! I can't believe you stood up to Agalia like that. She is one frightening witch."

Mahogany gulped. Hopefully, that little stunt wouldn't come back to bite her.

"Still here?"

"Gods, Ted," Mahogany gasped. "Learn to walk like a normal person, would you?"

Ted gave a sly smile. "Top of the food chain, miss. I can't help it if I'm light on my feet."

"Do Nancy Roberts and Agalia come here often?" Mahogany nodded to where they had disappeared into the darkness.

"You know Nancy? She won't like anyone she knows seeing her here. She enjoys her role-playing in complete autonomy." Ted glanced towards where the circle lay in the darkness. "However, to answer your question, they've come here the last couple of Tuesdays."

"You saw them here last Tuesday?" Mahogany asked, her heartbeat quickening.

Ted nodded. "They were here most of the night. I let them stay after the park's closed because they don't disturb the stones like the local teens do."

"Thanks, Ted. You've been wonderful. I'll bring Bazgul again soon." The demon spider hopped onto Mahogany's shoulder, and she jogged back to her Vespa.

"And bring your ghost back, too. I want to show him the circle," Ted called after her.

"Poor Steve," Guy said. "When do you think he'll realize Nancy dumped him?" He gazed in the direction Nancy and her new plaything had disappeared.

"Soon, I'm sure." Mahogany started the engine. "He doesn't know it yet, but it's the best thing that's ever happened to him."

Chapter 30

"Where have you been?" Evelina stood, hands on hips, a glare in her violet eyes. "We just finished hanging the prints so they could dry and develop."

"I had to take care of a few things," Mahogany said, kicking her boots into the corner. "Where's Neema?"

"She nipped upstairs for a shower," Evelina said. She offered her hand to Bazgul, and he hopped into her open palm. Her stern glare softened as she petted his hairy back.

"Someone's murdered Priscilla Wembley." Mahogany rubbed her hands over her face. Could this day get any longer? "Or at least she's dead, but I'm pretty sure someone poisoned her."

"Someone murdered the librarian?" Evelina's hand froze over Bazgul's back, and he lifted his head, nipping at her fingers.

"What? When? How?" Tony said, getting to his feet from the kitchen table.

"This evening. I just found her in the library," Mahogany said. She placed her backpack on the kitchen island and sat on one of the bar stools.

Evelina blanched. She scratched Bazgul's head absently, and the demon purred cheerily.

"Priscilla left me a message about some research." Mahogany pulled the manila envelope from her bag and laid it on the island.

Evelina frowned. She set Bazgul on the island and grabbed the envelope. "What kind of research?"

Mahogany shook her head. She hopped off the bar stool and went to the fridge, searching for something to quench the sudden dryness in her mouth.

"Jeez!" Evelina said. "What if the murderer were still there, like at the brownstone? You need to be more careful."

"Says the Fae who interviewed a potential murderer alone," Mahogany gave a dry laugh. She grabbed the milk bottle and tipped it to her lips, drinking deeply. "Also, Nancy has an alibi for the night of the murder."

"What? How do you know that?" Tony said, moving to stand next to Evelina.

"I stopped by the stone circle to call the police about Priscilla. I didn't want to call from my cell. Nancy was there, festooned like a Hot Topic reject with..." Mahogany hesitated, catching herself before she let slip that Agalia was there. "Wearing this horrid black dress. Ted confirmed she was there last Tuesday."

"So we're back to no viable suspects." Evelina dropped the envelope and sighed. "This sucks."

"Also, when Guy and I first searched Mike's evidence box, we found a photo." Mahogany took another swig of milk.

"What kind of photo?" Tony pulled open the envelope and examined the contents, his face pinched in concentration.

Mahogany tapped the printout in Tony's hand. "The police found this photo at the murder scene. The murderer placed it in Magic Mike's hand, except someone altered it."

"Altered?" Tony said, meeting Mahogany's gaze.

She nodded and retrieved the image on her phone.

"Oh, that's dark," Evelina said, her eyes widening.

"Who are these people?" Tony pointed to the crossed-out faces. "Why are they important?"

"That's Magic Mike, and that's Kassandra Frost." Mahogany pointed to the two figures with black marks over their faces. "The one with the circle is Dorcia Frost."

A creak on the stairs took their attention from the photo. Neema stood frozen, her foot hovering above the next step.

Mahogany's gaze ran up Neema, taking in every inch of the woman she knew and didn't at the same time. "Hello, Dorcia," Mahogany said.

Beside her, Evelina gasped, and Tony gave a low whistle through his teeth.

Evelina took the printout from Tony and held it aloft, comparing Neema to the teenager trapped in time.

The color drained from Neema's face. "How?"

"You better sit," Mahogany said, and motioned to the kitchen table.

Neema nodded and took a seat. Her shower-wet hair fell over her shoulder, leaving a damp spot on her t-shirt. Near her left temple, a tuft of white hair announced it was time to touch up her roots.

"The hair," murmured Evelina, her eyes darting between Neema hunched at the table and the photo. "It is her." She leaned toward Tony, pointing to Dorcia. "Same white patch."

"It's called poliosis. I've had it since childhood," Neema said. Her gaze locked on Mahogany. "I guess it's time to dye it again." The corners of her mouth rose in a sad smile.

"You need to start at the beginning. What happened to Aurora Kingsley?" Mahogany sat across from Neema at the kitchen table, the milk bottle still in her hand.

Neema sighed. "We were all friends." She nodded to the color printout in Evelina's hand. "Inseparable. Then we graduated from high school and went to train with masters in different areas to hone our magical crafts. That's when everything changed."

"What changed?" Tony asked, moving around the kitchen island to sit next to Mahogany. He smiled slightly, but she didn't have the energy to return it.

"Aurora started dabbling with demon magic," Neema said. "She got it into her head that she could summon a greater demon and control it."

Evelina gasped. "That's impossible. No one can control a greater demon."

Neema smiled sadly again. "We tried to talk her out of her insane idea, but she'd convinced herself that she could summon and control a demon. She'd become delusional."

"What happened?" Tony asked.

"She summoned a greater demon, and it possessed her." Neema shook her head. Her wet hair slipped from her shoulder and trailed down her back. "Thaddeus, Mike, Kassandra, and I tried to save her. To banish the beast, but in the end, it killed her. We couldn't separate them without harming Aurora. They'd bonded, their souls intertwined."

"That's what demons do," Evelina said, scratching Bazgul's head again. She walked him to his cat tree and placed him on the top platform. He peered out the window, interested in the goings-on outside.

Neema nodded. "To save Aurora and her family's reputations, we staged her death to appear like an accident."

Tony looked around, puzzled. "I don't get it. Why would she and her family's reputations be in jeopardy?"

"The Guild has prohibited demon magic because demons, especially greater demons, are almost impossible to banish. They go around causing trouble," Neema said. "Anyone caught playing with cursed magic gets their powers taken by the Guild. It's not a pleasant outcome for magical Folk. We tried to cover it up." She shrugged. "We were kids and didn't do the best job. The city police investigated, and the district attorney tried to bring charges against us for murder."

"Then you moved across the country and changed your name?" Mahogany asked.

"I needed a fresh start," Neema said. She picked at one of her fingernails, not looking at Mahogany.

"What about your sister and her husband? Were their deaths related to the demon?" Mahogany asked.

"The investigation concluded someone had tampered with their brakes, but the police never found who was responsible," Neema said.

"So, where do I fit into all of this?" Mahogany sat back, crossing her arms over her chest.

Neema sighed. "I've already told you. A Fae traded me a Changling for a remedy, and then I saw you and fell in love. Open and shut."

"That's it?" Mahogany said.

"That's it." Neema's blue eyes burned into Mahogany's.

A strained silence fell over the kitchen.

"Well, the photo ties this group to the murders," Evelina said, shattering the tension. "Whoever placed this in Mike's hand was sending a message. Kassandra and Magic Mike are marked off, literally and figuratively, and Neema is next on the list."

"What kind of list?" Tony asked, frowning.

"A revenge list, of course," Evelina said. "Someone who blames them for what happened to Aurora. See? She's been left alone." Evelina's eyes glowed. She tapped Aurora's image, holding the printout for Tony to see. "Holy crap. I think I just figured it out."

"We still don't know who's behind the murders," Tony said, studying the image again.

"Oh, right." The light faded in Evelina's eyes. "That's the important bit, isn't it?"

"What about Thad?" Tony asked, looking from the printout to Mahogany.

"He took the photo," Mahogany said, her eyes leveled at Neema.

"That ties him in too," Tony said. "What about the letters he sent?" He turned his gaze on Neema. "What was Thad trying to warn you about?"

Neema's face wore an unreadable expression. "I knew you'd taken Mike's letter from my desk."

"I did, but someone stole it from Tony's before we read it properly," Mahogany said. "Then yesterday, I intercepted one."

Neema sighed. "I had been hiding for nearly twenty-two years. Then Thad wrote Mike was on his way to blow my cover. Mike said his guilt was too much, and he wanted to come clean." She shook her head. "I don't know how they found me."

"The murderer must have followed them," Tony said. "Which means someone has incredible patience to wait all this time."

Evelina shivered. "The whole thing gives me the creeps."

The room fell silent, each person lost in a tangle of thoughts. Then, the timer over the oven chimed, bringing them back to the present.

"The photos are ready. Let's see what we have," Neema said, getting to her feet and heading into the living room.

Much like Thaddeus Spike's room at Tipsy O'Lush's, Neema, with the help of Tony and Evelina, had fastened yarn in a zig-zagging pattern across the living room. Photo paper dangled from the string using chip clips, close pins, and paper clips.

"Wow, there must be nearly fifty images here." Mahogany said, appraising their handiwork.

Evelina began inspecting the images. "It looks like some are duplicates from Thad's room."

"You were in Thad's room?" Neema swung around to peer at Evelina, her eyes wide.

"It wasn't like that. He's not my type," Evelina said. "Mahogany and I broke in."

"Well, in that case, I can relax." Neema rolled her eyes and inspected the swaying images.

"Didn't we hang the photos in the order we developed them?" Tony said, moving across the room to the far wall.

"Yes." Neema nodded. "That means these photos are older," she said, motioning to the pictures nearest the kitchen. "We started over there and worked our way over here."

Tony examined the images at the far side of the living room as Mahogany, Evelina, and Neema navigated under the strands of yarn. Guy passed through them, his face screwed into a grim expression.

Tony's gaze landed on one image held to the yarn at the corner by a safety pin. "This might be what we're looking for," he said.

Everyone gathered around and peered at the image. A figure cloaked in a black hoodie held the jeweled anelace over their head, ready to strike. Magic Mike stood in the brownstone's study facing the fireplace, unaware of his fate.

"Poor Mike," Guy said. "He had no idea."

Mahogany muttered, "Let's hope he didn't suffer." She gave Guy a wan smile, knowing he had lingered on the brink of death for an hour or more before dying with her hand on his chest.

"I can't believe we're looking at an almost murder." Evelina shivered, and Tony put his arm around her, pulling her close.

Mahogany frowned as an all too familiar lump caught in her throat. Guy and Neema glanced from Tony and Evelina to Mahogany, eyebrows raised.

"Well, we have the murderer caught in the act, but we still don't know who they are," Mahogany said.

"However, we know for sure that Thad didn't do it," Neema said, her voice filled with relief.

Chapter 31

Mahogany sorted the photos and put the image of Magic Mike and the murderer into the manila envelope with Priscilla Wembley's research. She placed the other magically gathered images from Thad's camera on the coffee table.

"Do you think whoever murdered Priscilla did it because of this?" Evelina tapped the legal-sized yellow envelope.

"It's possible." Guilt settled over Mahogany like a shroud. First the break-in at Tony's house and now murder. Ever since she'd walked into the brownstone, darkness had followed her, reaching its horrible tentacles into every aspect of her life.

Evelina's eyes widened, and she placed an arm over Mahogany's sagging shoulders. "This isn't your fault. You had no way of knowing the murderer would go after Priscilla."

Mahogany nodded but said nothing, afraid her voice would crack and release a flood of emotion.

"What I don't get," Tony said, "is why circle Neema's face like a warning? To build dramatic effect? Why wait to kill her? And what did the librarian do? What about Thaddeus? Why hasn't the murderer tried to kill him already?" Tony asked, his brow drawing together in a puzzled frown.

"Maybe the murderer doesn't know what they look like. It's been two decades," Evelina said. "Thad isn't in the picture, and, no offense, Neema, you've put on a few inches around the waist, and you dye your hair. Maybe they aren't sure who you are."

"Tony has a point. What's with all the waiting and scheming? If this is about Aurora, and someone wanted to pay us back for something, they would have had an easier time picking us off one at a time," Neema said. She'd made a last turn with the screwdriver, securing the mirror inside the camera again. "Let's hurry and get this back into evidence before the police miss it."

Mahogany nodded. She headed into the kitchen and used the spectare to place the camera in its evidence bag before resealing the red tape around the lid on Mike's box.

Tony stepped forward and helped Mahogany maneuver the box back through the port-o-hole—their arms intertwined. The warmth from Tony seeped into Mahogany's skin, making her heart flutter.

Once the box was back in evidence, Neema pulled the port-o-hole from the tabletop and took it into the living room.

A sudden shrill chime made them all jump. "Sorry." Evelina fished her phone from her purse. "My alarm. I need to get some sleep before work."

"You set an alarm telling you when to go to bed?" Mahogany said. "Isn't that kind of backward?"

"Not if you're a night owl. It's a reasonable time management device." Evelina dropped her phone back into her purse. "I need to go. Eric warned if I'm late again, there will be Hades to pay."

"Me too," Tony said, stretching, his back cracking. "I have to open the store tomorrow, but..." His eyes darted between Neema and Mahogany. "Don't take this the wrong way, but I feel like I shouldn't leave you two alone. The murderer has already made it clear they're willing to take innocent people down in their twisted quest."

Neema gave a sly half-smile as she returned to the kitchen. "No need to worry about us. We're more than safe." She gestured to the herbs stewing on the windowsill. "I've brewed a hefty protection spell. Speaking of which, I have a great idea." She opened one of the kitchen cupboards, retrieved two glass vials, and filled each container with some of the windowsill concoction.

"I thought that was for a customer," Mahogany said, nodding toward the bowl.

"I never said who it was for, only that it was a full moon spell," Neema said. She held out the vials. "Tony, you're right about being on guard. This person will hurt anyone in obtaining their goal. We all need protecting."

Tony and Evelina took the vials. "Keep them close. The closer, the better," Neema said.

"I'll sleep with it under my pillow," Evelina said.

"Me too," Tony said, slipping the vial into his pocket.

"When you're out and about, have it on your person," Neema said.

"What about me?" Mahogany said. "Shouldn't I get some too?"

Neema brushed her words away with a flick of her wrist. "You don't need it. I placed a protection spell on your necklace years ago."

Mahogany's hand went to the silver pentagram charm. "Years ago?"

Neema gave a smoky cackle. "Why do you think you never scraped your knees as a kid, learned to ride a bike without falling, or never once cut your finger while cooking? Did you think you were naturally graceful?" She laughed again, this time joined by Evelina.

"Yeah, right," Evelina giggled. "As if."

Mahogany stared open-mouthed at the older woman. She had thought of herself as exceptionally graceful. However, now that Neema and Evelina had pointed it out, she was pretty clumsy. She always avoided severe injury, but just.

"It's late. We all need sleep," Neema said and clapped her hands, her smile slipping from her lips.

Mahogany glanced at the clock over the oven. Two o'clock announced its steady green stare. "Neema's right. It's late." She walked Tony and Evelina to the door. "We'll talk later today and figure out what to do next."

"Make sure you keep the place locked tight," Tony said, "and call if anything freaks you out."

"My knight in shining armor," Mahogany said, trying to flirt, and immediately regretted her comment.

Tony smiled, and he and Evelina headed to his car.

Mahogany yawned and locked the door behind them.

"Well," Neema said, "that was the most truth I've told anyone in over two decades."

"Good for you," Mahogany said and headed upstairs. When she got to her room, the needle of the magical compass spun widely. Mahogany picked it up from her nightstand and sighed. She hoped it wasn't another murder.

Before the morning sun had driven the moon from the dawning sky, Mahogany crept from the sleeping house, ripe with Neema's contented snores.

"Where do you think the compass will take us?" Guy asked as Mahogany pushed her scooter to the street before starting the engine.

"I have a pretty good idea," Mahogany said, clipping the bone needle compass to the Vespa's handlebars.

Minutes later, they arrived at a cottage that appeared ripped from a Thomas Kinkade painting. A steep, thatched roof sloped to meet white stucco walls. Thick wooden windowsills cut into the squat cottage's walls, their glazing rippled with age. A small garden brimming with a lush rainbow of blooms lined the front of the cottage.

The Tony dream, with its rich garden, flashed in Mahogany's mind, and her stomach gave a quick dip. She shook her head, clearing her thoughts, and checked the compass. The bone needle pointed straight at the cottage's bright red door adorned with a crescent moon knocker. "This is it."

"Where is 'this'?" Guy asked, tailing Mahogany over the stepping stones to the narrow porch.

A cardboard box just outside the front door grabbed Mahogany's attention. Along with crumpled receipts and fast food wrappers lay a framed photo of a smiling girl of about eight. Her cheeks happily sandwiched between a man and a woman, all wearing matching knit hats.

"Isn't that the photo from the library?" Guy said, his mouth drawing down in a frown.

"Priscilla Wembley," Mahogany said. She took in the house again. Purple monkshood grew in luscious clumps with silver-green leaves of moonlight sage. Several stone wolves lay among the foliage–their heads thrown back, frozen in mid-howl. Unmistakably the home of a lycanthrope.

"Why is the picture in the—"

The front door flew open then, cutting Guy's words short. A dapper woman of about forty held the doorknob in one hand and a cream-colored clutch in the other. She wore a high-colored pink silk blouse and black cigarette pants that ended just above her ankles. On her feet, a pair of black flats adorned with a black bow at the toe announced she had places to go. Her brown eyes were puffy and red-rimmed.

Mahogany blinked at the familiar face, her mind attempting to parse the situation. "I'm sorry," she said finally. "I thought this was Priscilla Wembley's house."

"It is," the woman said, shutting behind her. "You're the girl from the herb shop. Misty, Marjory—"

"Mahogany."

"Right." The woman gave a tight smile and sniffled.

They stared at each other for a long moment. The woman's gaze trailed over Mahogany from her curly pink Afro to her beloved turquoise boots. "Can I help you?"

Mahogany shook her head, trying to make sense of the situation. "If this is Priscilla's house, why are you here?"

"I'm Priscilla's sister." She held out her hand. "Ivy. Ivy Wembley."

Mahogany took Ivy's hand, her eyes locked on the woman's face. Ivy's hand was cool and dry. "I take it you're staying here during your visit?"

Ivy's watery eyes grew wide. "Oh, you haven't heard. Priscilla died last night."

Mahogany's mouth dropped open, and she covered it with her free hand. "That's awful. I'm sorry for your loss. Priscilla is, er, was a lovely person." Mahogany released Ivy's hand and folded her arms over her chest. "May I ask what happened?"

"Nicely done," Guy said and gave a silent clap. "You should be on the stage."

"The police are still waiting for the autopsy results, but it's looking like an allergic reaction." Ivy shifted from one foot to the other. She pulled a tissue from her clutch and dabbed at fresh tears. "I must be going. I have lots to do before heading home."

"Of course," Mahogany said, her thoughts snapping momentarily to the box of tea she'd taken from the library. "I'm sorry to have bothered you." She stepped aside to let Ivy pass.

The older woman started down the walk, then hesitated and turned back to Mahogany. "Was there something you needed from my sister?"

Mahogany shook her head. "Not really. She was helping me with some research and I thought I'd stop by and thank her."

Ivy blinked at Mahogany, tears clinging to her eyelashes. "Isn't it a little early for a house call?"

Crap, Mahogany thought. "I'm an early riser and I often ran into Priscilla on her morning runs. I figured it was safe to stop by."

A small smile lifted Ivy's lips as if she was reliving a fond memory. "Priscilla loved her morning runs."

Relief spread through Mahogany. She didn't know if Priscilla was a runner. Most werewolves loved hiking and outdoor activities, so she'd taken a chance. "She sure did." She regarded the red-eyed

Ivy. "You didn't mention Priscilla was your sister when you came into Haughty Hemlock," Mahogany said. "I mean, it seems like something one would offer when meeting new people in a small town where we all know each other."

Ivy smiled, but it missed her swollen eyes by a mile. "To tell you the truth, Priscilla and I didn't get along. With our parents dying last year, I wanted to make amends since we were the only two left, but that sadly didn't happen." She dabbed her eyes again.

"Is that why you're throwing out the photo?" Mahogany glanced at the discarded frame.

Ivy followed Mahogany's gaze, but said nothing.

Mahogany searched Ivy's face for an answer, but the older woman revealed nothing. "Why aren't you in it?"

"In what?" Color entered Ivy's cheeks, and her eyes narrowed.

"The photo."

Ivy's gaze went to the photo again, and her eyes filled with fresh tears. "I wasn't there."

One of Mahogany's eyebrows shot upward. "Oh? Priscilla made it sound like it was a family tradition."

"It was, but I'm nearly ten years older than Priscilla. I was away at school." She shook her head, tears spilling down her cheeks. "I became busy with my life at school, and after a while, they stopped asking me to come with them. It was like they forgot about me. The memory is too painful." She nodded to the cardboard box. "It's no wonder Priscilla and I are estranged. Were, I mean." Ivy sighed and strode to her car parked at the curb, heedless of the stepping stones. Her flats left dark impressions in the dew-covered grass. She wrenched the car door open and jumped behind the wheel. A moment later, she peeled into the street and out of view.

"Is it just me, or was she a bit off?" Mahogany asked as the sound of Ivy's car faded.

"Well, she did just lose her sister," Guy said. "A sister she didn't get along with."

Mahogany narrowed her eyes. "Maybe." She examined the door with its moon-shaped knocker and turned the knob.

"What are you doing?" Guy gasped.

"I still have work to do. I have items here I need to collect."

Once inside the cottage, Mahogany pulled a paper from her pocket and smoothed the sheet against her thigh as lines of text appeared. "This shouldn't take long. There are only two items here."

Mahogany located a cursed Celtic cross and a pair of enchanted earrings. As she made to leave, she stopped to browse the large bookshelf in the living room. Unlike the bookshelves in Mahogany's house, this one didn't contain books but row upon row of records.

"You know, Guy. I need some new tunes."

"Want to treat yourself after breaking into a grieving woman's house and taking some of her inheritance?"

Mahogany frowned. "First, it's my job. Second, Ivy didn't lock the door, so it's not breaking in. Third, something's off here." She turned and glared at the ghost. "Aren't you forever telling me to seize the day? That life is short?"

Guy shrugged. "Maybe." He floated through the door before she could respond.

"It's my job," she said to the empty room. She ran a finger down the spine of an album and glanced around the living room. "No,

Guy, the real question we need to ask is, why am I here?" She shook her head and headed for the door.

Chapter 32

Mahogany and Guy pulled up in front of Backmasking Records. Through a void in the patchwork of fliers and posters taped to the inside of the massive plate-glass window, Mahogany watched Tony behind the counter. She took a deep breath and headed for the door.

A bell over the door announced her arrival. Tony looked over. Whatever rote greeting he automatically delivered to customers died on his lips. A cheerful grin lifted his cheeks, making his rectangular eyes squint into crescent moons.

"Hey, Mahogany. What brings you over this way?" Tony asked, coming around the counter to greet her properly.

"I need some new music. Any suggestions?" Mahogany glanced around the store. Long, low tables ran the room's length. Bins of records and CDs filled the tables in orderly rows. A few customers browsed the offerings.

"Well, you've come to the right place. What kind of music are you into?"

Mahogany stared at Tony, her mind blank. She hadn't thought this far ahead. Coming into stores like this often caused her anxiety. Her gaze traveled the tables with their packed bins, and she suddenly became overwhelmed. Crap. What kind of music did she like? If she were honest that she loved Pagan rock like Faith and the Muse, would he judge her as a tasteless hack? He didn't seem snobby, but she didn't want to take any chances. She eyed his t-shirt. The album cover for Iron Butterfly's *Sun and Steel* stared back at her.

"I wanted to try something new." She pointed to his shirt. "I haven't heard of them."

Tony grabbed the bottom corners of his shirt and held it out for inspection. "Do you like 70s rock?" He smiled, his eyes holding a hopeful gleam.

Mahogany shrugged. "Maybe. I'm feeling adventurous." She returned his smile.

"Okay. CD or vinyl?"

"Vinyl, please," she said, hoping a record would be more impressive. She had purchased a compact record player a few years back after she'd found an old record collection in the attic. It had been the day she'd unearthed her beautiful turquoise boots.

"Follow me." Tony led her through the tables until he found the correct crate. He flipped through the cardboard covers until he landed on one matching his shirt. "We just got this yesterday. Someone cleaned out their grandparent's old albums and brought them in." He lifted the record from the bin and handed it to Mahogany.

Scuff marks covered the album's cardboard sleeve. The scent of old paper and dust hit her nose, reminding Mahogany of the study at the brownstone. She turned the album over in her hand, examining the song list. "*Beyond the Milky Way* sounds familiar."

"It's one of the album's singles. The other is *I'm Right, I'm Wrong*. *Sun and Steel* was Iron Butterfly's last album. It's a bit more experimental than their earlier work, but, well, I like it," Tony said. He shifted from foot to foot. "You know, if you don't enjoy it, you can return it. We have a very liberal return policy." He puffed out his chest and pretended to straighten a non-existent tie.

Smiling, Mahogany looked into Tony's hazel eyes. "I'm sure I'll love it."

He grinned, his shoulders relaxing. "All right then." He returned to the counter with Mahogany in tow.

As she bought the album, she screwed up her nerve. "I was wondering—" she took a breath, pausing. "Would you like to get ice cream at Diabolical Delights tonight?"

"Ice cream?" came a familiar, effervescent voice behind Mahogany. She turned, and her gaze landed on Evelina.

Evelina threw her shining golden hair over her shoulder and handed a CD to Tony. Mahogany stepped aside, making room for Evelina at the counter.

Tony took the album and removed the plastic theft deterrent from the case. "This is such a great album," he said, an appreciative smile lighting his face.

"I'm so happy you had a copy. I destroyed my last one," Evelina said, pulling her wallet from her purse.

Mahogany glanced at Evelina's new purchase: *Evidence of Heaven* by Faith and the Muse.

"Well, isn't he full of surprises," Guy said over Mahogany's shoulder. "I think I saw that album in your collection at home, but I'm sure Iron Butterfly is good, too." He poked a translucent finger through the record in her hand.

Evelina nodded at Tony, her eyes bright. "It's creepy in the best way."

"How the vocals interweave with one another and the drums," Tony said. He threw his head back, his eyes closed.

"So," Evelina said, turning to Mahogany. "What time should we grab ice cream?"

"Oh," Mahogany said, picking at the frayed corner of her new album. "It was just a thought."

"How does seven sound?" Evelina asked, glancing from Mahogany to Tony.

"It sounds great. I've wanted to check out Diabolical Delights since I moved here," Tony added. "I love ice cream."

"Well, it's going to blow you away," Evelina said, leaning on the counter towards Tony. "A couple of enchanters run it. Whatever flavor you desire, they'll have it, even if you didn't know it."

"I'll see you tonight. Text me later." Mahogany uttered a hasty goodbye and rushed for the door.

"Wow. That was stunning," Guy said. "The way she swooped in like that. Does she have a clue you're into Tony?"

"Guy, you can shut up anytime," Mahogany said, shoving her helmet onto her head with too much force.

"Sorry." Guy mimed, zipping his lips shut and throwing away the key. "But seriously, does she have a clue?"

Mahogany thrust the key into the ignition and wrenched it to the right. A second later, the Vespa's motor flared to life. She revved the engine, pulled into traffic, and headed to the Pandemonium Historic Museum.

***

"Where have you been?" Neema asked, not looking away from the clipboard in her hands.

"Running a few errands for the museum," Mahogany said, coming into the apothecary. She'd stopped by the museum and delivered the items she'd retrieved from Priscilla's. Agalia had cut her a larger check than usual for their timely delivery. Mahogany wondered if part of the extra payment might have been for her silence, for having caught Agaila and Nancy together the night before.

Neema's head snapped towards Mahogany. "Did someone else die?"

"No, not yet. I had to pick up a few things from Priscilla Wembley's place. I ran into her sister. Did you know the woman you sold tea to, the one with the stomach problems from the plane flight, that's Priscilla's sister?"

Neema's eyes narrowed. "No, she didn't mention it. She probably didn't think it was important."

"That's putting a mild spin on it," Guy said, settling himself in the aromatic herbs, and taking a deep breath.

"Ivy, that's the sister's name, told me that Priscilla might have had an allergic reaction to something she ate," Mahogany said. She set her new album on one of the glass counters. "Maybe your tea?"

"My tea?" Neema asked, her eyes bulging. "What in Hades would my tea have to do with any of this?"

Mahogany pulled the box of tea she'd taken from the library out of her backpack and placed it on the counter. "Priscilla was drinking this when she died."

Neema stared at the box, her face unreadable. "Where did you get that?"

"I took it from the library last night."

"Why, in the name of the Prophet, would you do a thing like that?" She walked across the apothecary and picked up the box. "Unless," she said, her voice a hoarse whisper, "you think the tea actually killed that poor lamb?"

Mahogany raised her hands and shook her head. "You didn't have any reason to harm Priscilla. However, you can't control what people do with your products after they leave the store."

Neema turned the floral printed box over in her hand. "This is the tea I made for Ivy. For her stomach."

Mahogany shrugged. "Well, they were staying together. She probably took it to work. Maybe whatever was bothering Ivy's stomach was passed to Priscilla. Could have been the flu and not food poisoning."

A small nod moved Neema's head, her gaze still glued to the box. "Perhaps. It wouldn't hurt to test it. See if someone's tampered with it." She started toward the kitchen. "I didn't peg you for an Iron Butter fan," she said as she walked away. "Also, I need you to polish the silver measuring spoons."

"Right," Mahogany said, rolling her eyes at Neema disappeared through the doorway. She'd just started on the third tiny spoon when the bell above the apothecary's door jingled. She pulled her gaze from her task to greet the customer.

"Detective?" Mahogany said, her heart skipping a beat. "What can I do for you?" Crap. She'd forgotten she was supposed to go to the station this morning to speak with Sawyer about the photographs Thaddeus Spike had taken of her.

Detective Teresa Sawyer's intense gaze scoured the apothecary's shelves. Several uniformed officers stepped through the door after her. "Mahogany, it's like you're this investigation's mascot." She gave the younger woman a wry smile. "I have a search warrant, and I need to speak with Neema."

Blood rushed to Mahogany's head, making her temples pound. "I'll get her. One sec." Mahogany entered the storeroom in the back corner of the shop. "Neema, Detective Sawyer is here to see you, and she has a search warrant." Mahogany's voice trembled with adrenaline.

Neema's cool veneer never wavered. If the thought of speaking to Sawyer threw her, she didn't show it. Neema handed the clipboard to Mahogany and smoothed her blouse over her curvy frame before heading into the shop.

"Neema," Detective Sawyer said as she emerged from the storeroom. "I'm sorry. I don't have a last name for you." She thrust a bundle of papers attached with a staple. "It's a warrant to search the premises."

"You don't have a last name for me, because I don't have one," Neema said, taking the papers from the detective. "May I ask what you're looking for?" From inside the storeroom, Mahogany could almost hear Neema's shoulders square.

"Have you ever heard of *Aconitum carmichaelii*?" Detective Sawyer asked, her gaze directed at Neema.

Behind the detective, the uniformed officers moved around the shop. Mahogany peeked through the storeroom's doorway. She hadn't noticed the officers carrying disassembled boxes under their arms. As they moved behind the glass display counters, they pressed the filing boxes into shape and filled them with herbs.

"We both know the answer is yes. Any herbalist worth their salt knows it. One of *Aconitum carmichaelii's* common names is monkshood. Another is wolfsbane. Gardeners grow the plant as an ornamental but it's native to Central China. Traditionally, it has medicinal uses, but the whole plant is poisonous. However, I'm sure you already know this," Neema said.

"We found one of your monogrammed tea bags containing a large amount of monkshood at the library. Do you know how that may have happened?" the detective asked.

Neema paused, but only for a moment. "I wouldn't know. I don't carry monkshood. There's no need to. While some brave souls still use it for particular complaints, I won't touch the stuff. If you found some in a tea from my shop, well, I can't attest to what people do after they leave here. Anyone could have tampered with my tea after buying it."

Mahogany's mind raced back to the library, the scent of mint and licorice. The spilled mug of tea. Priscilla Wembley's frozen face. The box of tea placed behind the computer monitor. The bell-shaped flowers filled Priscilla's lush garden. Of course, a lycanthrope would grow wolfsbane. Most myths about werewolves told that wolfsbane was a deterrent to the beasts. In truth, it was just another flower that looked nice in a garden.

The detective mulled around the store, poking at items with her gloved hands as Neema spoke. Next to the front door, a hefty stack of evidence grew as the officers added more and more boxes to the pile.

"Are you going to collect the entire store?" Neema asked, placing her hands on her hips.

Guy materialized, having been lounging elsewhere in the house. "What's going on? Why are you standing in a closet?"

Mahogany pointed through the door and into the store.

Guy floated through the wall and into the shop with a puzzled expression.

"These all need to be tested for the toxin or other potentially toxic substances." The detective pointed to the door connecting the store with the living quarters. "Don't forget the living quarters," Sawyer said to her officers before striding into the kitchen.

Mahogany's heart pounded. The photos and manila envelope! She'd left them out. What would the detective think when she found them? She was already in hot water for investigating on her own. Mahogany imagined the clinking of iron doors as the prospect of prison presented itself.

"Detective, please. You said you found my tea at the library? What does that have to do with anything?" Neema followed Detective Sawyer into the house. Neema motioned for Mahogany to stay put as she passed. The younger woman stopped, her gaze lingering on the doorway as Neema and the detective disappeared into the kitchen. Mahogany leaned towards the threshold, straining to hear.

"Yes, it appears someone was poisoned with your tea." The detective opened the drawers in the kitchen and rifled through the contents before walking away.

"Oh, the poor dear." Neema took a seat at the kitchen table. "It's not a quick poison. It takes an hour or more to work. When exactly did this happen?"

"Sometime last night," the detective said.

"Ma'am?" An officer brushed past Mahogany into the kitchen, holding a book in his hand. "You'll find this interesting."

Detective Sawyer took the book. A ribbon attached to the spine was tucked between the pages, holding the reader's place. The detective opened it to the marked page. "*Aconitum carmichaelii*," she read aloud.

Neema frowned. "That's not my book," she said. "I found it on the counter yesterday. I figured someone had forgotten it as they shopped."

The detective motioned to the officer, who removed a set of handcuffs from his belt.

"Neema," the detective paused and shook her head. "Neema, you are under arrest for suspicion of murder. You have the right to remain silent."

Mahogany came to the kitchen door, her jaw dragging on the floor when she saw Neema in handcuffs.

"It'll be fine," Neema said as the officer led her past Mahogany. "We both know I didn't poison anyone."

"Don't leave town," Detective Sawyer said, pointing to Mahogany. "Stay home. I don't want to run into you again, poking your nose into my investigation. When I've finished with Neema, I'll send an officer around to collect you for questioning. We still need to talk about Thadeus Spike's photo shoots."

Mahogany nodded, unable to speak as the detective and Neema moved through the Haughty Hemlock's front door.

Some officers continued searching the premises while others loaded boxes into a white van parked on the street. Mahogany groaned, noticing a small crowd gathering to watch the spectacle.

An officer passed her and climbed the stairs to the bedrooms above. Mahogany followed him, a bubble of anger rising in her throat as he rifled through her belongings. She wanted to scream and throw everyone out onto the street.

Guy appeared then. "Don't worry about the pictures. I know where Neema hid them." He eyed the officer as he searched the medicine cabinet, tossing items into another box. "They'll never find them. Well, unless they have a sledgehammer. They don't have a sledgehammer, do they?"

Mahogany sighed and took a heavy seat on her bed, wishing she were anywhere but here.

Chapter 33

Several hours later, the officers departed with most of the Haughty Hemlock's stock, leaving the shelves bare. Mahogany locked the door behind them and turned the sign from open to closed.

She sighed, headed into the kitchen, and surveyed the mess wrought by the searching officers. The chaos before her caused an eerie sensation to crawl over her scalp. Her home resembled the brownstone the night of the murders and Tony's after the break-in; drawers dumped of their contents, and books flung from the shelves.

"The letters!" Mahogany raced to the writing desk. The police had gracelessly wrenched open the locked drawer containing the letters from Thaddeus.

"They're gone," Guy said, blinking at Mahogany. "Do you think the police will use the letters against Neema and Thad? Like they were working together to get rid of Mike and me?"

Guy had a point. Thad's letters warning Neema further pointed to the two of them conspiring against Mike. The police might think them capable of murder to keep him quiet.

"This day stinks." Mahogany covered her face with her hands and took a deep breath. "I need to think, and I can't do that with this place looking like a pack of imps had an orgy in it."

Guy gazed at Mahogany. His mouth turned down in a frown. "I wish I could help."

Mahogany nodded. "Lucky you," she said.

His frown deepened. "Wait. Imps have orgies?"

"Don't even get me started. They had one in the town center on May Day a few years back. The stench was horrible." Mahogany eyed the mess on the kitchen floor. It was as good a place to start as any.

"Ew, say no more," Guy held up his hands in defense. "Maybe you could call Tony and Evelina to help you tidy?" Guy suggested.

"Guy," Mahogany said, pulling her phone from her pocket, "that's the first good idea you've had since you died."

"Hey, I resent that," Guy said, folding his arms over his chest and sticking out his chin. "I'm glad I can't help you." Mock indignation peppered his tone.

Mahogany's thumbs flew over the surface of her phone, tapping out a text message: Neema arrested. Place tossed by cops.

Seconds later, her phone chirped. Tony replied: Getting my shift covered. Be there soon.

A smile sparked across Mahogany's face. Maybe Evelina wouldn't be able to make it for a while, and she and Tony could have more alone time.

Her phone chirped again. This time it was Evelina who texted: On my way!

"Oh, well. Many hands make light work, or something like that," Mahogany said, pocketing her phone. She picked up the silverware scattered across the kitchen floor and placed it in the dishwasher before moving to the next pile. She worked her way through the kitchen, refilling drawers and sliding them back into their homes.

"Something's wrong with Bazgul," Guy said, startling Mahogany from her thoughts. His voice carried an urgent note that froze Mahogany's insides. The ghost stood at the kitchen window next to the back door, gazing at something on the ground.

"What do you mean?" Mahogany dropped a pile of pens into the drawer she was working on and joined Guy at the window.

Bazgul lay on the asphalt on his back. His fuzzy legs curled against his abdomen as if in death. Next to him lay a half-digested baby bird.

Mahogany jumped to the back door, yanked it open, and flew down the steps. She scooped Bazgul in her hands with the gentleness of a mother hen and cradled him against her chest. "Bazzy, what's happened to you?" she whispered.

Bazgul's limbs twitched. The scent of licorice and mint drifted off him.

"Priscilla Wembley," Mahogany whispered and spirited him inside.

"Priscilla Wembley?" Guy moved away from the window and followed Mahogany.

"It's the same scent from the library the night Priscilla died." Mahogany grabbed a kitchen towel, folded it to create a tiny cushion for Bazgul, and set him on the kitchen island.

"Poison?" Guy looked at the bowl of herbs in the window, then at the open back door. "If so, the murderer must have left the poison outside for Bazgul to find. There's no way they could have gotten into the house. Bazgul must have slipped through the cracks in the frame to get to the bird."

"What to do?" Mahogany said, her voice ragged with panic. "Think, Mahogany, think!"

Suddenly, the memory of Bazgul getting into an extra-large box of chocolates floated into view. He'd been so sick until—

"Bazgul, you need to vaporate. It's the only way to remove the toxins." Mahogany brought her face close to Bazgul's body, the scent of death coiling off him.

"Vaporate?" Guy had floated outside and peered at the baby bird. Slime and demon foam clung to its featherless body. "That's a word?"

"It is for demons. If Bazgul stays in his corporal form, the toxin will damage his tissues," Mahogany said over her shoulder. "Bazzy, do you hear me? You need to vaporate."

Bazgul didn't respond. His large mandibles quivered, foam gathering at his maw.

"Bazgul," Mahogany said, a sob hitching in her throat. "I order you to vaporate."

Still jerking, the giant demon spider dissolved into a reddish-brown mist. The mist hovered over the dishtowel, shifting and swirling.

"Is there anything we can do for him?" Guy said, appearing next to Mahogany.

Mahogany shook her head. "It's out of our hands. He has to do this on his own." She swiped at her hot tears, fury burning through her.

"What if he can't?" Guy said.

Too afraid to answer or even ponder the alternative, Mahogany lowered her head and let the tears come.

After an impossibly long few minutes, Bazgul retook his spider shape. His legs no longer folded under his body like any other dead arachnid. Instead, Bazgul lay on his hairy tummy, legs bent at a reasonable angle. The tips of his tiny toes rested on the countertop.

Tony trotted up the steps and into the kitchen through the open back door. He gazed around the disorganized space before his attention landed on Mahogany sobbing on the kitchen island.

"It's okay, Mahogany," Tony said, placing a hand on her shoulders. "It's not that bad." He glanced around the kitchen again. "Well, it's pretty bad, but if we work together, we'll put it right in no time." Then his gaze fell on Bazgul's motionless form. He pulled Mahogany into his chest and hugged her while she cried, her tears soaking through his shirt.

"I brought ice cream. I figured our outing to Diabolica Delights was a no-go, so I..." Evelina's bubbly voice died on her lips as she took in the mess before her. "Holy shit. What the hell were they looking for? Gold? Plans to overthrow the government?"

Mahogany pulled away from Tony. "It's Bazgul. He's been poisoned." She wiped her nose on her sweater sleeve, not caring how it looked.

Evelina dropped the canvas bag with the pints of ice cream and screamed. She dashed to the counter and peered at Bazgul. "Oh, Mahogany! I'm so sorry." She reached for Mahogany and hugged her tight while Tony put the ice cream in the freezer.

"What happened?" Evelina asked, breaking their embrace.

Mahogany shook her head. "Someone left a baby bird laced with poison outside for him to find." She wiped her face dry with the back of her hand.

Tony found a plastic food container on the floor and retrieved the bird. "Just in case another creature finds it."

She hovered near Bazgul for several hours, too afraid to leave him, while Tony and Evelina tidied as best they could. Mahogany's heart ached like nothing she'd ever experienced before. She excelled in grieving what she hadn't truly lost, like the family she'd been born into but couldn't remember. However, Bazgul was her oldest friend, and now he wavered near death's door. If he were to cross over—Mahogany shook her head. She couldn't bear to finish the thought.

She trained her tear-stained gaze on Guy, who paced through the kitchen, his right hand gripping his chin while the other lay folded across his stomach.

"Guy," Mahogany said, her voice low and hoarse from crying. Guy continued to pace. She cleared her throat and tried again. "Guy."

The ghost stopped his pacing and gazed at Mahogany, his expression expectant.

"I don't know if I can do this anymore." Mahogany stroked Bazgul's furry legs. "People are in danger because of the investigation. First, someone broke into Tony's house, then someone, maybe the same someone, poisoned poor Priscilla Wembley, and now Bazgul."

Guy dropped his hands to his sides. His face drooped with understanding. "I'll be stuck here as long as my murderer runs free," he said. "You've made it clear you want me gone."

Mahogany nodded. "I'm sorry I've been so awful, but..." she trailed off. "I would rather put up with your annoying presence than have another person get hurt." She gave him a woeful smile. "Plus, you're growing on me."

Guy nodded and returned Mahogany's sad smile. "Like a fungus?"

"Like athlete's foot and ringworm all rolled into one." Mahogany sighed. "I'm sure Detective Sawyer will have your murder solved soon," she added, her voice carrying a hopeful lilt.

Guy nodded and sighed. "I don't want my desire to cross over to cause any more deaths." He began pacing again. "I mean, the police have arrested the wrong people, but you're right. They've got this."

Mahogany closed her eyes, causing several tears to spill onto her cheeks, and took a shuddering breath.

"We also don't know for sure if Priscilla's murder connects to mine and Mike's murders. While the same person may have committed them, the modus operandi is completely different. Another person entirely might have poisoned Bazgul and Priscilla."

"Are you suggesting two different murderers?" Mahogany said. She dropped herself onto one of the bar stools next to the kitchen island. "Where did Neema hide the manila envelope?" Mahogany asked.

"In the fireplace," Guy said. "There's a secret cache in the flue, by the way."

"A what?" Mahogany moved to the living room and stood in front of the fireplace. "What do I do?"

"Inside the flue. If you press here," he pointed the toe of his dirty sneaker at a brick near the floor on the front of the fireplace, "it will unlock the cache inside."

Mahogany bent and inspected the brick. Nothing about it stood out. She pressed it experimentally, and it slid several inches into the fireplace, grinding as it went. Inside the flue, she heard a click.

Guy thrust his head into the bricks and said, "Yep, that worked. It's open."

Frowning, she pulled her phone from her pocket and flipped on the flashlight. She got onto her hands and knees and peered into the flue, training the light up the chimney. Guy's head peaked through the blackened brick next to a metal lip. Mahogany reached up and pulled the manilla envelope and photos free. As she did, something small and rectangular fell towards her face. Mahogany flinched as the corner caught her forehead before hitting the sooty bricks.

Mahogany twisted and focused the phone's light on the object. The tea she'd taken from the library lay innocuously on the cold, black bricks, but something had changed. The Victorian flora print had gone from pastel shades of pinks and violets bordered in silver to dark reds and purples outlined in black.

"What the," Mahogany said, picking up the box. She ducked back into the living room. It was as if the box had changed to reflect whatever sinister poison lay inside.

"Maybe Neema did something to it. Like a test for toxins that made the box react like that?" Guy suggested, scratching his head.

Together, they returned to the kitchen, where she washed the soot from her hands. She opened the envelope and ran her gaze over the black-and-white image of the murderer about to plunge the anelace into Magic Mike's back. In the background, the edge of an overstuffed bookshelf hovered to the right, while the enormous brick fireplace took up the right half. A portion of a velvet couch lay near the center of the frame, with Mike and the murderer behind him.

"You're not in this picture. What if you're about to murder Mike, and then Thad murdered you for revenge," Mahogany said, dropping the photo onto the island.

"Are you serious right now?" Guy said, the corners of his mouth drawing down.

"The murderer is tall and thin, just like you and Thaddeus." Mahogany narrowed her gaze at Guy. "You get all stabby with Mike, and Thad brains you with the Mother Shipton bust. Instant karma."

Guy placed his hands on his hips. "What if Neema took the picture while Thaddeus murdered Mike?"

Mahogany looked through the pictures again. "And then Thad healed Bazgul's bite with superior magic, so no trace of it remained." She put her head in her hands and groaned.

"Is that possible?" Guy asked.

"No," Mahogany said, her voice muffled by her hands.

Evelina and Tony descended the stairs and joined Mahogany and Guy in the kitchen.

"The upstairs is back to normal," Tony said.

Evelina retrieved the pints of ice cream and washed three spoons. "We all need something to fortify our souls."

Without argument, they dug in.

"How's the patient?" Evelina said around a mouthful of gooey chocolate ice cream.

"It's too early to tell," Mahogany said, looking at Bazgul's still figure, taking a bite of her coffee surprise. The rich flavors of tropical breezes, dark coffee, and snorkeling hit her, sending her senses reeling. The dark cloud of the day receded a little, loosening the knot in her chest.

Evelina petted the giant spider. "Poor baby." Her face twisted into a sudden mask of anger. "I want to kill the person who did this." She slammed her fist on the counter.

"This is impossible," Mahogany said, her teary gaze resting on Bazgul. "No one we've interviewed has a demon bite. We don't know who's telling the truth." She gestured to the doorway leading into the apothecary. "Especially, Neema. How do we even know she was here when Guy and Mike were murdered like she claims?"

"Too bad you don't have a security camera out front. We could see if anyone came and went," Evelina said, licking chocolate ice cream off the back of the spoon.

The frown pinching Mahogany's tear-stained face disappeared, replaced with a look of surprise. "That's it! Evelina, you're a genius." She jumped off the stool and pushed past Tony, her boot heels clomping over the Hemlock's floor as she raced to the store entrance. She kept going until she stood in front of Humbaba, directly across the street.

In Humbaba's large window, a set of long, scaly fingers held the corner of the dark curtain back, creating a slim crack. Two piercing jade-colored eyes stared through the glass at Mahogany.

Mahogany yanked on Humbaba's door and found it locked. She hammered on the glass with the side of her fist.

"Stheno. Euryale. I know you're in there. We need to talk," she said, her voice commanding.

The latch clicked, and with a soft scraping of metal on metal, the door swung inward.

For all of Mahogany's bluster, she hesitated before crossing the threshold. She took a deep breath and entered the viper's den.

The rows of fluorescent lighting floated above her and remained stubbornly unlit. Shadowy statuary towered in the gloom, and the earthy scent of clay made the air stuffy. Icy fear crept through her stomach and across her scalp.

Tony and Evelina hurried into the shop after Mahogany. Their expressions strained, their wide-eyed gazes darting around the shadowy interior.

"Yess?" a snake-like voice came from the shadows. Mahogany turned in its direction and squinted into the darkness.

"I need to know if you saw Neema in Haughty Hemlock the night of the murders," Mahogany said, her voice disappearing into the dim interior.

Stheno walked out of the shadows, her heels knocking their way toward Mahogany on the hardwood floor. A crown of red locks encircled her head and trailed over her shoulders.

"I was watching *Curb Appeal* on HGTV while I put the finishing touches on a fresh batch of lawn gnomes. Snooping is more to Euryale's taste," Stheno said, hissing her esses.

Behind where Evelina and Tony huddled together, something scraped across the floor, making them jump. Tony gasped, and Evelina swallowed a ball of air, making her burp.

Mahogany turned and faced Euryale. "Did you see Neema in the Haughty Hemlock the night Magic Mike and Guy were murdered?" Mahogany asked the scaly Euryale.

"Yess," Euryale said, dragging out the end of the word. "She toiled in the apothecary, and then she donned a dark coat and departed," Euryale said.

"What time did she leave?" Mahogany asked.

"About one in the morning. That infernal clock tower chimed only moments before," Euryale said.

"There's enough happening at that hour to spy on?" Tony asked, an eyebrow raised on his golden brow.

"You'd be surprised," Euryale said. She licked her lips, her tongue giving a reptilian flicker. "This is Pandemonium, after all."

Tony and Evelina took several tiny steps toward Mahogany, placing more space between themselves and Euryale.

"The other person," Mahogany said, closing her eyes.

"What other person?" Guy asked.

"There was someone else at the brownstone that night. Well, sort of. I saw someone running toward downtown after Bazgul and I got out of the house," Mahogany said.

"Could it have been the murderer?" Tony asked.

Mahogany shook her head. "Not unless they got a block ahead of me and transformed from tall skinny into short and plump with the gait of someone who hasn't run in a decade."

"Thank you," Mahogany said to Euryale and Stheno. "Sorry, I barged over here."

"Don't be. Please come by anytime. You would make the perfect model for our art," Stheno said, stepping toward Mahogany and taking her by the chin.

Mahogany stared into her jade eyes, mesmerized.

"Thank you again," Evelina said, taking Mahogany's hand and firmly guiding her toward the door.

"Ice cream," Tony said, pointing over his shoulder at Haughty Hemlock by way of explanation. "Wouldn't want it to melt." He held the door open while Evelina towed Mahogany onto the side-walk.

They slipped out of the shadowy store and back across the street to the apothecary. Mahogany gave a fleeting look at the Gorgon's shop. Two pairs of eyes peered at her from Humbaba's large front window, sending a shiver up her spine.

Chapter 34

Mahogany turned to Tony and handed him the manila envelope. "I can't have these here in case the police come back. Please take them. We need to add them to the murder wall."

Tony took the envelope. "Let's all head over there now, drop these off, and then go to the police station and see if we can't spring Neema."

Mahogany nodded. She placed Bazgul on his cat tree. "You'll be safe inside," she said, kissing the demon spider on the head. "Do not, for any reason, go outside. Neema's spell only protects you while you're in the house."

Bazgul gave a weak nod, rested his head on the tree's carpeted platform, and closed his eyes.

Mahogany looked at Bazgul before following Tony and Evelina out the door, locking it behind her. "I wish I could bring him, but he's too weak,"

Evelina placed an arm around Mahogany's shoulders and pulled her close. "Neema's spell has kept him safe this long. It will do for another night. He's over the worst of the poison now. He needs rest."

Mahogany nodded against Evelina's shoulder. "I know, but I hate to leave him."

They got to Tony's and gave the photo of the murderer and the printed articles a quick once over as they hung them on the murder wall.

"See anything new?" Mahogany asked as Tony pushed the last pin into the wall.

Evelina shook her head. "Maybe we need to go back to the brownstone and take another look around? Perhaps the murderer left something behind the police overlooked."

"Before we do that, let's see about Neema," Mahogany said.

They pulled into a small lot for visitors across the street from the police station and filed out of Tony's car. The station loomed large and imposing before them. Security windows and barred doors had replaced the once-inviting hotel. It made one wonder if they were trying to keep things out or keep them in.

"Hey, Guy. You have unlimited access to the building. Would you mind checking things out?" Mahogany said.

Guy nodded. "My pleasure."

They crossed the street to inquire with the officer at the desk about Neema as Guy disappeared through the wall.

"Be back in two shakes," Guy said, using Neema's expression.

The interior of the station held some remnants of the old hotel. A parquet mosaic stained in an elaborate pattern stretched across the floor. Light bloomed upward from art déco wall sconces. However, the crème de la crème was a massive crystal chandelier suspended over the front doors. However, these architectural flourishes didn't diminish the fact that this was a police station.

A thick sheet of plexiglass ran the length of the front desk. What once welcomed weary travelers was now bisected down the center, separating the officers from the public. A series of concentric holes in the plexiglass allowed visitors to speak to the on-duty officer.

"Well, hello there, Sergeant Ralph," Evelina said, her best smile lighting her face.

Sergeant Ralph Evans smiled warmly at Evelina. His short-shorn brown hair made his round face appear even more moon-like.

"Don't be silly, Evelina. Call me Ralph." His gaze drifted to Mahogany, and his smile faltered and fell away when his eyes met Tony.

"I don't think we've been introduced," Ralph said, his tone hardened, taking on a professional air as he sized up Tony. "I'm Sergeant Ralph Evans."

Recognition rippled across Tony's face, and Mahogany felt her scalp tingle with embarrassment. He gave Mahogany a slight nudge with his elbow, and she knew he would tease her later about 'old Raphie boy.' She groaned inwardly. Of course, Ralph would be on duty.

"Tony Applegate," Tony said and offered an amiable smile to Ralph

Ralph's expression remained neutral, and he turned back to Evelina, his smile returning. "What brings you into today?"

Evelina blushed on cue and smiled demurely. "We're on a mission," she said, tossing her smile aside. Her eyes narrowed, and she leaned towards the protective glass separating them and lowered her voice. "The new detective brought Neema in for questioning in a murder investigation. If you can believe that."

Ralph's gaze darted to Tony and Mahogany standing behind Evelina. The golden-haired fairy maneuvered herself between Ralph's line of vision and her friends.

The sergeant blinked, his eyes softening as he peered into Evelina's violet gaze.

Right, Mahogany thought. Ralph was a human, which meant he was susceptible to Evelina's kitchen witchery. He ate at Hot Brews every morning, which meant they might have a leg up on getting information out of him.

"You wouldn't know what's going on with Neema?" Evelina asked, her steady gaze burrowed into Ralph's blue eyes.

It was Sergeant Evan's turn to look bashful. "I don't know too much information about suspects. It's above my pay grade."

Evelina made a scoffing noise in her throat. "That's utterly ridiculous. I bet you'll become a detective in a few short years, and then you'll be back there doing the questioning."

Ralph's face lit up. "Do you think so?"

"I know so," Evelina said, nodding her head with the self-assurance of a snake oil vendor.

"Well, I might have heard something," Ralph lowered his voice as he spoke into the microphone mounted to his side of the plexiglass partition. "They're questioning her now, but we're releasing her on bail in the morning."

Evelina's eyes narrowed, and she nodded as if Ralph had just told her how to crack the vault in the Bellagio in Vegas. "Got it. Thank you so much."

Just then, a commotion broke out on the other side of the station. Shouts for an ambulance reverberated through the old building.

"Hold it! Hold it," shouted a balding man who jogged into the room from where Mahogany guessed the cells and interview rooms were located. The man approached Ralph and spoke in a low tone. Evelina's eyes narrowed as she eavesdropped. As Ralph reached for the phone, Evelina turned and ushered Mahogany and Tony out of the building. Guy joined them in the parking lot, appearing winded.

"I found her, but something's happened to Thaddeus," Guy said, his words coming in gulps.

"What?" Mahogany said as the heavy-duty door to the station closed behind them.

"He's dead," Guy and Evelina said simultaneously.

"What?" Mahogany and Tony asked together.

"The bald guy, Detective Marrow, told Ralph to get the crime scene guys to the station ASAP and call the coroner. 'Mr. Spike is dead'," Evelina said.

Tony and Mahogany stared at Evelina, their eyes wide.

"Wait, that's not the worst part," Guy said, flickering with emotion.

"What do you mean?" Mahogany said, shifting her gaze to Guy. "What could be worse than him being dead?"

"He died magically," Guy paused.

"Spit it out, Guy. Magically, how?"

Guy stared hard at Mahogany. "He's frozen." Guy leaned back after uttering the words as if Mahogany would spring forward in shock.

Mahogany blinked at her ghost, an unreadable expression on her face. "Frozen?" She shook her head. "Elaborate."

"Have you looked through your uncle's library for books on ghost communication?" Evelina asked Tony, her voice low. She stared at Mahogany as she conversed with empty air.

Tony shook his head. "There was one book that might have some clues. It's hard to tell. Most of my uncle's library reads like stereo instructions."

"A freezing spell," Guy said. "He's like a block of ice."

Mahogany leaned back on her heels, her mind reeling as she imagined the scene inside the station. "No wonder they were losing their minds." She tapped her lower lip with her index finger. "Neema's not safe. We've got to get her out of there."

Guy shook his head. "No can do. They are not letting her go anywhere. Detective Sawyer was in the middle of questioning her when the whole popsicle Thaddeus thing happened."

Mahogany stomped her foot. "She needs protecting. Can we get this to her?" Mahogany unclasped the pentagram necklace and held it out in front of her. "If it's protected me all these years, it'll hopefully do the same for her."

Evelina studied Mahogany, reluctant to take the necklace.

"You won't change my mind. If you don't take it, I'll figure out another way to get it to Neema," Mahogany said, her steely gaze making Evelina flinch.

"Fine, but let the record show I am totally against this decision." Evelina snatched the necklace from Mahogany and stomped back into the station.

"What about you? Now you're not protected," Tony said, his brow furrowing in concern.

"I'm not trapped in a cell like Neema. I'll be able to defend myself."

"Will you, though?" Tony asked, placing a hand on Mahogany's shoulder and turning her to face him. "Can you defend yourself against magic? Thad was a sorcerer, and he couldn't."

Mahogany studied Tony's eyes, concern knitting his brow. "What choice do I have? Sit around, let this play out?" She turned back to Guy. "How is Neema?"

"Alive. Fine," Guy said. "There aren't any windows in the interview room. No one can get to her there."

"But there are in the cells, right?" Mahogany asked. "That's how the murderer got the spell through?"

Guy nodded. "I think so. It's the only thing that makes sense. Unless an officer cast it," he added with a dismissive wave.

Tony shook his head. "I don't like it." He reached into his pocket and retrieved the vial with the protection decoction Neema had given him. "Take this."

Mahogany took a step back, shaking her head. "No way."

"Take it, or I'm going back into the station and tell them I murdered Guy and Magic Mike." All the warmth and welcome had vanished from Tony's face.

Mahogany, realizing that Tony was as stubborn as herself, relented and took the vial. She resigned herself to planting it back in his person as soon as possible.

Evelina pushed through the station doors and joined them. "Done. Ralph is taking it back to her now."

"How did you manage that?" Tony asked, his expression incredulous.

"Feed a human enough enchanted Fae food, and they can't help but do your bidding, at least for a limited time. The enchantment wears off after a couple of days." Evelina shrugged.

"Handy," Tony said. "All right, everyone. Back to my place to confer. We can't do more for Neema now. I want to know everything Guy saw and heard in there."

Chapter 35

They got comfy around the coffee table while reheated lasagna steamed on plates. Tony finished filling their glasses with wine as Mahogany relayed Guy's adventure inside the police station.

"This is taking forever," Guy said. His voice was an octave higher than usual.

"You're right. This is a time suck. There's got to be a better way." Mahogany huffed against the couch. Bits of slashed foam caught in her curls as they protruded from the cushion.

Guy began pacing the living room, muttering under his breath. As he passed the stereo, light static filled the air.

"Why does your stereo sound like it's possessed?" Evelina asked.

"No idea," Tony said, offering the stereo a suspicious glare. "It's not even on."

"I think it's Guy," Mahogany said, watching Guy pace.

Recognition dawned on Tony's face, and he leaped to his feet. "I get it now!" he whooped and clapped before dashing down the hall to the back of the house. Mahogany, Evelina, and Guy stared after him, eyebrows raised in puzzlement.

He came back a few moments later, hunched over a heavy tome. "The application of amplification permits specters expressions audible to those not haunted by the deceased," Tony said, reading the passage aloud.

"Gesundheit," Evelina said.

"That's it. The application of amplification." He slammed the book shut with a triumphant snap. A small plume of dust lifted into the air above the pages.

Mahogany and Evelina stared at Tony, their blank expressions expectant.

"English, Tony. Speak English," Mahogany said.

"Amplification," Tony said and pointed to the stereo. "Guy is affecting the radio with his presence. If we find the right frequency, we," he motioned to Evelina and himself, "should be able to hear him."

Guy stared at the stereo and waved his hand in front of it. Static cracked each time his hand passed in front of the equipment.

"If I could kiss him, I would," Guy said, gazing at Tony.

"Get in line," Mahogany said. "Try standing inside the stereo, Guy." Mahogany said.

"Good idea." Guy floated into the stereo, his bottom half disappearing into the device's black plastic and chrome buttons. Static blared from the speakers, and the living threw their hands over their ears. Bob, who'd been dozing on Evelina's lap, leaped into the air and bounded out of the room.

Guy jumped out of the stereo. "Sorry."

"Now, to find the right frequency." Tony kneeled in front of the stereo. "Guy, can you please try again?"

"Wow, a please?" He gave Mahogany a pointed look. "So polite."

"Oh, stop your bellyaching," Mahogany said. "You're so sensitive."

Guy's chin jutted, and he stepped into the stereo again, avoiding moving through Tony.

The stereo screamed static, and Tony spun the dial, moving through the FM stations. The static decreased in volume, only to grow to a deafening magnitude again.

"Try AM," Mahogany yelled above the ear-splitting white noise.

Tony nodded and pressed the AM button on the stereo's silver face. The static lowered in decibels immediately but persisted. He rotated the station dial more slowly. About a millimeter before 700 AM, the air fell silent. Tony released the dial slowly, trying to keep it perfectly aligned.

"Okay, Guy. Say something," Tony said.

"Hello?" Guy said. The stereo transmitted his voice through the speakers as if he were sitting in the room with them.

Tony whooped again and did a little dance. Evelina squealed and jumped up and down while Guy threw his hands over his mouth and laughed-sobbed. Mahogany smiled at everyone.

"Tony, if I were able, I would kiss you right now," Guy said, his voice trembling with emotion.

"I feel you, buddy," Tony said. "Okay, let's get to work. We don't know if this is a fleeting parlor trick or something we can rely on." He patted the top of the stereo. "What happened at the station?"

"Right," Guy said. "I found Neema in one of the interview rooms. She and Detective Sawyer were the only two present. The conversation was being videotaped." Guy paused. "Let me see. What exactly did they say?" Another voice came through the speakers.

"Neema?" Mahogany stood. "Guy, why do I hear Neema?" A surge of panic rose in her chest.

Evelina covered her mouth with her hand, her eyes going wide. "She's not here with us, is she?" Evelina said, voicing the same fear Mahogany had.

Guy peered around the room. "Not that I can see. I haven't seen another ghost since I became one. That was me." He shook his head. "Hang on." Guy shut his eyes, his eyebrows pulling together in a deep frown.

"Right," Detective Sawyer's voice came through the speakers. "Tell me about your relationship with Magoris Idrus."

"What about it?" Neema answered.

"How well did you know him?"

"We knew each other in our younger years, but I hadn't seen him in two decades or more," Neema replied.

"What would you say if I told you someone reported seeing the two of you arguing hours before his murder?" The sound of shuffling papers followed Detective Sawyer's question.

"He came into town, and we ran into each other," Neema said, sounding bored. "I invited him out for a drink. Magoris got drunk and became belligerent, dredging up the past."

"You mean Aurora Kingsley?"

"Yes, Aurora was always a sore spot with us."

"What did he say about Miss Kingsley?" Sawyer asked.

"He blamed me for her death. Mike, Magoris, rather, was in love with Aurora as a teenager, and she was in a relationship with me. Magoris resented me for it," Neema said.

Mahogany's jaw dropped. She couldn't remember Neema ever being in a romantic relationship. She'd assumed the older woman was asexual. Anything else hadn't crossed Mahogany's mind.

"Are you sure the argument didn't have to do with these?" More ruffling papers followed the detective's words.

There was a pause as Neema looked over whatever Sawyer had handed her. "Thaddeus sent these. If I had an issue with the letters, I would have taken it up with him, not Mike."

"Yes, but Mr. Spike's message seems like a warning to you. Would that have something to do with Magoris?"

"Oh, she's good," Evelina said under her breath.

"Magoris showed up and argued with me about Aurora." Neema's words carried a sharp edge Mahogany knew well. It was a tone she'd heard often as a teenager.

The detective's chair squeaked as she sat back. "A man travels across the country to interrogate someone he used to know about a relationship that ended twenty years ago? Try again."

"I have no control over who sends me mail, detective. Nor do I control where people travel."

"This concerns me," Detective Sawyer said. She tapped her finger against the something as she spoke. "It's suspicious, especially the bookmark on the page for monkshood."

"Detective," Neema said. "Suspicion is subjective. If you want to find something incriminating in an apothecary shop, you will find it, but that doesn't mean it's a sign of guilt."

"What I'm wondering is when my officers finish with your place, will they find anything linking you to Magoris Idrus or Guy Miller's deaths?" Detective Sawyer asked.

"If you want to find something that fits with the story you've constructed, then you will," Neema said.

"Is that an admission of guilt?"

"Certainly not. It's a statement of fact. People from the outside have come to Pandemonium for generations. What they see are a bunch of freaks and crazies. People have accused the residents of Pandemonium of witchcraft, sorcery, devil worship, and any other manner of poppycock. Search all you wish with your warrant. You will find no monkshood beyond words in a book nor any other dangerous plant used in connection with the murder of Priscilla Wembley. Or anything linking me to Magoris's or Guy's deaths."

"You seem sure of yourself," the detective said.

"I'm innocent of any wrongdoing, intentionally or accidentally," Neema said. "The burden of proof lies with you."

A soft knock on the interview room door interrupted them. A second officer entered the room and whispered to Sawyer, who then suspended the interview.

The voices faded from the speakers as Guy closed his mouth. "That's when they discovered Thad's body."

"You're like an invisible recorder. The perfect spy tool," Mahogany said.

"That's what that was?" Tony said, pointing to the stereo. "I'm floored."

"Oh, thank goodness. I thought they were both dead and using Guy's frequency to talk to us from beyond the grave." Evelina took a large gulp of her wine.

"Detective Sawyer knows about Aurora," Tony said.

"We can also assume she knows about the rest of the group in the photo Thad took three decades ago. How half of them died under suspicious circumstances," Mahogany said. She sat heavily on the injured couch. "They must be losing their minds over Thaddeus's odd death."

"Stupid human question time again." Tony raised his hand. "If this is a magical town, wouldn't it stand to reason there are magical Folk on the police force? Wouldn't they understand what happened to Thad?"

"It's complicated," Evelina offered. "There are a few magical Folk who are cops. Most are pariahs to the rest of the magical community. To become a police officer while also being of the Folk is seen as a betrayal."

"Historically, the police haven't treated Folk with much respect. Sometimes they led the mob with pitchforks and torches. However, the Guild of Myth and Magic does like to have a couple of local representatives keeping tabs on things. I bet they're doing their best to mitigate Thad's death. Coming up with some explanation for a person being frozen solid while in police custody."

Tony nodded and rubbed his chin. "Hey Guy, did you see anything around the time Thaddeus died?" Tony said. "Something that might give us a clue into what we're dealing with?"

"I was in the interview room when a uniformed officer came in. I followed her, and there he was. Frozen solid like a block of ice." Guy scratched his head. "Wait, there was something. A blue haze near the window at the top of the cell."

"Was the window open?" Mahogany said.

Guy shook his head. "It was glass with mesh inside it. Not the kind that opens."

"A visual spell then," Evelina said.

"Visual?" Tony asked. He added the clue to a Post-it note and stuck it to the wall.

"It's a spell where the caster needs only to see their victim to perform. These spells can be done with even a photo of the person, but they aren't strong enough to kill. A visual spell can be annoying, sure. Like giving someone a rash or making their hair fall out temporarily, but kill?" Evelina shook her head.

"You said you saw a blue haze hovering near the window?" Mahogany said.

Guy nodded.

"Did it look like Bazgul when he vaporates?"

The ghost considered this, his head tilted to one side. "Yes. Exactly."

"Another demon?" Evelina said, blanching.

Mahogany nodded. "Not a lesser one either." She paused, tapping her lower lip. "What if it's the demon Aurora summoned all those years ago?"

She stared at Evelina and Tony, their faces pale. She grabbed her wineglass and drained its contents in one large gulp. Mahogany then snatched the half-filled bottle in the center of the coffee table and refilled her glass until it nearly overflowed. "This is not good. Not good at all."

Chapter 36

"We need to check out your uncle's study." Mahogany stood and grabbed her wine glasses. "If there's a murderous demon on the loose, we'll need all the help we can get."

Evelina freed another bottle of wine from the rack in the kitchen. "I'm not sure all the books in the world will be enough for two humans, a stereo-amplified ghost, and a wingless Fae to defeat a demon." She opened the bottle and drank straight from it.

"Nestor defeated Ereuthalion," Mahogany said.

Tony shook his head. "Who?"

"Similar to David and Goliath," Evelina said, filling Mahogany's glass. "But Ereuthalion had Areithous's armor, which was pretty beefy."

"True. We'll just have to arm ourselves with knowledge and hope it's enough." Mahogany took a fortifying gulp of wine. "To the armory." She pumped her fist in the air.

Tony and Evelina blinked at her, their expressions blank.

"The study? We're arming ourselves with knowledge." Mahogany sighed. "It's a metaphor."

"This way." A slight smile lifted the corners of Tony's lips as he led them to the back of the tiny cottage. Well, at least it looked cozy from the outside. Several rooms lay at the back, which were unaccounted for from outdoors.

"A pocket spell," Evelina said. "Nice. I should have a Space Witch work their magic in my apartment. I'd love to have a bigger closet."

"Space Witch? Now there's a perfect name for a band," Tony said. He turned a metal dragon-shaped sconce on the wall ninety degrees and rapped on the door three times. A blue light briefly illuminated the gap between the door and the floor. "I love this part," he said and opened the door.

Instead of drywall and 1980s decor, the room Tony stepped into looked like someone had sheared it off of a medieval castle and slapped onto the cottage. Large gray stones made up the walls and floor. The scent of candle wax and lamp oil coiled in the air. Twenty or more thick oak shelves loaded with books leaned hither and thither against the walls, looking as if dust and luck held them together. A large, rickety wooden table stood in the room's center. Stacked atop were books so massive they covered half the table's surface. One lay open and inked upon the page was a detailed drawing of a griffin along with an entry written in a calligraphic hand detailing its aspects.

"Wow," Mahogany said, gazing around the study. "Your uncle went for authentic."

"It is authentic," Tony said. "We're in a Romanian keep 600 years ago."

"What? Can we take vacations to Romania anytime we want?" Mahogany asked.

"Sadly, no free Romanian vacations for us. The spell only extends to this room," Tony said.

"Figures," Evelina said, casting an apprising gaze around the keep. "Still, it's pretty cool that you have a time portal in your house. Your uncle must have been one badass witch."

Mahogany approached the table and turned the vellum page of the immense book. A sketch of a hairy creature standing on two legs, holding a staff, appeared on the right page. A detailed account of the beast, on the other. "Grugach?" Mahogany read the entry title aloud.

"They're like wild elves," Evelina said, moving to stand beside Mahogany. "Kind of primitive with loads of nature magic. Not something you want to run into alone at night."

Mahogany nodded. "There's a family of them living near the old mill at the edge of the woods." She ran her finger over the page, feeling the rise of the ink. "Is there a demon section?" Mahogany asked. She dropped the vellum page and gazed around the dusty tomes.

"Don't forget freezing spells while we're at it," Evelina said.

"Good question," Tony said, peering around the room. "If there's an organizational scheme, I haven't discovered it yet."

Evelina bit her lip and looked around the room. "This will take days, weeks even to go through everything here."

"Maybe I can help," Guy said. He glided into the room and disappeared into a bookshelf. Pieces of his t-shirt and locks of his messy hair poked out between the books.

"Nope. Nothing about demons here, but there is a promising recipe for goblin chili." Guy moved on to the next shelf which reached the ceiling. He had to make two passes to examine every book.

"No demons," he said, "but there's an interesting chapter on succubus on the top shelf."

Mahogany raised an eyebrow at Guy. "It appears Guy can speed read. He's checking for anything useful."

Evelina leaned in close to Mahogany and whispered, "Are you sure you want to get rid of him? I mean, he's pretty handy. We could use him when we start the detective agency."

Mahogany frowned. "What makes you think I want to start a detective agency?"

"No reason," Evelina said and glanced in Tony's direction, who was busy reading about griffins.

"Oh, a duplicate book," Guy said. "It's the same one Neema used for the camera mirror and one with a chapter of lesser demons right next to it."

"Finally," Mahogany said under her breath and advanced on the bookshelf, leaving Evelina and her sly smile. "Which one?"

"Here." Guy pointed to a thin, red leather-bound book. Mahogany slipped it from the shelf and flipped through it. "This only has about fifty pages. I've read picture books longer than this. Keep looking."

Guy nodded and passed through the rest of the shelves. He found ten demonology books, three with demon lore, two about remote spells, and one about elemental magic.

They gathered the pile of books and carried them into the living room to inspect.

"This one's written in Latin," Evelina said. "Anyone here read dead languages?"

"Try closing it and saying English," Mahogany said. She snapped closed another book and added it to the growing stack of rejects.

Evelina frowned and did as Mahogany suggested. "Oh! It worked!" She settled back and read the table of contents. "This might have what we're looking for." Her face lit in a hopeful radiance.

Tony and Mahogany turned their attention to Evelina, listening intently.

"The Deep Freeze Spell can render a target immobile from several miles away." Evelina looked from the book to Mahogany and Tony. "Several miles away?" she said, her triumphant expression slipping. "The Deep Freeze Spell leaves a residue of blue mist for several minutes after it's cast."

"That sounds exactly like what I saw in Thaddeus's cell." Guy's voice floated through the stereo speakers.

Mahogany nodded. "So, we're probably just looking at a wayward wizard with an axe to grind, and not a demon." Relief loosened the band of anxiety cinching her chest. "Does the book say anything else about the spell?"

Evelina scanned the rest of the chapter. "Just that it's an advanced spell."

"So, we're not dealing with a novice," Tony said. "Not as bad as a demon, but still not great."

They collectively sipped their wine.

"Okay," Tony said after a thoughtful moment. "We know we're dealing with a magical person. Not a demon."

"Which is excellent news," Evelina said.

"A person leaves evidence behind. Everyone, no matter how smart or careful, eventually makes a mistake," Tony said. He gazed at the murder wall. "We need to reexamine the clues."

"We've already been through them a million times," Evelina said, her tone petulant.

"Then let's make it a million and one. Two million if necessary." Tony handed the manila envelope to Evelina, and Mahogany grabbed the stack of photos they'd developed from Thad's camera. They worked silently for several minutes, mulling over the facts before them.

"Mahogany. You've been inside the brownstone." Evelina held the photo of the murderer about to strike Magic Mike. "Does anything here jog your memory? Something, anything, we can use to catch this psycho?"

Mahogany took the photo and studied it, thinking hard. Realization spread across her face, and she gazed at the fireplace in Tony's living room. The late afternoon sun spilling through the French doors caught the framed poster of Led Zeppelin hanging over the mantel. The broken frame's glazing projected a ghostly reflection of the room.

"I'm such a moron," Mahogany said, her gaze running over the photo in her hand. "I can't believe I didn't think of it sooner."

"What?" Evelina asked, leaning over the photo.

"There's a giant, gilded mirror hanging over the fireplace." Mahogany jumped to her feet and raced down the hall to the Romanian keep and its library. She located the book on mirror magic Guy had discovered and ran to the living room.

"We can try to reproduce the spell Neema cast on the mirror from Thad's camera and see if we can see the murderer's face." Mahogany eyes sparkled, and her cheeks grew rosy.

"How?" Evelina said. "None of us is a wortcunner, and Neema is still in police custody."

"No harm in trying, right? If it doesn't work, we try something different," Tony said, casting a wary eye at the murder wall.

Mahogany flipped through the book's pages until she found the spell. "According to the book, the spell works better on larger mirrors when applying the spell through smoke," she read.

"What do we need?" Evelina said, a doubtful frown creasing her brow. She grabbed the manila envelope and a pen to jot down the ingredients as Mahogany read them aloud.

"I have some of those here," Tony said, heading into the kitchen. He rummaged through his herb drawer and found star anise and rosemary. He grabbed a box of chamomile tea from a cupboard and an orange from the fruit bowl on the counter.

"Fantastic," Mahogany said. "The mermaid tears and mink oil will be at the Haughty Hemlock."

"Hang on a sec," Tony said, wagging his finger. "My uncle has an entire cabinet filled with potions and liquids. Maybe what we need is in there. Save ourselves a trip."

Tony dashed back down the hall. Evelina's doubtful expression slowly lighten as she scampered after him. A ripple of excitement surged through Mahogany at the thought of trying to cast a spell. Would it work? She hoped so, but doubt lurked in the shadows. Trying to keep her optimism in check, Mahogany trailed behind them.

She entered the study and gasped. A tall, glass cabinet filled with twinkling bottles had gone unnoticed as she searched for books.

"Here we go," Tony said, holding a set of bottles. "Mermaid tears and mink oil."

Evelina gave a happy squeal and clapped her hands.

"What are we waiting for?" Tony said. "Let's catch a murderer."

Chapter 37

W hen they reached the brownstone, the hour had grown late. Sodium streetlights cast their ghostly yellow glow, blanching the color from the cars parked along the wide sidewalk. For a moment, Mahogany, Tony, Evelina, and Guy regarded the house with its unassuming facade of sand-colored brick and large bay windows.

Mahogany adjusted the canvas bag on her shoulder with the ingredients and tools needed for the spell.

"Bazgul usually opens doors for me," she said, a stab of sorrow slicing at her heart. She hated the thought of her loyal companion home alone. He'd been so fragile when she'd left him.

"Not to worry. I've been practicing," Tony said with a reassuring smile. He pulled a small black case from his pocket and opened it. Metal picks of various sizes caught the streetlights and glinted. "After our chat at Tipsy's, I invested in a lock pick set. I've been practicing at my uncle's place, which is challenging since Evelina's aunt placed her protection spells."

He started toward the front door when Mahogany grabbed the back of his shirt, stopping him. "Let's go to the alley. Fewer probing eyes," she said.

The alley wasn't as well lit as the street. A few back porch lights drifted to the asphalt, creating semi-circles of illumination that traveled no farther. Household garbage cans lined the narrow passages, giving off the stench of last night's fish dinner.

"Here we go," Mahogany said, stopping. Three narrow wooden steps led to a white wooden door. Black and yellow police caution tape crisscrossed the faded paint, warning people away.

Tony tiptoed up the stairs. He inspected the lock and deliberated over his choice of picks.

Mahogany shifted her gaze up and down the alley, listening for the approach of anything that would foil their plans. She didn't want to join Neema in a police cell. Absently, she reached for her necklace and found her neck bare. She hoped Neema was still breathing. There was more she wanted to talk to her about.

At last, Tony made his choice and set to work on the lock. It only took him half a minute to ease the bolt out of position. "Wow, I mean, got it." Tony stood, stowed the pick set in his pocket, and opened the door.

The hinges, in need of oiling, squawked their protest. The trio cringed and waited for porch lights to switch on as the residents investigated, but the expected nosy neighbors were tending to other business.

"Remind me to add hinge oil to our list of breaking and entering tools," Evelina said as she and Mahogany stepped through the police tape behind Tony. The faint odor of coffee tinted the dark kitchen, lingering from when Guy and Magic Mike had occupied the house.

"I'll make a note," Mahogany said, brushing into Tony. She slipped the vial Neema had given him with its protection decoction into his pocket with the pick set. She refused to allow another person to be injured on her account.

Mahogany closed the door behind them and locked it. She didn't want anyone sneaking up on them. She was done with murderers catching her off guard.

They moved together through the house, down the hall, and into the study. Over the imposing brick fireplace hung a massive, gilded mirror.

Mahogany slipped the canvas bag off her shoulder and retrieved the book, rereading the spell. She placed the ingredients on the mantelpiece, along with a brass bowl filled with quick-light charcoal. As she measured and mixed the ingredients, a low buzz hummed in her ears. Mahogany shook her head, dispelling the tickle in her eardrums. Once finished, she carefully sprinkled the components over the briquettes.

A flash of movement reflected in the mirror caught Mahogany's attention, and she turned to find Evelina dancing from foot to foot.

"What's the matter with you? You're making me nervous." Mahogany adjusted the brass bowl on the mantel until she centered it under the mirror.

"I have to pee," Evelina said. Even in the dim, moonlit room, Mahogany saw a blush creep into the Fae's cheeks.

"You went before we left my place," Tony said.

"I know. I have a weak bladder when I'm committing a felony."

"You didn't have to pee when we broke into Thaddeus's room," Mahogany said, fishing a lighter from the bag.

"Maybe it was all the wine," Evelina said. "I'm bursting."

"I guess it's a good thing we're in a place with indoor plumbing," Tony said. "Mahogany. Do you know where the bathroom is?"

"Past the stairs on the left, and make sure you tidy up. If the cops find your DNA, we're toast," Mahogany said.

"Duly noted," Evelina said, scampering on tiptoe down the hall.

"How long did the book say this would take?" Tony asked, lifting his chin to the mirror.

"About twenty minutes," Mahogany said, holding the flame to the charcoal. "If it works at all." A burst of blue sparks sped across the surface of the charcoal, making the herbs glow and smolder. Mahogany watched, her eyes fixated on the smoke as it coiled over the mirror's surface. From behind, an invisible force pressed against her. The soles of her feet tingled, and the sensation climbed her body, creeping down her arms, and making her fingertips buzz.

Mahogany flexed her hands several times, and the electric feeling slowly dissipated.

"You all right?" Tony asked, raising an eyebrow at her.

"Yeah," she said, shaking her hands a few times. "Okay, now we wait." She sat on one of the velvet couches, tilted her head against the cushions, and gazed into the mirror.

A noise at the back door made her and Tony jump.

"What was that?" Mahogany whispered, sitting up straight.

"Stay here and watch the mirror," Tony said, and he crept back down the hallway on silent feet.

***

Evelina found the bathroom and raced in, pulling at her leggings as she kicked the door closed behind her.

The waning moon shed its dim light through a window high in the bathroom wall, giving her enough light so she wasn't plunged into complete darkness.

She sat on the toilet, sighing as relief flooded her. Her head drooped, relishing the feeling.

Suddenly, the room's temperature plummeted, interrupting the evening's warmth. Evelina's skin erupted in goosebumps, and she shivered.

Her head snapped up, the chill seeping into her bones. "Guy?" she whispered. The word left her mouth in a puff as it hit the chilled air.

No, she thought. No, this isn't Guy. This is something sinister. Something evil.

An odd crunching sound swept through the room, sending a thrill of fear up her spine. The moon's faint silver light caught the sparkle of something traveling across the bathroom's walls and floor.

Evelina raised a tentative hand and touched the wall nearest her. It was cold and slick to the touch. Icy even.

She stood, pulling up her leggings, her heart racing. The sparkle continued to travel the walls until it hit the door. Here, the effect was more pronounced. As it touched the hinges and doorknob, tiny icicles formed. Near the window, a faint blue haze appeared.

"A deep freeze spell," Evelina gasped.

She threw herself at the door and tried the handle. The cold burned into her hands like she'd touched an open flame. She screamed in pain and pulled her hands back, staring at them in disbelief.

Blisters covered her palms.

The frost on the walls continued to travel until it covered the bathroom in a layer of thick ice, trapping Evelina.

Tony crept down the hallway and paused, listening at the kitchen doorway, his gaze roving in the shadows, searching for the cause of the noise.

A pair of cats in the alley yowled, and a trash can rattled as they fought over a scrap of food. A rush of breath escaped Tony with relief, not realizing he'd been holding his breath. He waited for several more moments, but the house was silent again. He turned and started back toward the study when a creak sounded from the kitchen again.

Adrenaline surged through his limbs, and he peered around the dark space for something to arm himself with. A coat rack next to the front door grabbed his attention. Swiftly, Tony moved past the study to the front door, grabbed one of several heavy black umbrellas, and held it over his shoulder like a baseball bat.

He took a cleansing breath, trying to quiet his hammering heart, and started back toward the kitchen.

Tony poised himself against the kitchen doorway like a cop in an action movie, doing a room-to-room search for a perp. He held the umbrella tight in his hands. The crescent moon shed its pale light through the windows at the back of the kitchen. Elongated, ghostly shadows slunk long across the patterned vinyl floor. The faint scent of coffee and mint dusted the air. Beyond that, the room was empty.

He laughed as the tension in his limbs broke. "You're letting your imagination go wild. It's just the house settling," Tony muttered to himself. He dropped the umbrella to his side and started back to the study.

As he passed the foot of the stairs, the floor creaked behind him. He swung around, raising the umbrella over his head when something large and heavy crashed into the back of his skull, accompanied by a low metallic ring.

The words cast iron flashed through Tony's scrambled thoughts before he crumpled to the ground, unconscious. Blood bloomed from his wounded head, encircling his head in a macabre halo.

Chapter 38

M ahogany gazed up at the mirror, her anticipation growing as she waited for something, anything, to happen. She rubbed her fingers together, wondering at the source of the mysterious tingle that had surged through her body when she lit the charcoal.

"Hey, Guy. Where are you?" Mahogany whispered into the quiet study.

"In my bedroom." Guy's voice came from above her. His face appeared in the ceiling directly over where Mahogany sat, surprising a yelp from her.

"Jeez, Guy!" she said, clutching her throat. Her heart stuttered against her ribcage in an uneven rhythm. "You are going to give me a heart attack."

"Sorry," Guy said, smiling apologetically. His gaze shifted from Mahogany to the floor beneath her feet—to the place where he'd taken his last breath. "This house makes me uncomfortable."

A wave of sadness washed over Mahogany, and a sad smile touched her lips. "I'll let you know as soon as something happens," Mahogany said.

Guy returned her sad smile and disappeared back into the ceiling.

With a sigh, Mahogany peered up at the mirror. The smoke from the burning herbs coiled across the glassy surface, obscuring the reflection. Behind the fog, an image materialized, bringing Mahogany to her feet. Over her right shoulder, a hooded figure appeared out of the haze.

"Gods!" Mahogany stared wide-eyed at the magical reflection. It was the hooded figure Thaddeus had snapped a picture of the night Guy and Magic Mike were murdered. The same hooded figure who had attacked her while Guy died.

Mahogany gazed at her hands, flexing them. The tingle lingered as a ghost of a memory. How had she cast the spell? It should be impossible. She was human, but she had, and it was working, fast. She checked her phone. Only five minutes had elapsed since she'd begun the incantation. "Really fast," she murmured. Her heart quickened again. She was doing magic.

Mahogany peered into the mirror, intent on the magical reflection. She hadn't been present when Neema had developed images from Thaddeus's camera and didn't know what to expect.

She leaned from side to side, trying to get a better look under the black hood at the face of the murder, but had no luck. At the mirror's far left corner, another foggy image emerged, unfurling over the surface like ink in water. Unlike the snapshots produced by the camera's mirror, this image appeared like a slow-motion movie playing in reverse.

The smoky image revealed several police officers milling about the study as a pair of EMTs lifted Guy's and Mike's bodies into body bags.

Mahogany glanced at the study's ceiling, which thankfully remained devoid of Guy's semi-solid face. He didn't need to see his body placed in a black zippered bag like luggage.

The image rolled past Mahogany's reflection. Her gaze followed the coiling playback as it bloomed across the mirror's surface until it reached the hooded figure's reflection. Instead of merging with it, as she expected, the past image blanketed the murder beneath it. "What the?" She stared at the mirror, not comprehending the scene before her.

Panic bolted up her spine, and she peered over her shoulder. Staring back at her was the hooded figure.

The murderer raised an arm, revealing a large kitchen knife. Its sharp blade glinted in the moonlight. Mahogany gasped, dropping her phone. She stepped backward, and her knees caught on the coffee table. She lost her balance and fell backward onto the low oaken surface just as the murderer brought the knife down. Mahogany rolled to the right. The knife hit the tabletop with a metallic ting—the tip embedding into the wood with a sickening thump. Mahogany scrambled to her feet and bound over the couch nearest the door. Her boot heels hit the floor on the other side, and she raced across the study as the murderer struggled to free the knife from the coffee table.

Mahogany fled down the hallway and towards the stairs. Tony's prone figure lay crumpled at their base. His eyes were closed, and he appeared to be unconscious. Mahogany paused, but the murderer's charging footsteps got her moving again. She stumbled up the stairs, panic clouding her actions. All she wanted was a door to lock between herself and the murderous person trying to slice her into pieces.

She took the stairs two at a time. Behind her, Mahogany heard the figure jump over Tony's body and land on the foot of the stairs. Mahogany dove through a doorway to the right and slammed it shut behind her. Panicked, she fumbled over the doorknob, searching for a lock.

In the room, Guy stared at her wild-eyed. "What's going on?"

Mahogany returned his panicked stare, still fumbling with the lock. "Murderer," she croaked, her mouth dry.

"What? Here? Now?" Guy said.

As if in answer to his question, the hooded figure ran at the door, shoving it open a few inches with their shoulder. Mahogany screamed and pushed back, slamming it shut again. Again, the murderer thrust their weight against the door, but without the running start, the door didn't budge.

"Oh, shit," Guy said. "The murderer's here now. What do we do?" He peered around the room.

"I need to barricade the door," Mahogany said. "Lock it. Something."

Guy nodded. "There's a lock at the top." He pointed a ghostly finger at where the slide bolt lay.

Mahogany reached up with her left hand and slid the bolt home.

The murderer hit the door again, but the lock held firm.

"Where are Tony and Evelina?" Guy asked.

"Tony's lying at the foot of the stairs, and Evelina's peeing." She gulped at the air, trying to catch her breath.

"Peeing?"

"Too much wine," Mahogany stifled a sob. "What if they're both dead? Gods, this is all my fault." She thought of the vial of protection decoction she'd slipped into Tony's pocket and hoped it was powerful enough to keep him alive until they got help.

On the other side of the door, the murderer stopped pushing into the door, and silence fell over the brownstone except for Mahogany's ragged breath.

"You can't stay in there forever," came a sweet, melodic female voice.

Mahogany raced to the window on the opposite side of the room, slid it up, and kicked out the screen. She leaned out and looked down at the alley below. Nothing lay between her and the ground. The brownstone contained no awning or gutter for her to lower herself to the ground. She was trapped.

"Oh, I don't know. It's cozy in here." Mahogany called, reaching for her phone but finding it missing. "I bet I could make this a desirable home." Mahogany frantically patted her person, searching for her phone.

"What are you looking for?" Guy said, his face lined with worry.

"My phone." Mahogany's eyes were desperate. "I must have dropped it."

"Hang on." Guy floated through the floor to the study below, leaving Mahogany alone.

"You're too quiet. Is your ghost not in there with you?" the voice crooned through the door.

"Oh, he's here," Mahogany said, pleased her voice came out strong and unwavering. Considering how her hands shook, it was a small blessing.

"I hadn't planned on killing him or the librarian," the murderer said.

"Then why did you?" Mahogany pulled the dresser away from the wall. Its weight made her lower back scream in protest. She slid out some drawers to lighten the load.

"That twerp of an apprentice saw me. I couldn't have that. I needed to see my plan to completion. And the librarian made a great guinea pig for my poison."

"You could have used the spell on Magic Mike that you used to kill Thaddeus Spike. It would have kept him from photographing you in the act." She grabbed the sides of the dresser and heaved it across the floor. Even with several of the drawers removed, it still weighed a ton. Sweat sprung out on her forehead as the dresser butted against the door.

"Mike was personal. Of course, Thaddeus had to die as well, but I wanted to watch the life spill from Mike." Her voice seeped through the door like seawater through the fractured hull of a ship, slowly dragged to the ocean floor. "What are you doing in there?"

"A little redecorating," Mahogany said. "What was your plan, exactly?" She replaced the drawers, praying her burgeoning barricade would be enough to keep the murderer out while she plotted her escape.

"Revenge, but you must have figured that out by now," said the murderer. A metallic ting punctuated her words as she scraped the knife against the door, sending a thrill of fear through Mahogany, raising the hair on her arms.

"How's that working out for you?" Mahogany tested a trunk. She lifted one side of it, dragged it across the room to the door, and placed it in front of the dresser.

"Pretty well. However, I let my nostalgia get the better of me with Dorcia. I regret that now."

"How so?" Mahogany asked, looking for other items to put against the door. For a furnished rental, the room lacked amenities. Even the closet next to the room's only window lay bare. Mahogany didn't even see extra bedding.

"I used to love her when I was a kid. She was so nice to me when she dated my sister, but then she and her friends killed Aurora, and Mike broke her heart."

Sister? Mahogany's mind raced. "You're Aurora Kingsley's sister?" The pieces were falling into place but in an unexpected arrangement. "But you're wrong," Mahogany said to the closed door. "They didn't kill your sister. Aurora summoned a demon. That's what killed her."

The door shook in its frame as the murderer flailed at it with punching fists and kicking feet. "Lies! Aurora would never have done something so careless." The door thudded again as the murderer shoved their weight against it. "I shouldn't have let my emotions rule me with Dorcia."

Guy floated through the floor then. "Mahogany, I checked on Tony. He's alive but out cold. Evelina's stuck in the bathroom. It looks like the same freezing spell that killed Thad. The whole thing is under a foot of ice."

"Is she all right?" Mahogany asked, alarm raising the hair on her neck.

"She's fine. Sorry," Guy said, rubbing a hand along the back of his neck. "I should have led with that."

Relief flooded Mahogany. "I don't understand. If she's so murder-happy, why not kill them?"

Guy shrugged. "None of this makes any sense. Looking for rational answers is fruitless."

"Good point," Mahogany said. "What now?"

"By the way, your phone is on the study floor," Guy said.

"Terrific. A lot of good it will do for me down there."

"There's one more thing." Guy pointed to the barricaded bedroom door.

"I hear you whispering. Is your ghost back? His skull gave the most satisfying crack when I slammed Mother Shipton's bust into it. Not the best use of the Prophet, but she came in handy."

The corner of Guy's lip raised in a snarl, and he squared his shoulders.

"Be right with you," Mahogany said. "What?" She stared at Guy, her eyes frantic.

"That woman out there is Ivy Wembley," Guy said, "and she just mocked my death."

"Ivy Wembley? The librarian's sister?" Mahogany frowned. "She said she was Aurora Kingsley's sister."

"The demon summoner?" Guy asked. "This makes no sense."

"I felt him lurking nearby a minute ago," Ivy said. "Did he identify me this time?"

Mahogany remembered her encounter with Ivy that morning outside Priscilla's house. Her cold, dry hands. The discarded photo. Another piece of the puzzle clicked into place.

"Guy says you're Ivy Wembley, Priscilla's sister." Mahogany pulled the bedding from the small twin mattress. "But he's wrong. Ivy Wembley doesn't exist. Priscilla didn't have any siblings, did she?"

The mock sound of distraught sobbing made its way into the room, followed by a laugh so sinister it could curdle milk. Mahogany shivered.

"What gave me away?" Ivy said, her voice dripping with venom.

"It didn't occur to me this morning, but Werewolves run hot, but your hands were icy. When I shook your hand, something bothered me, but I couldn't place it. Then there's the family photo in the trash. A grieving sister would never throw away something so special."

"Astute observations, Mahogany. You'd be surprised how easy it is to forge identification when one knows magic. The police fell for my false identity without question. But you're wrong about one thing—families forget people. After Aurora's death, I became invisible. Nothing I did garnered my parent's attention. They died with Aurora all those years ago. Just a couple of living ghosts, but you wouldn't know about family, would you, Mahogany?"

Anger rose in Mahogany's chest, driving away the fear. She fought the urge to charge at the door and tear the impostor Ivy apart. "This is an uneven relationship with you knowing my name." Mahogany tied the ends of the fitted and top sheets together and gave them a hard tug, funneling her anger toward a more productive endeavor. The knot held.

"You are too right. A proper introduction is in order. I'm Ysabel, Ysabel Kingsley."

"Hey, Guy," Mahogany said, her voice low. "Are you up for an experiment?"

"You sure you want to play around right now?" Guy whispered back, pointing to the barricaded door.

Mahogany rolled her eyes. Only Guy would whisper when only she could hear him. "I need you to pop into my phone and call Detective Sawyer, or the fire department, the president, anyone who can help us get out of this and arrest the vindictive bitch out there."

"Do you think it works like the stereo?"

"Have a better idea?"

Guy flung a worried look at the door. "I shouldn't leave you alone."

"You could stay and watch me get murdered. Maybe we can haunt Pandemonium together."

"Right." Guy gave a determined nod and floated through the floor, disappearing into the study below.

"How's your creepy little friend?" Ysabel asked. "After the bite he gave me, the least I could do was return the favor."

"So, he bit you? Bazgul wasn't sure. Demons pack a debilitating punch, even the lesser ones." Mahogany closed one end of the sheet in the closet door and threw the rest out the window, where it dangled down the side of the house. "It must be bothering you if you kept coming back to buy more tea from Neema. How did you hide the bite? That must have been pretty tricky." Mahogany peered out the window. The sheets reached just past halfway down the brownstone's side, leaving a six-foot drop to the alley below.

"Boots, don't fail me now," Mahogany muttered, throwing a leg over the windowsill.

"Okay, less talking and more stabbing." Ysabel threw herself into the door. It rattled in its frame but remained shut.

Mahogany looked at the door and then at the waiting alley below. She gave the sheet a test tug. It stayed anchored inside the closed closet door. "Now or never, girl," Mahogany said to herself.

Ysabel threw herself at the door again, screaming in frustration. "I will kill you. I will kill you all for Aurora!"

Mahogany gripped the sheet with both hands and wrapped the excess around her calf to help slow her descent. "Just like gym class," she muttered, lowering herself out the window until the sheet held her full weight.

Inch by excruciating inch, the alley grew closer until her leg dangled free, and only her hands gripped the sheet. Mahogany carefully twined the sheet around her right forearm and let herself slide until she dangled on the last foot or so of the fabric. Aiming away from the trash cans below, Mahogany let go of her makeshift rope and fell.

The last several feet to the alley came up faster than she expected. When Mahogany's boot heels hit the asphalt, she reeled backward, stumbled, and fell hard on her tailbone.

Pain shot up her spine, and a scream bubbled in her throat, refusing to pop. She sat there for a few seconds, reeling from the pain, before pulling herself onto her knees and crawling up the back steps to the brownstone's back door. "Tony, Evelina, I'm coming." Her voice, hoarse with pain, barely made it past her lips.

Using the wooden railing on the side of the steps, Mahogany pulled herself to the standing position. The pain in her posterior seared with the heat of a branding iron.

She tried taking a step, but her legs wouldn't hold her. Mahogany caught herself on the railing as her knees buckled and lowered herself onto all fours. She reached up and tried the knob, which didn't budge.

Mahogany cursed herself for locking it and tried to call Guy. It hurt her back to talk, and she winced but tried again.

Guy stuck his head out the back door. "What happened to you?"

"I broke my pride. Any luck with the phone?" Mahogany winced again as she spoke.

"Yes," Guy said, nodding, an enormous smile on his face. "I did it. I called the president."

A sob escaped Mahogany.

"Sorry, no time for jokes. I dialed 911. Did you know cell phones work the same as a stereo for ghosts?"

Mahogany hung her head. Another sob welled in her throat. "You're insufferable. You know that?"

A thud at the upstairs window grabbed their attention, and Mahogany and Guy peered up as Ysabel Kingsley glared down. Her prim face wore a mask of rage. Her tidy 50s chic had vanished. She screamed and ducked back through the window. Her footsteps charged through the house to where Mahogany waited, defeated.

"Mahogany, you're brilliant. You're the strongest and the bravest person I've ever met. Thank you for solving my murder," Guy said. "Now get up and move your ass!"

"Tell Tony and Evelina I'm sorry," Mahogany said, falling to her side.

"I said move!" Guy screamed.

Guy's tone ignited Mahogany's resolve, and she pulled herself up. She hobbled down the stairs and grabbed a pair of large river stones from a once-thriving begonia planter. She lifted the smaller of the two, took aim, and hurled it at the back door's window. The glass pane shattered, and she hobbled back up the stairs, reached through the void, and unlocked the back door, swinging it open.

Ysabel Kingsley reached the foot of the stairs as Mahogany entered the kitchen. Their eyes locked through the hall separating them, and Ysabel snarled. Mahogany tightened her grip on the rock. Her regret mounted as she realized she'd brought a rock to a knife fight. She took a single step before the front door burst open. Detective Sawyer, clad in a bulletproof vest and flanked by officers, stood at the ready. An armory worth of guns barreled down on the wild-haired, knife-touting Ysabel.

"Drop the weapon," Detective Teresa Sawyer said, leveling her sights on the crazed woman.

Ysabel turned and let out a despair-filled scream, dropping the knife. A shimmer flashed around Ysabel and was gone.

Mahogany let out a breath she hadn't known she was holding and let her knees buckle, the rock slipping from her fingers.

Chapter 39

"Ysabel was just a kid when everything happened," Neema said. She, along with Mahogany and Evelina, sat around Tony's hospital bed. Guy stood near Tony's feet, his torso sprouting from the blankets where Mahogany's phone rested.

They had all made it out of the brownstone relatively unscathed, mostly thanks to Neema's protection spell. Ysabel had hit Tony with a cast iron pan, knocking him unconscious. He'd sustained a concussion with no permanent damage.

Evelina's stint in the brownstone's bathroom had been uneventful, yet claustrophobic. Ysabel had aimed a freezing spell at her, but it had backfired, freezing the interior instead, trapping her inside. The ice had proved to be an excellent sound insulator, blocking her shouts from being heard by the rest of the house. The burns on her hands had been superficial and were nearly gone.

The Guild of Myth and Magic had stripped Ysabel's magic and erased human memories of Thaddeus Spike's mysterious death. All they knew was what the coroner's report stated as the cause of death—heart attack. Any knowledge of the freezing spell had vanished, along with the icy bathroom at the brownstone.

The fall had broken Mahogany's coccyx. Her treatment was a donut-shaped cushion and 800 milligrams of ibuprofen every six hours for the next two weeks. Without her pentagram, she had been susceptible to injury. Mahogany figured it was a small price to pay for Neema's safety, at least until she got the whole truth from the woman about her abduction; then Mahogany would decide whether to kill Neema herself.

After Guy's phone call had led to the capture and arrest of Ysabel, the police had released Neema and ushered to her to the hospital.

"So, Aurora summoning a demon created a ripple her family never recovered from. That's so sad," Evelina said, brushing her golden hair behind her shoulders. "Imagine being so affected by the death of a loved one that you brooded over it for two decades, planning your revenge."

"How did she find you?" Tony asked. A massive bundle of white bandages encircled the crown of his head. Wires trailed out from under a blue hospital gown, where they attached to a series of beeping machines that measured his vital signs.

"Do you remember the article in Popular Potions that came out a couple of months ago?" Neema asked. "It featured a picture of me in front of Haughty Hemlock. Since it's a local publication, I thought nothing of it, but one made its way to Ohio, where Magic Mike found it."

"He recognized you after all these years?" Mahogany shifted on her donut. Her fractured tailbone gave a dull ache.

Evelina shook her head. "I've seen those magazines in airports, ferry terminals, and train stations. If someone grabbed one and read it as they traveled, who knows where it could have ended up?"

Neema nodded. "After my sister's death, we all knew we were marked. We hid out across the world. I changed my name and started a new life with a new family." She nodded to Mahogany. "Mike and Thaddeus kept in touch for years under heavy magical encryption. When Mike found me, he told Thaddeus he was tired of hiding and wanted to come clean about what had happened with Aurora and the demon. All the years of hiding had exhausted him. Thaddeus tried to dissuade him. It wasn't just his life. It was all of ours. We were all at risk if the truth came out. There was a reason we covered things up." She sighed. "Mike was always stubborn. Once he'd decided something, there was no changing it."

"After the police arrested you, we spoke to Euryale and her sister, Stheno. Euryale watched you leave the night of the brownstone murders. You were there," Mahogany said.

"Mike and I planned on meeting in the park at one o'clock, but when he didn't show, I got a bad feeling, so I went to the house. When I saw you go inside with Bazgul, I knew something horrible must have happened."

"You knew he'd died because I had shown up," Mahogany said.

Neema nodded. A heavy sadness filled her eyes.

"Why didn't you say something to me?" Mahogany asked, folding her arms over her chest.

"Say what? I was just out for a late-night stroll?" Neema shook her head. "If I had known Magic Mike had been murdered, and the culprit was still there, I would never have let you go inside. I saw you and Bazgul get out right before the police arrived, so I ran."

"Why were you meeting Magic Mike in the middle of the night?" Evelina said.

"It was about a binding he had planned with Guy. Mike needed another wizard to make it official," Neema said. "A witness."

"Mike was binding Guy to someone? Do you know who?" Mahogany asked, peering at Guy, who rubbed his chin thoughtfully.

"He wouldn't tell me," Neema said. "Typical Mike."

"Why not have Thaddeus witness it?" Tony said.

"Thaddeus was against Mike engaging in any spells that could bring notice to him or us." Neema gestured to herself and Mahogany. "The Guild frowns on unsanctioned bindings."

"Stupid human question time again." Tony raised his hand. "Why would a binding do that, and how was it unsanctioned?"

"Because it was a one-sided binding," Neema said. She tucked her hair behind her ears. She'd dyed it the morning Sawyer had arrested her, erasing the budding white streak from the front. "The person being bound to Guy didn't know about the ritual."

Mahogany looked at the ceiling. Wizards were so irritating. She counted herself lucky she'd never met Mike. Mahogany sensed they wouldn't have gotten along.

"So, Magic Mike bound Guy to someone without their permission or consent?" Mahogany said, still looking at the ceiling.

"Yes," Neema said.

"What does that mean, exactly?" Tony asked.

Neema turned to him and spoke. "Usually, when Folk perform a binding, it's protecting someone. A binding works better if both parties are privy to the arrangement. However, it's not unheard of for someone to bind themselves or another to an infant, if that infant is in magical danger."

"Mike performed the binding without a witness, which means he knew he was in danger and couldn't risk waiting," Mahogany said. She leveled her gaze at her ghost. "Guy, do you remember anything about the binding? A name? Something?"

Guy shook his head. "Like I said, all Mike told me was the bindee's name had something to do with the forest. Or was it cold weather? Hail, or maybe it was sleet? Dying from blunt force trauma messes with the old neurons." He tapped the side of his head. "I remember Mike mentioning being afraid that we could be in danger if I knew the person's identity."

"Maybe that's why you're still here, Guy? The binding is keeping you from crossing over," Tony said, gesturing to Mahogany's phone at the foot of the hospital bed.

"That's a possibility," Guy's voice drifted out of Mahogany's phone.

"You should have crossed over right after we solved your murder," Evelina said, her forehead wrinkling.

"Do bindings last after death?" Mahogany frowned at Neema. "Shouldn't death break a binding?"

"It's rare," Neema said. "However, hauntings are rare unto themselves. Yet, it's possible that a firm binding may have trapped Guy here until he completes his mission."

"But we don't know what his mission is," Evelina said.

Neema sat back in her chair and let out a long breath.

"What?" Mahogany asked, casting a wary eye on Neema.

"I'm just tired," she said, brushing Mahogany's words away. "It's been a long couple of days."

The doctor walked in then, ending their speculative conversation.

"I'm sure he'll find his way soon," Neema said. She pushed her chair back and got to her feet. "We should let you rest, Tony. Come on, ladies. You can come back tomorrow." She left the room and headed for the elevators.

———※———

"When are you going to tell her?" Thaddeus asked. His spectral form floated next to Neema as she exited Tony's hospital room.

"When I have to," Neema said.

"She'll find out on her own eventually, and when she does, she'll be upset," Thaddeus said. "Furious even."

Neema nodded. "I'll tell her before that happens, but first, I must find out what other dangers lurk out there."

"That mist that killed me. I've seen it before," Thaddeus said.

Neema nodded again. "Aurora."

"Is it possible Aurora's demon is still out there, trying to get revenge?" Thaddeus said. His spirit flickered and faded for a moment before solidifying.

"I don't know, but I'm going to find out," Neema said. "Your time is near. Please send my love to Mike, Kassandra, and James."

"I will," Thaddeus said, and he vanished.

———※———

Across town, in her sparse apartment, Detective Sawyer clutched the phone in her hand. "Thank you for returning my call, Professor Hume. So, is the anelace authentic?" She tried to ignore the stacks of boxes piled about the place. She kept telling herself she was too busy to unpack, but she knew that wasn't the truth.

"Yes, yes," came a deep male voice over the phone. "14th-century England, to be exact. It's a beautiful relic. Where did you say you found it?"

"It's part of a murder investigation. It's over seven hundred years old. Is it possible that whoever crafted the dagger left their fingerprint in the blade that would still be visible today?" Detective Sawyer studied a photo of the anelace.

"Oh, uh, that's terrible," Hume sputtered. "Most castings took place in sand, and fingerprints don't last in that environment. It's possible with clay molds, but having it visible hundreds of years later is unlikely. The smith should have polished off any imperfections in the final sharpening or they should have worn off through use."

"Thank you, professor. I appreciate your time," Detective Sawyer said.

They hung up, and Sawyer brought the photo of the jeweled anelace close to her face.

She'd run the blade's fingerprint through CODIS, but the database returned no matches. Until she ran the fingerprints found at the library after Priscilla Wembley's death. A single print on the librarian's desk matched precisely the one embedded in the anelace's blade. How could a fingerprint made in the 1300s match one left today? She'd run the print a dozen times, and the results came back the same every time.

The detective placed the photo in a folder labeled Pandemonium and then dropped it into a side drawer of her desk, locking it. Ever since she'd transferred to this odd little town in Oregon, something had been off, but she couldn't place her finger on precisely what it was.

A vague memory of a dream niggled at the base of her brain. Something to do with a life-sized ice sculpture. The detective shook her head and let out a dry laugh that cracked in the quiet of her house, echoing off the bare walls. If she was going to make Pandemonium home, she would need to unpack.

———

"We'll see you tomorrow," Evelina said and squeezed Tony's hand.

"Rest well," Guy said, before stepping out of the bed and away from Mahogany's phone.

"Thank you, Guy. If you haven't crossed over before I get out, I hope I get to see you one day."

Guy smiled and headed for the door.

Mahogany stood, wincing at the pain in her backside, and grabbed her phone and cushion. "Don't watch too much television," she teased.

"I have a lot to catch up on. Season seventeen of Love Island is out now," Tony said and smiled.

Evelina stood and caught up to Mahogany, slipping her arm through hers. "When are you going to ask him out?" she asked from the corner of her mouth.

Heat rose in Mahogany's cheeks. She peered over her shoulder at Tony. The doctor had his full attention.

"What are you talking about?" Mahogany hissed. "I thought you two were a thing?"

Evelina snorted. "Not likely. I like my lovers with more breasts and no penis."

Mahogany gazed at Evelina, her mouth agape.

"I mean, I've made a few exceptions in the past, but he has to be magical, if you know what I mean." Evelina shrugged.

"What about Diabolical Delights? I was asking him out and you swooped in and stole my thunder."

Evelina blushed. "You were floundering, and I thought if I made it into a group thing, it could relieve some of the pressure. My plan was to have something come up right after I got there, leaving the two of you alone."

"Thanks, doctor," Tony said, and the doctor headed to finish her rounds.

Evelina released Mahogany's arm and gave Tony a last wave before heading out the door.

"When will you tell them the mirror's spell worked?" Guy asked, a frown puckering his brow.

No one had been in the study when the spell took hold in the mirror, and she had failed to mention it once everyone was out of harm's way. Neither Tony nor Evelina had asked about it, either.

"Major rain check on the ice cream outing," Tony said.

Mahogany stopped in the doorway, her heart hammering against her ribs. "Rain check?" There was that hook in her chest again. She rubbed it absently.

"When I get out of here, let's go for real. You still need to tell me about old Ralph Evans and your horrible dating experience."

Mahogany smiled, warmth filling her. "It's a date."

Acknowledgments

A lifelong lover of mysteries and whodunnits, it was only a matter of time before I tried to write my own. However, I didn't write this book alone. There are scores of people who had their fingers in the batter, and for which I am eternally grateful.

I want to thank my parents for always encouraging my love of writing. Without their words cheering me on, I would have given up long ago.

Matthew, my husband, talked me off several ledges where I wanted to scrap the whole thing and start over. Without his steadfast humor and unwavering confidence that I had something not only worth writing, but something that others would want to read, this book would not have seen the light of day. Thanks for all the juggling of my fragile author ego in breaking the news that I couldn't do it all on my own.

To the beautiful Jewel, who read a very early and very messy first draft and gave me the invaluable advice of "More Bazgul." Yes, my dear friend, there will be more Bazgul. Heck, he might even get his own book one day.

Thank you to my editors Olive and Geetha at Fantastic Editions Editors. Their sage advice made me want to throw in the proverbial towel (editing can feel like an insurmountable task), but I made it through with their assistance.

A giant thanks to Suzy and Marcus for their fun ideas and beautiful designs with the book cover.

While writing this book for National Write a Novel Month 2021, I began my streaming journey on Twitch. It is safe to say that Twitch has one of the best writing communities around. We live by the motto, 'We Rize by Lifting Others.' A loving shout out to SailingOcelot for your lovely voice and kind words. To AngelFea87 for keeping me company on almost every one of my streams. BlueMoonKraken for always noticing if I'm having a good hair day. Thanks, buddy, I appreciate it. To SwiftnessAuthor and itanshi for the great conversations. To the sweet shirevenge, the queen of Stitch memes who makes me feel loved. And to AllyAlexisGhostWriter for all the laughs.

Some of my more staunch yet less vocal support has come from Patreon. Thank you to my few, yet dedicated patrons who have made the difference when it counted most. I appreciate all you've done for me.

To my Wattpad friends and fellow authors who read the first draft of this book cover to cover, I am forever appreciative to you for your support and lovely comments, especially Gauravaaditya Kulkarni for leaving me my first review!

I know I'm forgetting a few important someones. Please forgive me and know that I still love you.

About the Author

C ynthia Varady (she/her) is an award-winning short story writer and creator of the Pandemonium Cozy Mystery series. When not writing, you can find Cynthia playing video games with her son, whipping up off-the-cuff baking recipes (many of which are edible and some might say, quite tasty), reading mysteries and comedic fiction, and cuddling with the family cats, Storm and Snowy. *The Girl with the Uninvited Ghost* is the first book in the Pandemonium Cozy Mystery series.

You can contact Cynthia at wordslinger@cynthiavarady.net, or visit her website at CynthiaVarady.net